Pamela Jooste was born in Ca[ ]
She is the author of three crtic[ ]
and Min, Like Water in Wild [ ]
Man's Daughter, her first[ ]
Commonwealth Best First B[ ]
Region; the Samlam Literary [ ]u, and the Book Data
South African Booksellers' Choice Award. At the time of
going to press, *People Like Ourselves* is shortlisted for the
South African *Sunday Times* Literary Award for Fiction
2004.

Praise for *People Like Ourselves*:

'Subtle and affecting ... with a fluid charm that belies the
keenness of her observations'   *Big Issue in the North*

'The changes that post-Apartheid South Africa has gone through
are well documented but what of the individual lives? ... Moving,
intelligent and interesting'   *Ireland on Sunday*

'An intelligent look at the new South Africa'   *Mail on Sunday*

'An acidic, instructive and measured account of a bewitching
country'   *Irish Tatler*

'Pamela Jooste has not needed to evolve, [as a writer because] she
arrived on the shelves a fully-fledged writer and her ability to
change her style and narrative shows a braveness and control of
her craft which is awesome ... Jooste has produced a novel of
supreme elegance and fine observation. While Jooste remains
popular on the book club circuit it is time she was recognised as
one of this country's best serious novelists. One who manages to
blend storytelling with humanity, observation with wit and
intelligence with accessibility'   Jennifer Crocker, *Cape Times*

'Known for her accessible, light, yet very sharply observant writing
about South African people, set against the complexity of our
multi-cultural society and turbulent political past, Jooste's books
have become firm book club favourites ... Praised by critics for the
"wonderful South Africaness" ... and insightful portrayal of
ordinary people'
Angela Zachariasen, *The Eastern Province Herald*

'Few novelists have written about the new South Africa in this accessible, humorous and insightful way, to reveal a daring and provocative vision of life after truth and reconciliation'
Gorry Bowes-Taylor, *The Cape Times*

'Jooste has a talent for reaching into people's hearts and pulling out the universal truths we can all relate to'
Jacqui l'Ange, *Oprah Magazine, South Africa*

'Jooste knows how to scratch beneath the surface as she looks at people like ourselves living lives that are fast becoming redundant ... As always it's a great read' *Pretoria News*

'Read it – a South African book quite unlike any other – but expect to feel vulnerable, uncomfortable and challenged ... Madam, maid, gardener, executive, former liberal, entrepreneur, socialite, rebellious teen ... they are all there – those we know and those we think we know, but don't. Yes, people like ourselves, all caught up in our own lives in the new South Africa ... It's the first time Jooste ... has truly delved into the scary reality of the present and she has done so with brilliant candour'
Debbie Derry, *The Eastern Province Herald*

'A dry, clear-eyed, thoroughly elegant exploration of the brave world of contemporary Johannesburg society' *Shape* magazine

'A perceptive and wry look at the brave world that is the "African miracle" today ... It is a new world in which anything can happen, and nothing turns out the way you expect'
Pace magazine

'A wry but powerful look at life in Johannesburg in the "new South Africa" ... this is an immensely readable book that captures so much of our times' *Your Family*

'A very grown up and uncomfortable observation of where we are after liberation. There's very little child-like innocence in this examination of how very different our personal histories are'
Style magazine

Also by Pamela Jooste

DANCE WITH A POOR MAN'S DAUGHTER
FRIEDA AND MIN
LIKE WATER IN WILD PLACES

and published by Black Swan

PEOPLE LIKE OURSELVES

Pamela Jooste

BLACK SWAN

PEOPLE LIKE OURSELVES

JULIA

Douglas and Julia are on the brink of divorce. It's been coming for a long time, like an oncoming train approaching much faster than it appears to be at first, becoming increasingly ominous the closer it gets. Douglas hasn't been officially told yet but he must know divorce is inevitable. Even so, when the moment comes, he won't be the one to say the words out loud because, unlike Julia, Douglas has not been practising them.

Divorced women, the ones who feel wronged, are happy to tell you the way it will be. They mean well but it's of no real help. Every divorce, like every marriage, is different. It takes on the colour of all that precedes it. It really can't help itself.

In Julia's case the idea, she discovered, had been with her for quite a long time. There it was, in her head, living an independent, parallel life of its own, sitting around waiting for the day she'd wake up and

9

recognize it so she could call it forward and it could make itself known and then, one day, she did.

Julia doesn't hate Douglas. She's known him far too long and too well for that. She doesn't loathe, detest or despise him. This is the way those other women talk. You won't hear anything like this from Julia. For her, it's quite simple. The man she married has vanished. He's not there any more and he would, she's quite sure, say the same about her.

Nothing turned out the way it was meant to. Not one single thing has worked out the way they intended. Once life was good to them. They got where they are the long way round but for a while they did have one another. She remembers that this is what it felt like in those days and so this is what she believed. Then there was Kimmy and they loved her. She stood at the very centre of their world and there's nothing at all they wouldn't have done for her. There were things to look forward to and then, in no more than a split second when they weren't paying proper attention, it all came to pieces. Or, at least, that's what it felt like.

All that Julia has left now is fragments of the life she once took so for granted and so precious few of those she feels she could hold them in the palm of one hand and they would carry no weight at all.

Money, or lack of it, is a part of the problem. You can ask Adelaide. Adelaide's their maid and she knows all about it.

Julia's asked Douglas goodness knows how many times to keep their private affairs private and not to discuss them when Adelaide's around but it never does any good. When Douglas has been brooding on something it takes very little to ignite him and then he goes off in a firecracker fury. It makes no difference if Adelaide's there. There are times, she's quite sure, he wants Adelaide to hear.

'Do you think money grows on trees?' Douglas says. 'Haven't you any idea how much it costs to run dishwashers and washing machines and tumble dryers and what, by the way, has become of washboards and laundry done by hand and hung out to dry in the sun?'

He's not talking to Adelaide. Adelaide just happens to be there. Julia's the one he's talking to.

What does she think the wash lines behind the white wall in the back garden are for? Did he have them put up because he thinks they're aesthetically pleasing? He did not. Why does she think she has two hands?

'Show me your hands?' he says and Adelaide shakes her head, in that sad slow way a compassionate woman reserves for a person mentally impaired, and offers her hands up for inspection.

'For heaven's sake, Douglas,' Julia says. 'Is this really necessary?'

Adelaide says nothing at all. She's not in a position to. Adelaide is in Julia's debt. She owes her a favour.

Adelaide has a grandchild staying with her, a girl, aged six, in return for which Julia expects at least a greater show of willingness on Adelaide's part.

For this concession, Adelaide is willing enough to go through any reasonable charade this 'master' or 'madam' has resolved upon for that particular day. She knows them by now. When he's done his play-acting and she is flush-faced, glint-eyed and silent they will either stalk off in different directions or take their quarrel to some other part of the house.

11

Having played her part as a prop in their ongoing marital conflict she will be left to get on with her work and for a while after that they'll avoid her in the way one avoids that person who has seen far more than they should.

Adelaide doesn't mind. While they're in the middle of a quarrel, each of them desperately looking for new things to snipe at the other about, the question of her granddaughter will not be uppermost in their minds, but even in the midst of adversity Julia is diligent.

'It's definitely not a permanent arrangement,' Julia says. 'Just as long as you understand that.'

No matter what has happened in the interim Julia says this at least once a day just to make sure Adelaide is not so imprudent as to slip into complacency.

Julia has spelled it all out very clearly. One has to. If you allow this kind of thing on your property, you run the risk of opening a floodgate. Besides which, there are 'Conditions of Employment' now. Aside from a salary laid down by the Domestic Workers' Union, Adelaide's 'Conditions' include a room, a shower and a lavatory she's compelled to share with Gladstone when he's on the premises. There's no condition that allows for a six-year-old girl, with a fly-by-night mother.

Adelaide's daughter is an actress in soap opera, which doesn't mean she has quite made the 'big time' yet. If she was in England or America it would be very different and it would show in her pay packet but this is not England or America. It's dog eat dog for actresses these days and 'actress' is what Adelaide's daughter puts down under the heading 'profession' when she fills in her Unemployment Insurance Fund card. If, when you work, most of your paying work comes from the State broadcaster, as hers does, the pay isn't good but you have to start somewhere.

She does, though, have a part in a series that comes on in the prime slot right after the news. It seems to her, because the news has a certain sameness about it and is never entirely satisfactory, that when it's her turn to take over the screen she makes it shine with a special kind of radiance which the whole country depends upon.

In the townships her star quality is recognized. She knows this because people come over to talk to her or call out to her on the streets but it's not only in the townships she's known. In the kitchens and staff quarters of the more affluent areas the volume of the TV is turned up when 'soapie' time comes and when she appears on the screen people sit back in their chairs, they cluster around the television, they notice. They put their own lives on hold while they wait to see what is happening in that glamorous other world so very different from anything they know, which is meant to be paralleling their own.

In doesn't matter that in offscreen life she still has to make ends meet the same as everyone else does. These several years, in her multiple personalities in *Generations, Backstage, Isidingo – The Need*, she's no longer the single mother of a six-year-old daughter whose schedule is inclined to clash with her own and never mind what stalwart leftovers of the Struggle may tell you. This is the true place where freedom lies. This is the adoration of the masses. Here's where the power is, in this national addiction where, for a few minutes each evening, her turn comes around and she

13

shines like a light and everybody loves her and what can be so very wrong with that?

Adelaide's daughter has progressed in life and developed a taste for all the good things it has to offer. She doesn't wear overalls and a headscarf. She likes her clothes labelled and if she could wear the labels on the outside that would be just fine with her too. She knows where she's going and she's ready. Even before she's even really quite on the way there she already looks the part because one thing is certain, from where she is now there's no going back.

Adelaide's daughter has come a long way. She doesn't have to hold up her hands to be inspected by a crazy man playing games with his wife.

What does she think they're there for, asks Douglas, those twin pink-palm appendages stuck on the end of her arms? For drinking his tea and eating his bread? They all know she manages that well enough but if she wants to keep her job she'll have to do better than that.

None of which worries Julia the way it did once. She can switch herself off. She can switch Douglas off too. She can stand quite still and watch and listen while his voice buzzes through her head like a chain saw vibrating so hard it makes her teeth chatter, until it reaches a pitch that's quite perfect, when it's nothing at all but white noise.

Julia hasn't wasted her time in this marriage. There's one thing she's learned and it's this. The man you're about to divorce no longer has the power to upset you the way a husband once did.

Julia can look at Douglas now and think about him with a shoulder-shrug, the way Adelaide must do.

This is Mr M. This is his house. He's lord and master here. He can do as he pleases. He can say what he likes and who's there to stop him? He'll go as far as he can and then, just before it's too far, he'll turn it all around into a joke and pretend that's all it was in the first place.

'Can't you take a joke, Adelaide?' he'll say. 'Don't you want to be educated? You don't know what it costs to keep a place like this going. I know you don't know. That's why I'm telling you. It's no good looking to the "madam" to tell you. She wouldn't know. If she were the one earning the money she wouldn't be spending it so freely and you can take that look off your face. I'm not blaming you. I'm telling you, and the reason I'm telling you is because you're a sensible woman. You know what it is I'm saying.'

This is Douglas' way these days. At first Julia minded. When they were alone she'd argue back. She'd tell him if he had something he wanted to say to her, he should say it directly and while he was at it, he should stop picking on small things and say what it is that's actually on his mind. She knows very well whatever it is has nothing to do with the price of electricity, but he doesn't like it when she talks like this. Perhaps he's afraid she wants to talk about Kimmy. If only he knew. She can put a brave front on a great many things but not that, not yet, perhaps never.

He turns away, switches off and she gets nowhere at all. Everything goes on just as before until one day she simply stops doing it. She knows Douglas isn't going to change but it doesn't trouble her any more. That's the kind of thing of concern to a wife. There's really no place for it in the grand scheme of things of a woman about to divorce.

'If you've decided and there's no going back then why are you putting it off?' her friend Caroline says. 'Why don't you tell him and get it over and done with once and for all?'

But now she's made up her mind that awful sense of urgency that's been driving her for so long is no longer there. The outcome is inevitable. This leaves her free to do things in her own time and in her own time she will do what she has to. She knows that Caroline won't understand but how could she? Caroline is looking at things one way and Julia is looking at the same things but in another way altogether.

People say a bad marriage is like sitting in a bath waiting while the water gets cooler and cooler but sitting there anyway because you know how cold it's going to be when you eventually decide it's time to get out. Julia has been sitting in this bath for quite a long time now. She can endure the chill just a little while longer.

Her thoughts turn to Rosalie. How can they not? Rosalie, after all, once stood in this same place where she stands now but it was different for Rosalie. Everyone knows that. Douglas was mad with love for Rosalie when he married her and Rosalie was very many things in her day but she was never second best.

Anyone in the 'know' could have told you, if asked, that Douglas should never have married Rosalie. It was clear from the start there was only one way it could end and that was in disaster but even after all the things Rosalie did to him Douglas never once demanded divorce. When he eventually conceded that it was inevitable it was only because his mother put pressure on him.

'I can't compel you to do anything,' Alice Merchant said to her son. 'All I can do is "suggest" and what I suggest is that you realize this nonsensical farce has come to its end. All you can do now is have the papers drawn up and put a legal end to it once and for all. There's no need to make more of a fool of yourself than you already have.'

It's a hard thing to bear when your wife, with the honeymoon barely behind her, runs off with another man the way Rosalie did and even worse when that man is a Jew.

If anyone was to blame, and of course someone must be, then in Douglas' mother's opinion it must be the Rosenberg boy.

'She was restless, of course,' Alice had confided as much to Cuckoo Bannerman. 'I knew that but I thought things would work themselves out. The early days of a marriage are often like that.'

Cuckoo Bannerman, who had, herself, to deal with a very different and far easier kind of girl for a daughter-in-law in the person of Caroline, was not going to let her friend Alice off the hook quite so easily. It must, she said, be faced that some of the blame lay with Alice herself. The minute that foolish girl Douglas married latched onto young Rosenberg, Alice should have intervened.

She should have made it her business to have a word, to Douglas, to Rosalie herself if necessary. She should have put a stop to it before it even got started.

What happened in the end was that she'd left it too late. Rosalie had become like a desert dweller slaking her thirst in every kind of troublesome activity the Rosenberg boy chose to lead her into and the Rosenberg boy, they both knew, was up to his neck in politics. Where did Alice imagine it was likely to end up?

Their families were business people. It was no concern of theirs, never had been, who was scrabbling over control of the country. With them it was always 'business as usual' and their 'business' had never been politics. That was up to the Afrikaners and the blacks and to people like the Rosenbergs and that was where it ended. Someone should have made it abundantly clear to Rosalie that this was the case.

'I've never really been able to get through to her,' Alice said. 'That's the trouble.'

If Douglas had married Julia, which was what they expected, there would have been no need for a conversation like this, of the kind that has to take place with the sliding doors drawn closed so the servants can't hear.

There was nothing for anyone who came after Rosalie except leftovers and Julia knew what she was getting but she took it anyway, and the sad thing to remember now is how pleased she was and how grateful.

She can't imagine now how much she once used to worry about absconded Rosalie, whose departure Douglas had taken so badly. This too has passed. Resentment, she seems to recall, is a bit like dancing on thorns. It comes at you in small sharp jabs and embeds itself. It makes you bleed all right but not so copiously that anyone else would notice.

ROSALIE

If only she knew. Over all of these years, Rosalie has not given any of them more than a passing thought. She doesn't think about them for long months at a time and then something will nudge her into remembering and they blur through her mind for an instant, but they never linger long enough to take on any shape or form and then they're gone.

London is where Rosalie belongs now. In the top-floor flat in this fine three-storeyed house, the third in a short, curving, pastel-coloured crescent of houses. Duck Egg, Paris Grey, Ochre, Ink and Pollen. So pretty to look at and window boxes filled with hyacinth, pink and lilac and white, and brass-knockered front doors of Venetian Red and Brilliant Blue.

This is her place now. The almost still life she steps out into each day is her life. Even with her eyes closed she can see it.

The red-haired girl on the corner leans out of the street-level window to talk to her lover. Her words float over the steps that wind down to the locked front door of the basement flat below. (The Spanish woman with her beautiful luggage has gone back to Madrid where her husband, at short notice, will have to re-arrange his life to accommodate her.)

Dappled ivy creeps up the steps. It curls over the spiked railing that separates the girl from her lover and they stand there, fixed, drenched in pale light that pulls out the blue from the panes of stained glass that frame the window above.

The girl's laugh is infectious. Her lover (perhaps her still aspirant lover), slim-hipped, in jeans and a black leather jacket, is caught in her word-web. She, this girl, is quite wonderfully fresh leaning out of the window, enchanting to look at in an old-rose rib sweater with the silver glint of a belly button ring where it rides up too high.

How natural and uncomplicated it all seems to Rosalie. Why should she wish herself anywhere else? Why is it her London friends once said she'd never stick it out because she'd got too much involved in Africa and would never belong here again?

The cats know her here and that's a good sign, a sign of belonging. The red-collared tom who lives down the street has become her familiar. He waits for her at the corner, struts beside her for a step or two then detaches himself in that insouciant way that comes to cats naturally, and goes back on the prowl.

If there's to be an extension of life (my God! she hopes not), if she's ever recycled she'll come back as a cat. She'll come back as that cat. She will learn that same ease of detachment and this time she'll do it successfully.

Rosalie's flat has one big comfortable room at its heart, a room filled with colour, with rich rugs of complicated oriental design, with overstuffed pillows dotted here, there, all over the place, a table she works on and many shelves and tables of books. It overlooks the street on one side and on the other the patchwork of other people's gardens. On long summer evenings, when the light diffuses and the heat lifts up off the pavement stones, she can pull up her windows and in wafts the smell of honeysuckle, jasmine, verbena and evening primrose.

Once, a long time ago, she wrote to her mother about Paradise. That was when she'd been living in the so-called 'City of Gold' for almost a year, nearly all that time married to Douglas.

Johannesburg, in the first flirtation, lying in a summer drift of jacaranda with its roots safely planted in gold, is not really Africa at all. Everyone says this. Things go well here, people are happy, life is good and it's easy. Up here, on the Highveld, the air is clean and thin, it floats so light and easy into your lungs you need hardly bother with the business of breathing at all.

'People say this is Paradise,' wrote Rosalie to her mother, who lives in Bathampton. 'But we'll see about that.'

She thinks now that Paradise, after all that long search, lay a whole lot closer to home than she knew.

People said she'd hate coming back to the confines of London. She had the impression she was meant to long for the heat and the space and the brilliance of the

African light but she doesn't at all. People said no matter how hard she tried, she'd never fit in but that's another, very different kind of story. They warned that after the life she'd had, so extraordinary, and in such a tumultuous place, that so many people herded so tight together on such a small island would drive her demented but that too was wrong.

It's a paradox, she discovered quite quickly, just how easy it is to leave the mainstream behind, the cars and the buses; the streets clogged with people in perpetual motion and in two turns of a street find a quiet corner in just such a place. What could suit her better than somewhere exactly like this, where people have spent so much time and put such effort into smiling politely even as they withdraw from each other?

From time to time her neighbour, Silvie, who lives on the ground floor with her Senegalese lover, telephones and asks if she might come up for a coffee. There's milkmaid abundance about Silvie, who's an opera singer and looks exactly as you might imagine an opera singer to look. She comes up the stairs, sure-footed enough but she comes out of guilt. She thinks she owes Rosalie something because Rosalie is the only one in the house who never complains about the endless scales and fragments of song. The others, an osteoporotic psychoanalyst and a lapsed priest, are huffy about it and make sure she knows it. The current interchanges, such as they are, have become pretty icy which is why Silvie feels a sense of indebtedness to Rosalie, so absorbed in her own world that no one else has the power to bother her.

Rosalie, who's increasingly uninterested in the location of cups, filter jugs, sugar or the condition of the milk in her fridge, is passive about these visits. She's content to leave Silvie in the kitchen and let her get on with it. The Senegalese lover is a street performer. He does break dancing on the pavements outside Camden Lock market but not for ever. He's destined for higher things and there are auditions in the offing.

This is what Silvie says and she says other things too.

A strange young man is coming and going from the lapsed priest's flat. He comes on a Piaggio with learner plates affixed at the back and a sticker on the side pleading for Exmoor, which is apparently endangered.

Rosalie, with her coffee from Fortnum's, high-pedigreed in its day but murky as a mill pond now and long past its sell-by date, listens intently but hears only in snatches.

The psychoanalyst appears not to sleep. She walks in the night and Silvie can hear every squeak of the floorboards but does she complain? Of course, she does not. A situation like theirs calls for high degrees of tolerance. This is what she tells her Senegalese lover, naked, on top of the kitchen ladder, with the ceiling in view and a broom handle in his hand.

'He could pound on the ceiling as hard as he liked,' Silvie says. 'It wouldn't help. In fact, it would only make things worse. All she'd do is pretend not to hear and then take it out on us in some other way.'

How beautiful they must be together, Rosalie thinks, milk white Silvie and her chocolate man to whom the night comes as a gift, sent special delivery and not as a torment.

MOTHERS

Julia is becoming more and more like her mother, the bridge player, who keeps her mouth shut but even so has no trouble at all making her opinions known. This is something Douglas has been noticing lately. Isn't the accepted wisdom that you take a good look at a girl's mother before you marry her so you know in advance what you're going to end up with? Douglas never knew Rosalie's mother.

'Who are her people?' was the first thing his own mother demanded to know.

Young men can be so easily misled and sexual attraction, if not firmly directed, is such a dangerous thing.

He didn't know, didn't care. He thought then there was a lifetime for all that kind of thing.

'We are her people,' he said rather grandly. 'At least, we are now.'

But Douglas, who should have known better, should have known he would not be the man to decide this. His mother would see to all that.

He couldn't have cared if Rosalie's mother turned out to be an axe murderer with a prison record twelve miles long but he knew Julia's mother all right and so did his mother.

You would have expected Julia's mother to harbour some resentment against Rosalie, the rank outsider who ran off with the prize, but if she did, she didn't show it. No one knew better than Julia's mother that thing called 'the luck of the draw'.

She would say nothing to poor Alice, who'd so badly wanted 'someone more like ourselves' for her Douglas, who, despite being such a capable woman, managed to be the one who got landed, take it or leave it, with the girl who caused all the trouble.

In Julia's mother's opinion, which she confided to no one, the jury was still out on the question of which of the girls drew the luckiest card. Rosalie who'd married Douglas or Julia who hadn't, or at least not quite yet and only time would tell that.

Rosalie met Douglas' friends. Caroline, in those days newly married to Gus Bannerman, who cut such a fine figure on the polo field out at Inanda. 'Old Johannesburg money.' It was tagged onto his name like a title.

She met Julia who, Douglas told her offhandedly, had 'been around' his entire life and Julia's brother who was thinking of throwing in his lot with Douglas and might bring some money into the business.

Rosalie met Douglas' mother, her new mother-in-law,

poor Alice Merchant, the one who'd been presented with a *fait accompli*. Rosalie had no idea what to call her. Nothing seemed to fit and as she wasn't invited to call her anything, for the short duration of her marriage she called her nothing at all.

Rosalie put aside the hiking boots that had taken her right across Africa for that meeting. She wore sandals specially bought for the occasion but such humble offerings carried no weight with Alice. Alice herself was shod in beautiful shoes fashioned from calf leather hand-made by a conspicuously handsome Italian cobbler who'd come out as a prisoner during the war and decided to stay.

'Even in this age of jet travel we're still a very long way away from England.'

These are the first words Douglas' mother speaks to Rosalie and it's abundantly clear she does not speak simply in terms of geography. This is all she says for quite a long time and as none of them knows quite what to say next, no one says anything.

In that lengthy silence sits Alice, neat and totally self-sufficient, making it perfectly obvious that what she's busy doing is sizing up the exact enormity of this problem her son has seen fit to land her with.

A maid brings tea and biscuits and Douglas' mother is firmly in charge. She pours tea. She offers milk. She offers lemon slices. She hands around biscuits, which nobody takes. There are napkins available, glassy with starch. She rings for the maid and asks for additional hot water.

'You can make a good life here if you set your mind to it,' she says. 'There are nice places to go, the people

26

are charming and as Douglas' wife you wouldn't have to start from scratch. You'd never think it was Africa.'

Rosalie has by this time seen Africa. Her hiking boots alone will attest to this. She has come overland and seen for herself those all too apparent ills that gnaw at its heart but she has never seen anything quite like Alice Merchant before.

Rosalie's opinion after that meeting is that here, they all know each other rather too well. She doesn't think it's a good thing. Perhaps they are too far away, too cut off from the rest of the world. That's what makes them so self-absorbed. Perhaps someone might open some metaphorical window and let in a great gust of fresh air. Rosalie's feeling is that it's needed and needed quite badly.

'I suppose there just aren't enough of us to go round,' Douglas says. 'You have to make do with what's up on offer I'm afraid. If you look at the population figures, you'll see for yourself.'

It's the Whites he's talking about, of course. But this, she realizes by this time, is something that always goes without saying.

None of this would need to be explained to Julia. Her problems, when they come, will come from another, very different direction altogether.

Julia came ready-made into a world where she already knew anyone who was ever likely to be of any importance to her, and understood very well the way it all worked.

Douglas had always been 'one of the family' even before eventually, belatedly, he married her and the

27

occasion not quite what any of them had hoped it might be.

Which is not to say that Douglas' mother did not do her best.

Julia's mother was involved too. She had to be. She was after all the mother of the prospective bride and had, at least, to be consulted. But a woman who looks first to the dates of upcoming bridge tournaments jotted down in her diary is not the kind of woman to give the sort of wedding Alice Merchant had in mind for her son.

Douglas marrying Julia at last was an 'inevitable adjustment'. It was the right thing to do. The one thing they could all comfort themselves with was that at last it was happening.

This was how Cuckoo Bannerman put it to Alice Merchant. It was, Alice knew, her way of trying to make things better and what else was there to be said? The whole sorry business of the first marriage was her son's fault. There was no consultation with her. No one else could be blamed.

So, Alice kept her chagrin to herself and got on with the job even though she knew very well that no matter how hard you might work at it a second wedding can never be quite the same as the first wedding was.

Her old friend, Cuckoo Bannerman, who knew better than most how these things could best be 'managed', offered to help her. Her contribution was the use of her house, 'Stonehenge', the famous old Bannerman mansion up on the ridge.

'Isn't that wonderful?' said Douglas' mother to Julia's.

Julia's mother, when left to herself, stared down at

her cards with the eye of experience and was happy enough to leave it to them. Julia, in a dress of pink silk faille, was married. Caroline was there, very much the new younger wife anxious to prove herself and Gus in his prime, before that terrible accident, in those days when people were still anxious to seek him out to ask for a few words in private, which meant a favour.

Around Julia's neck were her grandmother's pearls and pearl earrings to match. In her hands was a blush of pink rosebuds. There was a mountainous wedding cake swagged with iced blossoms and Dan Hill's dance band dressed in blue tuxedos with silver lapels.

The rumour was that Johannesburg people who weren't invited to the wedding went to their beach houses. They disappeared to the Berg. They lay low by the trout streams in their fishermen's huts, so that afterwards they could look at each other and say, in truth, that they were out of town on that day and couldn't possibly have made it, much as they might have liked to have been there.

It wasn't being left off the list for Julia's wedding that mattered so much. What was important was the invitation to the Bannerman house.

An invitation to the Bannerman house that didn't mean money up front for a fundraiser, for literacy, for a mobile dispensary for sick township animals, for prevention of violence against women, was a trophy not to be sniffed at.

Cuckoo Bannerman knew this and so did Alice.

Even so, the wedding day was a day with a peculiar feel about it and then the 'feel' lived up to its promise, the sky darkened and the hail came down. It flattened the garden, it pitted the bodywork of the cars in the driveway which were so closely packed there was no time and not enough warning to move them elsewhere. Down it came, clattering on the paving, sending guests running for the safety of the terrace and the famous Summer Hall, furnished like a room, that stood open to the garden but was only ever used when the weather was fine.

There they stood rain-soaked like survivors of a shipwreck, men in black ties and women in evening gowns with hems muddied and shoes ruined and the music all but drowned out by the terrible clatter.

Afterwards it was the hail everyone remembered and Alice, magnificent in mauve, who, with Cuckoo's help, had so nearly pulled off a 'coup', made light of it, but she minded.

DIVORCING DOUGLAS

It is daybreak, first light, and Douglas, alone in the marital bed, is peacefully sleeping. Julia stands barefoot, on the veranda, the tiles under her feet still warm from the previous day's baking. They smell of clay, as if in the night they remembered where they came from, as if the sun teased them into remembering the kiln in which they were baked.

You can see the cascade of Julia's hair and the outline of her body, still slender, draped in a silk dressing gown found years ago on a visit to England, tucked away at the end of a rail in an Oxfam shop.

Her body records certain events. In her own eyes, in the eyes of a dispassionate outsider, it's clear she's known something of life. Her body will tell all the obvious things. Her appendix is gone, somewhere along the way her tonsils were removed, at some point she broke an arm and at some other point she bore a child.

The things her body can't tell are how good the raspberry jelly was slipping down the place where the tonsils were once rooted. It can't say what a trophy the plaster cast was, signed all over with messages from her friends. Her body can't tell the way Julia took to motherhood with a tenacity that might have seemed rather alarming if anyone cared to examine it too closely.

Julia is made for motherhood. Everyone says so. Once she sets her mind to it Julia will be a wonderful mother. She will love, support and fulfil her responsibility toward her child, no questions asked. Julia's child will be the luckiest child imaginable. Who could wish for a finer start in life than having the good fortune to have Julia for a mother?

In the end this is not the way things turned out.

Julia's considered that perhaps she's not, after all, the stuff good mothers are made of. She's made every mistake in the book and then added one or two more, just for good measure, and made them peculiarly her own.

She never did learn the knack of knowing where her skin ended and Kimmy's began. Isn't this what you're meant to do, or do they only tell you this later, once the damage has already been done? She's intruded. She's intervened and she's interfered. Somewhere along the way she's learned to make herself immune to unhappy faces, tears, anger, curses and ultimately rejection.

There's never been any doubt about 'Who's in charge' or 'Who's right'. That's Julia's job, it's the job she asked for and all things considered, in her own way, she's done it terribly well but there was a price tag attached and in the end they all paid for it.

Kimmy is who she is. She's turned out the way she has. Her track record isn't good. Julia can't be proud of her, which is not a nice thing. What's even worse is that she can't be particularly proud of herself.

There is some light here at least although it's not very bright. The truth is that once you've managed with such conspicuous success to estrange yourself from your daughter any other breaking of bonds becomes easier to do.

Divorcing Douglas can be nothing compared with that moment when she knew she must let go of Kimmy.

Julia hasn't told her mother about the divorce. That moment will come and when it does, contrary to what Douglas may think, her mother will not derive any particular pleasure from saying 'I told you so'.

In fact, in reality, her mother didn't give her any forewarning at all, thinking the whole thing self-evident. In her mother's opinion, which she did not express to Julia, marriage as an institution is no safe place for a bug-eyed girl who's happy enough to grab anything she can lay her hands on with no eye for quality at all.

Marriage has to be forged from far hardier base materials if it's to work. At least it must if your aim is survival. Julia's mother knows this perfectly well but what point was there in passing it on? Julia's mother knew it was a discovery Julia would have to make for herself.

In their shared bedroom, on his side of the bed lies Douglas half-asleep, half-awake in that safe, transitional world where anything's possible. He dreams of lamb sizzling on a not-too-clean spit. The smell enters his dream, the thick smell of lamb juice, of lemon, of garlic, of oregano and his nostrils flare slightly at the familiarity of it and the promise it offers.

Douglas, protected by sleep, not yet adrift in the hard, waking world, safe from Julia, may lie in his bed and dream as he pleases.

Today is Saturday and Douglas plays golf. At least this is what he tells Julia.

In due course he will wake, shower, drink a glass of fruit juice, eat a slice of whole-wheat toast, dress in golf shorts and shirt, take his golf bag down from its place in the garage. Today, he will go out of the house and with him will go the man smell of after-shave, lemons and a certain salty manliness, which is, or so Julia is persuaded, what keeps him attractive to women.

Douglas is still attractive to women. Her friends can't resist telling Julia so but he's fishing in the wrong end of the pond. Everyone knows it and much younger women are his speciality these days.

It's nothing new, a phase, sometimes shaming but it can be endured. It's certainly not the end of the world. These are the days when men are overly attentive to waitresses young enough to be their daughters and to the pretty girls down at the gym, the 'personal trainers' who, for a price, will put them through their paces and keep them in shape.

It's simply another time of their lives and there are plenty of other women who have the same problem. They make jokes about these men of theirs who simper at waitresses and puff and pant and sweat copiously trying to keep up with their bouncy young 'trainers' but there's not very much they can do about it.

The young women themselves are not all that important. For the most part they never stay long. They're there, then they're gone. There's always someone else scenting a comfort zone and an easy ticket to the good life who's willing enough to step into their shoes. There was a time when Julia lost sleep over this but not any more. These girls are like any other fixture. If you live with it long enough, your life goes around it so that eventually you don't really notice it at all. Not unless someone is silly enough to move it so it gets right in your way and who would be foolish enough to do such a thing when the old established life is so easy? Some men might, but not Douglas.

There was a time when all this seemed important but not any more.

Julia has no more secret grudges, against Rosalie or anyone else. That time is past, which is not to say that the time for secrets has gone altogether. Julia's secrets of the present are far more interesting than the past ever was and multiplying at a rate that sometimes alarms even her.

These are the things she's thinking about, standing barefoot on the terrace, enjoying the last of the night breeze, waiting for morning to come and then the light in Adelaide's room comes on. It spills out across the back lawn and Julia is still as a statue, complete in herself, belonging only to herself, for the last time that day.

Soon, Douglas will wake. The digital clock at the bedside will show five-thirty. Precisely at six,

Adelaide will step from her room. Her overall, her apron, her headscarf, her person smelling of Sunlight soap and some other, earthier undertone, and her arm will stretch out and the light in the room will be switched off. There's no need for it now, in the summer, and Douglas will have one thing less to complain about.

JULIA

There's something nobody knows about Julia, not even Caroline. She's been seeing a psychoanalyst. She decided to do it after Kimmy left. She has in the past tried for marriage guidance counselling but Douglas refused.

'Get yourself sorted out first,' he said. 'If you manage that then come back and talk to me again and maybe we can do business.'

Douglas doesn't believe in outside help. She learnt that the hard way with Kimmy but she perseveres. She still goes to 'Tough Love'. On Tuesday evenings she goes to the meetings to talk to other parents with problems similar to her own.

She goes along by herself and they come in pairs, seeking comfort, some of them holding hands trustingly, like young lovers. She slides in at the back of the hall, hoping that no one will turn up who knows her and knows why she's there.

'I don't know why you keep it up,' Douglas says. 'You may not believe it but Kimmy's doing just fine.'

Through everything that's happened Douglas has refused to break contact with Kimmy and Julia resents him for that. She wants solidarity. She wants inclusion but as it's she, herself, who has elected to stay out in the cold, there's not very much she can do about it.

'Your idea of "fine" and mine probably don't bear much relation to each other,' Julia says. 'Everything Kimmy's done, everything she ever did was always perfectly "fine" as far as you're concerned. As it happens, I feel differently.'

'Well, you go then,' Douglas says. 'I've told you a hundred times that Kimmy's fine, Kimmy's happy. All she ever wanted to be was just an ordinary girl and that's what she is now.'

'Is her life what you'd call ordinary?' Julia says. 'I don't think so.'

'She'll be all right if you leave her to get on with things,' Douglas says. 'She's like me. She's not perfect. Have you ever thought that maybe, just maybe you're the one who's the problem? Perhaps your expectations need to be adjusted. Have you ever thought about that?'

She thinks of it all the time. She thinks of it when she's worn out with thinking and doesn't want to think of anything at all. If things were only better between them, if she knew how to tell him, she'd tell him and it would be the greatest relief.

At some time in their relationship while she wasn't watching Douglas got older. His face, she sees, has become florid, his jowls more pronounced. His neck has thickened and sits closer to his shoulders and when he thinks himself unobserved his shoulders slump slightly.

Julia has passed on every word that he says to her analyst.

'I don't want my daughter to be perfect,' she says. 'I just want her to be happy and have what I consider a normal life. She doesn't have that now. She's living in some kind of commune in Melville. I've told her that when she's cleaned up her act and I'm satisfied she has she can come home. She's made it quite clear that's not what she wants. She goes her own way now. Does what she likes. It's just so typical of Kimmy.'

It seems to Julia that this must be a story her analyst has heard times without number but at the current charge-out rates she thinks she has at least bought the right to have her say and get it out on the table. If she has nothing different or better to offer than anyone else she makes no apology. At least her pain is her own; she can vouch for that and if she needs to pay someone to listen to her then that's what she'll do.

If you put your ear to the ground and could tune in to what those other women, those women like Julia, talk about in the shopping malls, the coffee shops and the hairdresser's, the stories you hear will not be so different. This is, after all, the bittersweet background music to life in this place where husbands won't toe the line and demanding children think adults live only to serve.

All Julia wants to be is the best she can be. She doesn't say perfect. That's Douglas' word. What Julia wants, her analyst says so, is something that falls short of actual perfection; what she wants is to be appreciated and above all to be loved.

A nervous tic, says her analyst. That's how she should look at it. The whole construct of her life is no more than a nervous tic that drives her onward, ever onward, seeking these goals that remain forever elusive.

She, for it is a 'she' (Julia has never been able to entrust her real, true, innermost feelings to a man), has a further suggestion as well. She says she suspects that Julia has been playing the role of 'Julia' for such a long time now that somewhere along the way, she has lost her true self.

'Perhaps you might loosen up a little and try and be a little less hard on yourself,' her analyst says. 'You might even offer to meet your daughter halfway? Have you thought of it?'

'Sometimes,' says Julia but from where she is now even halfway seems a long way to go.

KIMMY

Kimmy has nightmares. She dreams she is being sent back to her mother's house. She doesn't want to go. There's a horrible sick kind of feeling in the pit of her stomach. She knows she's dreaming. It must be a dream. In some deep down part of her, her waking self has already begun to offer comfort in much the same way she always comforted herself when she was a child.

'You'll wake up in a minute. It can't go on for much longer. It's only a dream.'

The trouble is, she can't wake up.

A terrible feeling of foreboding takes hold of her. It's a feeling so strong it tugs her from even the deepest recesses of sleep and pulls her back from that very same place in which at one time, when she was a very small child, she used to curl up and hide to seek comfort.

No matter how hard she tries she can't wake herself up.

Her dream feet move her forward towards her mother's house. She can see the house clearly. It stands all alone, no house to its left, no house to its right. It's dreamtime and everything else has simply melted away. All that remains is this one house and everything inside her urges her to turn back before it's too late but she can't.

'Pleasantville', that's how Kimmy tried to joke off the house in that time she still lived there, that wild time when she was making her way through the pills and the raves, waking up in a pile of warm bodies on strange beds in places that were never the same.

She remembers those wake-ups and having each morning to reassemble the room, slowly, piece by piece, like a jigsaw until it made sense.

'What about your folks?' the other kids sometimes say.

'No problem,' says Kimmy even though that isn't true. 'My folks live in "Pleasantville". Didn't you know? Everything there is just perfect. In fact, it must be just about the coolest place in town.'

At her mother's dream house the colours are deeper and darker than anything real is. You can see that at once. At the instant the gate slides open to let you in you can see this is not a good place. It's a bad trip, the worst kind. You can tell that just by looking at the colours.

Here, every petal on every flower in the garden is colour coded, unblemished and stays perfectly still in its place. The green of the trees, of the lawn, of the shrubbery is graveyard green, almost black. The pool is black. The stone girl with her feet sunk among waxy immobile lilies is too frightened to move.

Kimmy doesn't want to go into the house. Birds chirp her along as if to say 'don't be silly' but she thinks they are wind-up birds and not real. This is a beautiful house, a picture book house. We are all lucky to live in a place like this. Can't you see for yourself what a beautiful place this is?

Kimmy's parents fight all the time. She hates it but she hates it even more when they don't fight. When they don't fight her heart pounds, it's hard to breathe and her mouth is dry. She sits at the work desk in her room. She lies on her bed. She takes her seat at the dining room table where, most nights, her father's place is conspicuously empty.

She doesn't think it was always like this. She isn't quite sure. She can't remember. It was too long ago. She can remember something though. The door to her parents' bedroom stands open. Her father is singing opera loud in the shower. 'Just listen to that,' her mother says. 'Have you ever in your life heard anything so awful?' When she shakes her head her mother's hair is like gold with lights caught up in it and she laughs in a very nice way and Kimmy in those days used to laugh with her.

Then it was not like that any more. It was different.

For a long time now she's had to listen to the rise and fall of their voices behind the closed door of their bedroom. It made her afraid of the night, which was something she'd never been. She learned then that the night changes things but if she could only make it through she knew it would all be different and better in the morning.

In the morning her mother will be cheerful and smiling. Her breakfast will be on the table. Her mother will say her father's already gone. He had to leave early. Her mother will ask about homework and look in her diary to work out the day and see who's on lift club.

Her mother will be herself again and the woman of the night will be gone.

She doesn't know what happens in other people's houses. For all she knows it's the same everywhere but something inside her tells her it's not the kind of thing you can ask.

'If there's anything you're not quite sure of, darling, anything at all you want to know, all you have to do is ask. You must never be afraid to ask. Asking is very important because that's how we learn things.'

Julia is determined that Kimmy will be a child with an enquiring mind, unafraid to seek satisfaction, but Julia's encouragement, her exhortations come too late.

Kimmy already knows there are some things you can't ask. How can you ask any child, any adult, your own parents, if in other people's houses parents turn into roaring monsters during the night and then turn back into themselves again the next morning?

Kimmy becomes a bed-wetter. She doesn't want her mother to know. She is ten years old. She thinks she can dry the wet bits with a hairdryer but they're too big and too soggy for that. It's very quiet at night where they live. At least it is once the hissing and shouting stops. Her mother may hear the hairdryer. That's what worries Kimmy but she can't very well simply leave it. Her mother will walk into the room and there'll be the smell.

Kimmy pulls the sheets from the bed and takes them as quietly as she can to the washing machine in the laundry and forces them in. She knows that in the morning the maid will find them and know what she's done but if the maid just pays attention to her work and couldn't really care what goes on around her, like her father says they all do, perhaps the maid will not tell.

She knows even as she thinks it that this is not going to work. Whatever she does to hide it, her mother is bound to find out in the end. Her mother always finds out everything.

'It's all right, old girl,' says her Dad when it happens. 'It's just a little accident, that's all. It's not the end of the world.'

'It's not "all right",' says her mother. 'It's very far from all right. She's far too old for this kind of thing. Can you imagine if we'd sent her to boarding school? Can you just imagine how dreadfully they'd have teased her for being such a baby? Her life would have been an absolute misery. Thank God we decided to keep her a day girl.'

Kimmy tries not to sleep. Half sleep is better because then you know when you have to pee and are not so asleep you can't make yourself get up and go to the lavatory but half sleep has its own problems. You can't hide in half sleep. That means she'll be awake when her father comes home and finds the dining room light still on, shining down on the place setting for one while the dinner, shrivelled to nothing, cringes under the cover on the hot tray.

She tries not to drink anything.

'You must drink lots of water.' This is her mother's dictum. 'Human beings are made up mainly of water, you know. You should drink gallons of water. It's very good for you. It'll give you the most wonderful skin.'

Her mother has wonderful skin but it blotches the livid dark rose colour of a birthmark when she gets angry.

Kimmy sips at her water glass. When her mother gets up from the table because something in the kitchen is not satisfactory, or the 'maid' hasn't answered the bell quickly enough or to give an instruction that the 'master's' dinner must be left on the hot tray, Kimmy pours her water into the flower vase.

She wakes up in the night with a tight knot in her stomach and her tongue cleaving to the roof of her mouth. Her eyes scratch. The door of her parents' room is slightly ajar. All is quiet except for the familiar night noises. She still pees in her bed.

Her father gives her a night-light. It's beautiful. It has a cavalcade of bright coloured fish that swim endlessly past.

'Cheer things up a bit,' he says and he plugs it in and gets it going for a test run and sits on her bed beside her and puts his arm round her shoulders and watches it for a while and says: 'It's OK, old girl. Nothing to look so down-in-the-mouth about. Not the end of the world.'

She doesn't know if her father doesn't like the dark either. She knows he doesn't like not having company. On those days when he comes straight home after work the first thing he shouts when he comes through the door is: 'Hello! Anyone home?'

If her mother is out shopping, or having coffee with Caroline or doing her turn behind the counter down at the thrift shop, he'll go to the kitchen and ask the maid if the 'madam' is home.

'No, master,' the maid says. 'But Miss Kimmy's here. She's in her room.'

It's always the same. Kimmy, in her part of the house, which is only a family room away from the kitchen, can hear it. She can sit still as a statue and mouth the words silently. Is the madam here, no master but Miss Kimmy's here, she's in her room.

She hates it. No one talks like this, not any more, except her parents. No wonder they can't keep a maid and when one leaves the next one in the line is always an old woman who will still 'master' and 'madam' them. If embarrassment can kill, then Kimmy is destined to die of it and she will die gladly. How can she ask her school friends to the house? What will happen if one of her parents is there and they hear how they carry on and tell the whole school?

She's fed up with the maids too. 'Call me Kimmy,' she says. 'If I call you Patience/Grace/Irene, why don't you call me Kimmy?'

They won't and her mother doesn't like it that she even asked them.

'It's not fair,' her mother has told her. 'It's nice that you try to make friends with them but they're not your friends. Not really and anyway, they have friends of their own.'

Her mother doesn't make an issue about this but Kimmy knows. In the matters of her own house Kimmy's mother knows when she has to intervene and

47

when she can safely leave matters to take their own course.

Kimmy spends a lot of time with her mother although she doesn't know if she'd recognize her voice without the drone of the car engine behind it. Kimmy can go nowhere unless her mother takes her and fetches her and Kimmy's life, her dance classes, swimming practice, tennis lessons, is full.

'I don't know if you realize exactly how lucky you are,' her mother says. 'It seems to me sometimes that you take things too much for granted. Don't you know how many other girls there are who can only dream of having a life even remotely as privileged as yours is?'

Kimmy doubts that.

The school counsellor has spoken to Kimmy's mother about Kimmy.

'I have to bring it to your attention, Mrs Merchant,' she says. 'If I didn't I wouldn't be doing my job. Here it's not just the academic results that are important. It's the whole child we're concerned about.'

Except at Kimmy's school there are no 'children'. Life is short and fast and some phases have to be gone through at a gallop. At Kimmy's school from the age of ten girls are already 'young ladies' and referred to as such, as if their life-path can be set as easily as that.

The problem, the counsellor says, is with 'socialization'. Kimmy isn't nearly as interested as she should be in developing friendships. It's something that must be looked into. One of the most important life skills is being able to get along with others. Kimmy lives too much in a world of her own.

'It's hardly surprising,' Julia says. 'She is, after all, an only child.'

'She's not the only only child in our school,' the counsellor says very gently and Julia, the blusher, feeling an implied reprimand as if it was the whip of a lash, blotches crimson.

'I'll speak to her,' Julia says.

'Perhaps you might like to get her into some kind of outside counselling?' says the counsellor but Julia says 'no'.

'In our home we deal with things in our own way,' says Julia, rising. 'Thank you for your concern and your interest.'

Kimmy's parents fight about Kimmy.

'I've got a good mind to pack up and leave you to your women and take Kimmy with me,' says Kimmy's Mum to her Dad.

'The door's open,' says Douglas. 'You're free to come and go as you please but Kimmy's not going anywhere. She stays here with me.'

Kimmy has worked it all out. The main quarrel is about money. That's what gets them going fastest. How hard her father works making it. How quickly her mother runs through it.

'He wouldn't dare say a word about it,' her mother says to her best friend, Caroline. 'I'd hate to know how much his little bits on the side cost him. Plenty, I should think, and how much of a fool does he take me for? Am I supposed to be actually shopping at the thrift shop while he's splashing money around giving his women the time of their lives?'

Her father's women are what come next on the 'fight

list' that Kimmy's made up. The ones that keep him away from the dinner table and out so late at night.

'Pay no attention to Mum,' her father says after the fight's gone this way. 'It's a work thing and sometimes I have to work very late, that's all. The rest of it's in her head but you know that, don't you? You're not as silly as Mum is and don't you worry about that either. She'll get over it. You'll see.'

She knows very well she'll 'see' nothing at all and her father's women stay on her list. Those women she's not supposed to know anything about.

Then there's Kimmy. The way she's worked it out she comes third.

'It's hard to be a single parent,' her mother says in that light, bright voice of hers in front of guests, in front of Kimmy, in front of Douglas. 'I've always felt that a child really does need two parents. A girl needs a father but Douglas is always so busy, of course. We all know that.'

There'll be a fight about that too but that will come afterwards, after the guests have left, or when they're on their way home in the car from an evening at someone else's house.

'It's not about you, sweetheart,' her father always says about this one. 'It's about something else altogether. You know how Mum is.'

'Yes,' Kimmy says. 'I know how Mum is.'

Kimmy has begun taking things. Small things at first, a peanut and raisin health bar from one of the girls at school. It's amazing to her how much bewilderment this can cause. One minute it was there, the next minute gone and the evidence eaten.

'Sorry,' says Kimmy, so rarely asked about anything, when asked about this. 'I don't know anything about it.'

It's such a small thing. What comes in its wake is much larger. There surges up inside Kimmy the incredible power of pulling it off.

It's easy to steal small things from the market vendors, especially things she could easily pay for if she wanted. There are no electronic scans at the market and the last thing Kimmy, in her school uniform, in her pretty designer street clothes, looks like is a thief and there's a sense of satisfaction in that as well.

While the stallholders watch the black kids like hawks certain of their prey, just waiting to swoop, Kimmy slides what she wants into a pocket. She can slip something into a book bag with a sleight of hand that would make the magician David Copperfield proud, even though she cannot yet make whole aircraft disappear the way he did on television. Who at her house is interested in a hoard of cheap trifles that are the kinds of thing all the kids like these days? Any one of which could be Kimmy's just for the asking.

The watch is a mistake. She doesn't know why she did that but even so the store detective isn't totally unsympathetic. She doesn't call in the police. She sends for her mother.

'Next time you won't be so lucky,' Julia says.

'There won't be a next time, will there, old girl?' says her Dad but he's wrong.

* * *

The next time the probation officer explains it to them. She's a nice enough woman, wearied out with children of privilege like Kimmy and her well-dressed disbelieving parents who always thought there was one set of problems for themselves and one set for the 'others'.

There's the juvenile court, the probation officer, the Head Teacher who regretfully must issue a 'final warning' and give notice that if such behaviour persists there will, regretfully, no longer be a place for her at the school. These are the things that mount up one on top of the other and eventually send Julia to 'Tough Love'.

'If you think I'm going with you, you can put it right out of your mind,' Douglas says. 'I'm not going anywhere and that's final.'

'Yes, you are,' says Julia. 'Just for once in our married life, you are actually going to support me on something.'

'It's a phase,' Douglas says. 'She's looking for attention, that's all.'

'Yes, she is,' says Julia, who knows things for what they are when she sees them. 'She's had all the attention she could possibly want from me. It's a terrible thing to have to do something so drastic to get noticed by you.'

'That's not fair,' Douglas says but Julia is not in a mood to be fair.

'Where were you when the call from the police station came?'

'Come on, Jules,' Douglas says. 'That's got nothing to do with this.'

'It's got absolutely everything to do with this,' Julia says.

Julia has been waiting for Douglas to come home. Kimmy has been waiting too.

'You're not going to go into your room and close the door in my face,' Julia says. 'Not this time. If you're old enough to go out thieving and have me called to a police station to talk you out of trouble, you're old enough to sit up with me and wait for your father to come home.'

Julia's had two whiskys one after another in rapid succession. It's not Julia's way. Julia, in fact, drinks hardly at all. When she does accept a drink she ices it down, waters it down, lingers over it until by the time she's finished with it, it can almost certainly be officially classed as a non-alcoholic beverage.

But not tonight.

'It may be a long wait,' Julia says. 'I'm sick and tired of keeping that to myself as well. Your father, in case you hadn't noticed, isn't too keen on what other people call "home life".'

Kimmy feels sick. When she was very small, when it first began, she used to put her hands over her ears to shut the sounds out. She would like to do it now but she can't.

Then suddenly, without warning, Julia gets to her feet.

'I will not wait,' she says. Not to Kimmy, not to herself, not to anyone in particular. 'I will not wait one second longer. I simply refuse.'

She slams her glass down, goes to the telephone and opens the directory that lies beside it. She lifts the receiver and dials a number.

Kimmy, still in her school uniform, disgrace upon disgrace, taken to the police station in the uniform of such a well-known school where all the girls are 'young ladies'. This will certainly count against her when the Head Teacher hears about it.

'Gillian?' says Julia into the telephone mouthpiece. 'This is Julia Merchant. I know Douglas is there.' There's a pause. 'Don't even bother to deny it. Just tell him, if he's interested, that I've just been to bail his daughter out at the police station and just before the whole of Johannesburg hears about it, I would like him, just once, if it's not too much trouble, to be here when he's needed.'

It is here, or very close to this point, that the Tuesday meetings begin and Douglas, out of shame, out of guilt, goes along with his stone-faced wife.

'It's just her way, sweetheart,' is what he says to Kimmy. 'It's not the end of the world. Just be a good girl. Do what I do, lay low for a while and she'll get over it.'

If he would listen to her, Kimmy could have told him that 'she' won't 'get over it'. Not this time.

Julia is back in control. That's what 'Tough Love' does for you. The days of non-helping rescuing love are over. From now on Kimmy can make as many mistakes as she likes just as long as she understands she must bear the consequences.

'I will never stop loving or caring for you,' is what Julia tells her. 'But what I'm going to do from now on is stop shielding you from things. From now on whether you like it or not, you're going to learn that

54

rules apply to you too. If you choose not to stick by them, then you must pay the price.'

'Come on, Jules,' says her father. 'That's enough.'

'Yes,' says Julia, 'it is enough. It was enough a long time ago.'

This is where Kimmy finds herself. In that same place she always sticks fast. Right in the middle between her mother and father who are locked so securely in their long-term battle that neither of them really has half as much time for her as they imagine they do.

This is Kimmy back where she started. This is the same place the nightmare always begins.

DOUGLAS

The name of Douglas' building business is Merchant and Merriman. There's not a Radebe or a Dlala or a Zwane in sight and that won't do these days. All it shows is visible resistance to transformation. All it means is that there's someone who isn't trying hard enough. These names and names like them are something that needs to be seen on the letterhead. They're a presence that should be apparent at site meetings, at board meetings and in a company's private box at the rugby.

His friends at 'Old Eds' say it's time to 'black up'.

'You should have made old Gladstone your Chairman,' they say. 'He certainly looks the part. He's been with you forever. Much better than pulling someone in from a recruitment service.'

He asks if they know that Gladstone's barely literate.

'So what?' they say. 'So are you most of the time and

isn't it just what you need in an MD or even a CEO? The last thing you want is someone who actually writes the Chairman's Report or can read the financial statements.'

Everyone's doing it. It won't kill him to keep a sense of humour and do the same. If he can't find the real thing he can probably get away with a 'token'. It'll cost him a few bob and a company car but that's the way things are going these days, it's worth the investment and why kick against it when eventually he'll have to buy in because there's simply no choice?

Douglas says he hasn't done badly so far. As far as he knows, under the new Constitution you're still entitled to run your business in the way you think best. When the Department of Labour come knocking at his door to ask why he hasn't replaced himself with a black managing director he'll deal with the matter and do it in his own way. Until then it's Merchant and Merriman. That's what it was named when the company was incorporated and that's how it'll stay.

There's a building in Didata Park with that name on it. Even when business isn't good, it's reassuring to have a building with your name on it. This is what Douglas thinks on bad days, after meetings with the bank, after consultations with the accountants and confrontations with the Union. This is what Douglas thinks as he leaves the building at night, going across the low-light foyer past the banks of glossy-leaf plants, seeing himself reflected in the sparkling sweep of the entrance foyer's glass.

You can tell things about a person by the way that they walk. Douglas knows this, and Douglas' walk still has about it the self-assured strut of success, retrieved from memory, faithfully reproduced and flawlessly choreographed. The night guard at reception – the one with the coal-black face of North Africa, the 'makwerekwere' as the local people derisively call them; those who have come here looking for work and a good life – may see it or he may not.

'Good night, Jackson,' says Douglas.

'Good night, Mr Merchant,' says Jackson.

He doesn't smile and he doesn't look up. The two-way instant response radio cradled in the palm of his hand crackles with static and the incomprehensible accents of no-speak.

It's real. The bricks around him are real, granite face bricks. They come pre-stressed. The tiles tap-tapping under his shiny bright shoes (cleaned with chamois leather and Dubbin, courtesy of Adelaide) are as real as you like. Tomorrow his name on the building will still be there in its rightful place, defiant of bankers, accountants, contracts that don't get rubber-stamped through just when you need them most, Government go-betweens who come 'guaranteed' but withdraw if the price isn't right, and the imperious demands of the Union.

JULIA

Julia's been paying her analyst's bills out of the money she got for her jewellery. This is because Douglas refuses to pay, any longer, for medical insurance. 'Money down the drain,' he says. All he has now is a 'Dread Diseases' policy.

'That's all we really need worry about,' he says but it isn't as simple as that. The instant they came off medical insurance he started ferreting around in her doctor's bills and that wasn't good. Julia could laugh at his queries about the wine-shop account, or the super-market bills or the embarrassing reminders from the specialist delicatessen where she buys the imported cheeses and chocolates and speciality breads she's so fond of serving. She can almost bear his increasingly snide remarks (perfectly straightforward observations, all the rest's in your head, is what he says) about the cost of her hairdresser, her cosmetics, manicurists and podiatrists but when it comes to her visits to various doctors and chemists she must draw the line.

She has needs the 'Dread Diseases' policy won't cover and they're not the kind of needs she's likely to tell anyone and especially not Douglas who won't understand because, so far, nothing has happened to him bad enough to shake his faith in his own invincibility. Not even Rosalie quite managed that although she had a good try.

Is it wrong to wish an almost but not quite classifiably Dread Disease on your husband just as a life lesson? Sometimes when Douglas eases himself in beside her in the very late hours of the night or those other, even later times when the clock has already turned toward morning, this is what Julia thinks about. She lies very still and listens while his breathing evens out as he decides she's asleep and he's home clear, not clocked in, it's then that she wishes it. She wonders how high he would rate the benefits of a 'Dread Diseases' only policy then?

Julia sells her jewellery in a shop in downtown Johannesburg close by the railway station. It's a hole-in-the-wall kind of place. You'd think she might have chosen somewhere a bit more salubrious but that wouldn't be possible. How can a woman with a life as impeccably structured as Julia's walk into any one of the places she'd normally go with a bag filled with jewellery for sale? If only life were as easy as that but even so, there's a bright side and the place she's found comes recommended by her greengrocer, Andreas, a Greek of the old-fashioned kind. The sort of man a woman like Julia can turn to when she finds herself in need of information like this.

Some years ago Andreas gave Julia a tip for the Durban July and it worked, nineteen to one, but that was a foretaste, a token of friendship to show she was different from his other customers, that there was something in her that he recognized.

Douglas wants Julia to get a job but what could she do? The only thing she can see herself doing is working as Dr da Costa's secretary. Once upon a time Dr da Costa's secretary was a woman quite a lot like herself but there was that business with the black boy and then her husband shot himself and she had to go out and find something to do.

Julia does not feel the insistent prod of 'have to' in her own case although there are certainly days when Douglas, in his high-windowed office in Didata Park, feels differently. Dr da Costa's secretary was left with no money at all. There was an auction of furniture at her house. What people couldn't understand is why she stayed home on that day. She should have gone out. They felt bad, seeing her there, in the home she'd made for herself and her husband, standing by herself in the middle of her things with all that bad business still fresh in her mind while one thing and another was bid for and sold.

It's Julia's fear. Sometimes when she roams her house in the half light alone, she walks through a house peopled by ghosts of those people who have come for her things and Douglas is there too, saying: 'I told you so' and she is powerless to change any of it.

It may come to that but not quite yet and almost certainly not today.

*   *   *

She hasn't told anyone, not even Caroline, what she's been doing although she has thought about it. Caroline is the one who'll find the thing to say that will put everything right.

'Why not?' she'll say in that neat voice of hers. 'Who wears that kind of stuff any more anyway? You'd have to have it all re-set if you wore it at all. It's so out of date.'

Nothing would persuade Caroline to part with the out-of-date pearls she inherited from old Mrs Bannerman. Large wild pearls perfectly matched. A rope to hang down in a loop or three times around her neck as a choker and a diamond and sapphire clasp designed to finish it off. It's all very well for Caroline to talk.

'You're right,' Julia will say. 'Who wants a whole lot of stuff locked away in a safe?'

It's not a 'whole lot'. It was never a 'whole lot'. They both know it. There are one or two nice things and that's all. If Julia were Caroline, owned Caroline's pearls, never mind the sapphire and diamond clasp which came from Asprey's via the Bannermans, she wouldn't be worrying about the dwindling resource she finances her own secret life with. She wouldn't be wondering who it is this time that Douglas dreams about in that complacent half world between sleeping and waking. She wouldn't be asking herself why she keeps a maid who's really too old for the job just because she knows perfectly well she has nowhere else to go.

This, she thinks, is what her analyst means when she says she's been playing 'Julia' for such a long time that somewhere along the way she's managed to let go of her actual self. The woman Julia used to be would have dealt with these things. She would not have had these problems.

There's something else too. It's not just her analyst. Julia has been going to Dr da Costa as well, the visits so far paid for by an inherited eternity ring being sold. Next year will be lucky if it gets here and finds things unchanged, never mind eternity, and no one is likely to notice that the ring's gone and there's no need to account to anyone for the money. It's the mixture of guilt and glee, the cash in her hand, that makes her reckless.

She said nothing to her analyst. She told Caroline a lie. Not a big lie but a lie just the same. On that public holiday weekend, which stretched to a week, when Douglas went on the golf tour to the South Coast, she didn't go to the Magaliesberg Spa for a break. She booked herself into the Sandton Clinic, just for removal of eye lines and the pucker around the mouth, which is usually the best and most modest beginning.

She would like Douglas to notice but never to know. She might not have dared it, it smacked so of defeat, but everyone knows about Dr da Costa with his nice Latin looks and his German man friend and his red Maserati and they know he's discreet. His secretary is the most 'introduced' person in Johannesburg. She's always meeting people she knows for the very first time, too polite to acknowledge acquaintance until she's acknowledged first and there's no chance of that.

Julia, standing barefoot on the still sun-warm tiles of her veranda in the cool of pre-dawn, has moments when she'd like to swap places with this not-ever-met-before secretary. Perhaps then someone would say: 'Douglas Merchant, this is Julia Merriman.' Then she could say: 'Imagine meeting you here, like this, for the very first time.' And then, maybe, they could like each other again and start over.

When she drives into town to the funny little shop to sell jewellery she thinks about Michael Rosenberg. She hasn't thought about Michael Rosenberg for a long time but can one do what she did and step into what were once Rosalie's shoes and pretend you cannot remember who Michael Rosenberg is? She thinks if he knew, Michael would think how laughable is Julia Merchant, driving into town in her conspicuous car with her next offering, her grandmother's out-of-date ruby dress ring nestling in a pink Kleenex tissue in that small safe place between the cups of her bra.

No white person goes to the station side of town. It's so in-your-face African now, with its taxi terminus, hawkers, dealers, food vendors and rot and rubbish everywhere and the shudder and thunder of trains coming in and going out. Chicken heads for sale, chicken feet, raw chunks of meat attracting flies in the sun, an emaciated daddy-long-legs of a man made haggard by Aids although no work for Aids sufferers, so he'd deny it if you asked him.

There are people everywhere. A sea of people and Julia is in that sea, at the deep end of the ocean and drowning, so perhaps she is, after all, not in her right mind doing this but she does find the place again and she does sell the ring. She's given cash in banknotes that have seen something of life and aren't quite clean.

When she gets home to her house with the

shampooed carpets, the gleaming silver, the electronic garage door with that discordant squeak that needs oiling, she remembers thinking about Michael Rosenberg.

He came in and out of her head in a flash and in the grand scheme of things, she supposes he did her a favour and took Rosalie from Douglas but aside from that he was no one important. He was just a strange-looking young man from the wrong side of town who played at cricket and small-time politics and walked with such confidence into their lives and changed everything.

MICHAEL

Michael is no longer the Michael that Julia knew. He's not the Michael that Rosalie knew either.

Times have changed and Michael's made good. A security guard in black uniform stands at his gate. He has boots and a truncheon, epaulettes on his jacket that make his shoulders look larger and a cap with a cap badge on his head.

Ordinary people don't live in the street where Michael Rosenberg lives. He's come a long way since those days of the small fry, although the people who live here are ordinary enough. Behind the walls, the electrified fences and old-established trees in this road are the rambling houses of Government officials and Embassies bought in quick deals from the bolters who saw a new Government coming and threw in the towel. It's this new élite who feel the need for protection. Michael himself can take it or leave it. He's happy to offer employment to the guard (there's still a faint gnaw of conscience about who has and has not) even though he doesn't have all that much left that's worth taking. The departing Mrs Rosenbergs have taken good care of that side of things.

It's what he deserves, he thinks. This is what comes of growing up, getting older, getting married, taking over your late father's business and putting together a few deals that make money. That was the first real point of resistance and he should have resisted but he couldn't say 'no' to his mother, with his father so ill, and after that it was easy.

The next thing that happens is a nice enough girl you think is no trouble. Then she's your wife, a woman with opinions, asking for a better house in a nicer type of suburb and what can you say? You can say the suburb she found you in is more than good enough for you and for her too as far as you're concerned but she's not going to listen. He sees now that a ring on a finger is all it takes to tune the nicest of women right out of your wavelength. That's what he landed himself with but he doesn't blame his wives (there were two). He isn't first prize. He's not exactly Prince Charming. He's always known that. He knows he's not handsome but at least he's ugly on the grand scale. That's something that sets him apart and it's amazing how amenable women can be when it comes to a bright man like him, with a good sense of humour who's good-hearted, has an eye for a deal and is not shy with money.

You can say what you like about Michael, people have and they do. Some of it, but not very much, has to do with his abortive little two-step with politics in those long ago days. Most of it is about how exactly it is he's made so much money and made it so fast (first high-walled townhouses, then full-scale 'security' villages, then the shopping complexes with tight-secure parking and then the casinos).

They can say what they like but there's one area in which no one can fault him. Michael Rosenberg is a wonderful father. It's as if in finding his children (he has two) unfolding before him at last he's finding himself.

The political days are long gone. The world has moved on. All his passion these days is reserved for his children. The fact that they spend weekends and part of school holidays at his house is a good enough reason to have a guard at the gate. He would have twenty security guards; he would have a battalion if he could ensure it would keep his children from harm. If he has any private nightmare it's that something might happen to them.

'You're paranoid,' says his ex-wife, Liane, his children's mother. 'You don't know what you're doing. Children need to experiment; they need to have space. They should at least know what freedom is. Visiting you is like going into prison. Five-star prison perhaps, but prison is prison.'

'So? I'm paranoid,' Michael says. 'Indulge me. These are the only two children I'm going to have. I think that gives me a licence to be a little bit paranoid and if it's paranoid for a father to look out for his own children I'm happy to be paranoid. I take it as a compliment.'

Liane has that exasperated look of those paid upfront for their time. Those who openly look at their watches to note when exactly the allotted time has run out.

'Certify me if you like,' Michael says. 'As long as you leave me in peace to go on doing what I know is the best thing for my own children without forever bitching about it.'

'You can't keep them wrapped up in cotton wool for the rest of their lives.'

Here she stands, in the door of her good-address townhouse. Slim-hipped Liane with her apple-hard breasts and the mask of her make-up always firmly in place, smiling with that smile the Botox injection keeps from her eyes.

Hot water for breakfast, salad for lunch, grilled fish for supper and the ongoing love affair with the scale in the bathroom. Who can have a decent conversation with this exclamation mark of a woman always half on the lookout to see where the next kilojoule might be coming from?

'I know about over-protection,' he says. 'But for as long as I can, I will watch out for my children and I'd be grateful if you'd do the same.'

Michael likes the idea of his children, the most perfect, most beautiful children in the world. Mandy, aged ten, and Tracey, aged twelve, safely, securely asleep under his roof with the guard, muffled up against the night, at his gate and the infrared alarm system activated.

The guards are human; you don't expect them to be foolproof. As far as the foolproof systems are concerned, though, when you put them to the test they're not always quite as foolproof as they're cracked up to be. Perhaps because the criminals these days are not the fools people once took them for. They too have moved with the times. If you have infrared beams they come looking for you in scuba diving suits the rays cannot penetrate.

You go to the best place for a security system, that one everyone recommends. You say 'state of the art', money's not important here, we're talking about lives. You pay a fortune and this is what you get for your money.

'My God! A man by my bed, I thought I was back in Mauritius. All he was short of was a snorkel and a fish in his hand.'

As for the systems, most of the time the best you can do is return them, after the event, when the police have been and the insurance company notified and what do you do then? Tell the manufacturer that 'fool-proof' is not what it used to be and ask for your money back?

What does a man need other than a place with a bed and a chair, a table to work at, a sink with a tap and a bath with a gas geyser which, if you're lucky, will gush out hot water at the strike of a match. Isn't that the sum total of need? Just a roof to give shelter and if there's any choice in the matter and if it's no trouble to anyone, preferably one that doesn't leak like a sieve. (He has a childhood memory of his mother running round the house with metal basins all shapes and sizes while the rain slammed down on the worn-out roof in Cyrildene.)

Women, we are told, feel something kindred with other women but if there's a white woman in Johannesburg who would warm to a story like this, Michael hasn't met her yet.

The matter of the children always comes up.

'I know your mother's a wonderful woman but I'm not your mother and I'm glad you like your old neighbourhood where you were brought up but excuse me for mentioning it, it's not what it once was.'

That's what the wives say. They're right, it isn't what it once was and how can he tell them he likes it even better the way it is now because it's so willing to keep step with change it will walk alongside it even if that means decay. How can he say how much he likes the sassy way the old places in Bez Valley stay standing, how they seem to know that being graceful has no place around getting old and giving in at the seams. That's good enough for the buildings downtown on Hollard Street and on Main and on Loveday, the totems of that other life and that other extinct society. Self-preservation not pomposity is what counts here, where each day people primp themselves up to tackle headlong this thing we call life.

He likes the unisex hair salons (straightening treatments at special rates) and the houses with too many children spilling out of their doors and the casual, unremarkable way a goat can walk down the street or the confident crow of a cock in the morning.

'Africa in the backyard is fine with me,' says Liane in those early days of their marriage. 'On the doorstep it's a different story and we don't need this. I don't need it, your children don't need it and if you're really honest with yourself, you don't need it either.'

He doesn't blame her. Who can blame someone for wanting more, for wanting better, for wanting the best, for wanting it all? Wasn't that, says Liane, what 'they' were struggling for in the first place?

'Well, they've got it now,' she says. 'And they're welcome. If it makes you happy to see it, it makes me happy. Just so long as they do it in their part of town and we do it in ours.'

Men shouldn't pick their wives. Their mothers should. He knows there's nothing in the vast new legislation that makes provision for this but there should be.

How is it a man can head like a homing pigeon for exactly the right woman, then marry the wrong one and do it not once but all over again?

There are things only a certain kind of woman can understand and here, like it or not, the free-flying spirit of Rosalie imprints itself on his inner self for an instant, then is gone. To such a woman he could say in that old certain voice that seems to have left him, that this, at the end of it all, is what he'd lived for and wanted. Now that it's here what else can he do but rejoice and love it unashamedly in all of its brazenness? He should weep for joy to see the beauty of such ordinariness. He may be a man reluctant to speak about love but when he sees it, he knows what it is.

There's nothing that touches him in the way the old houses do and the paper and plastic thrown in the street. No security guards necessary here. Nothing worth taking and everyone knows everyone else anyway.

He likes the way those people live who are living here now, who make the best of what they have and live out their lives with humour and style, that little bit of 'sass' they take out on the street.

Two marriages later, in all his unloveliness, what his heart yearns for is someone who can feel what he feels and have enough sense to leave it unsaid.

No good looking back except sometimes at night when he goes out of his way to drive through that old neighbourhood under trees grown tall and then what can he do but remember her?

She's standing in the garden on a hot day. He's coming down the road, a young man in a state of perpetual excitement of every possible kind. All of life is exciting and he sees her before she sees him and he can't wait to reach her. There's something he's been thinking about, some things he's been wanting to say and when he says them he'll say them in that voice full of certainty that was his voice then and he's walking fast. He can't wait to start talking. He can't wait for the look of her and that moment his eyes meet with hers and are home. He can't wait for the touch, for the smell of her or the feel of her body but that was a long time ago and it was like that and then again the memory won't hold steady and maybe it wasn't really like that at all.

He looked for her for a very long time, in this place of his slow night drives down the memory road of that pushy, unlovely, young man he once was. He looks for her still sometimes, in shame and regret and he knows that it's pointless but he simply can't stop himself.

JULIA

In the privacy of her bedroom with the door firmly closed against Adelaide (never alone, never alone, not even in her own house), Julia takes the money out of her bra. She sees herself in the full-length mirror, reflected back again through the open door in the mirrored wall of the bathroom 'en suite'. She sees herself watching herself and what she sees is a blond head, voluminous with hair. A young woman's head, she can smell the jojoba shampoo, she can see her own face and it occurs to her as she tugs the bank-notes out of her Victoria's Secret bra (those streetwise, grubby notes, unseemly, embarrassing, thank goodness her friends can't see her now) that Julia is changed. Someone has tried to make, out of a Brussels lace bra, a nip and a tuck, Crème de Mer for face maintenance and Pearl Silk hair highlighter, the woman who once was Julia, and has made a botched job of it.

GLADSTONE

Although they have worked together for over eight years and she's the newcomer, Adelaide has no time for Gladstone. Mr M has told her she better get over it. If anyone doesn't get on with anyone else and someone has to go it will never be Gladstone.

The job on the property is Gladstone's 'old age' job. He's been with Mr M from the beginning when Mr M was a youngster just starting out and Gladstone was young too with juice in his veins and had done it all before and knew how to get a job on a building site done and get it done right.

Mr M has a whisky bar he likes to open up for his friends. He has a key, so does Gladstone.

'You talk about wasting money,' Julia says when her hormones are flowing in a certain direction. 'I'd like to know what it is you call this?'

'I call it one of life's pleasures,' says Douglas. 'My

pleasure, which, when you consider that I'm the one paying for it is not, I would think, all that much to ask.'

When the whisky's flowing Mr M likes to tell how he and Gladstone started out with nothing but a few bob he raised from his father and some money Julia's disaster of a brother put in and took out again in a hurry and a pick-up to load labour in. You could do that in those days. Everyone knew you were doing it but nobody cared. You could drive up in your pick-up, you didn't even have to stop, just slow down, put your head out of the window and shout how many you needed. Six. Eight. Show with a flash of your fingers and watch them push for a place. 'Take me, boss. Take me. I'm a very good worker. I'm strong. Take me.'

That's how he got hold of Gladstone.

'Built like an ox,' Mr M says. 'Older than the others but he could work as hard as any two of them put together and a "boss boy" mentality which was the thing that I liked about him. He's not afraid to open his mouth, not even to his own kind.'

Gladstone takes his orders from Mr M and Mr M only. 'Suits me,' says Julia. He has a place too if he'd like to live 'in' the way Adelaide does. The second servant's room is his any time he wants it but he doesn't want it. He likes to live in Soweto and come into town every day in his suit and his hat to his job.

'He looks like a bloody banker,' Douglas says. 'They all look like bloody bankers these days but he's a good boy. He's been with me all these years, I told him I'd look after him and I will.'

TULA

There are chickens in the back of the big house where her grandmother works. They're called Silkie chickens. Tula knows this. Tula knows a great many things. She knows things even people in the big house don't seem to know. 'Gladstone' is a made-up, white name and not worth a spit. 'Gladstone' is really Mr Malipile. This is what she must call him. He has told her so himself.

Her mother told her that if the people in the big house ever get around to speaking to her she must call them Mr and Mrs Merchant and even if they look surprised she mustn't let that stop her. She must just keep on doing it. They may be her grandmother's 'master' and 'madam'. They will never be hers.

If they know so much and are so important they might at least have known what Mr Malipile's real name is. Tula hasn't said as much. She thinks Mr

Malipile has seen in her face what she thinks. It doesn't matter, he says. There's so much they don't know and it's a little too late to think about teaching them now.

It's Mr Malipile who told her about the Silkie chickens. They're there for decoration, not to eat, and you couldn't eat them anyway, even if you wanted to. Under their white feathers they have black skin. Mr Malipile showed her this. He caught one in his hands and held it out and called to her to come over and have a look. The chicken didn't seem to mind. It just sat there in his big hands as if it was safe on its nest and when she came over Mr Malipile stroked back the bird's silky white feathers so she could see the black skin underneath.

He says the chickens may be no good to eat but they're good for something just the same, which is to show that things are not always what they seem from the outside.

She isn't really interested. The only reason she came out of her grandmother's room when he called her was because the room is small and she's bored. Her grandmother says she can only come out when the house people are away but what can her grandmother say if she goes out when she's called by Mr Malipile.

Today is Saturday. She thinks maybe her mother will come and fetch her today. Her mother says she will come when she can and when she was smaller she used to ask when that would be. She didn't ask because she wanted to cause trouble. She only asked because she wanted to know but she doesn't ask any more because it makes her mother angry.

'I'll come when I can,' her mother says.

Her mother has a make-up mirror with lights all around it that work from a plug you stick into the wall. In front of it is a plastic tray divided up into places for cheek colour, places for lip colour and eye make-up and nail polish. There's special cream colour for the skin and powder to put over it and every kind of pencil you can think of. There's a special box for false nails and another for eyelashes and her mother sits in front of the mirror with a gown pulled over her shoulders and a stocking over her hair and puts on her new face. All around the mirror, stuck on the wall, are the pictures of stars and models pulled out of magazines and Tula knows them all, Naomi, Iman and Halle Berry who is surely the most beautiful woman in the world and the biggest star of all. She must be because Oprah Winfrey said so right on air, on the Oprah Show.

The way her mother talks about them they might just as well all be friends together. There are pictures of her mother too, from the TV magazines, and she may not have a father but she has one thing no other child she knows has and that is a TV star for a mother.

She thinks her mother will fetch her today. Sometimes she has to work on Saturday but not always. If she doesn't have to work today perhaps the phone inside the house will ring and it will be her mother saying she's coming to fetch her. It won't be a long phone call, so there won't be any trouble over that. It'll just be her mother phoning to say her grandmother must have her ready because it's Saturday and she's coming to fetch her.

She doesn't think her mother will come in at the

back gate because she's not that kind of woman. She says so herself.

'Do I look to you like I was born to know anything about "back gate", "servants' entrance" kind of rubbish? Didn't anyone tell you the days of slavery are over? No more "master" and "madam" and "yes, sir" and "thank you, miss".'

This is what she said to her mother when she brought Tula in the first place. Then she had to say she was sorry, she didn't mean it. 'I'm sorry. You know how I am. You know how I get. My mouth runs away with me. I say things I don't mean. It's new times, that's all. I didn't mean it against you.'

Tula knew then, when her mother who never says 'sorry' for anything, says sorry in such a hurry and changes her voice to a very small little-girl voice, that she was going to ask to leave Tula there and maybe leave her there for a very long time. But she worked that out anyway when she saw her mother packing her clothes in a case, pushing them in any which way because she was in a hurry.

The 'summons' people have come to the door again today.

'I'll pay you when I can,' says her mother. 'I'll make an arrangement.'

That's what she says to them. She tells Tula it's nothing to worry about, she couldn't care less. They can wait for their money. One day when she's a big star they won't be sending people around to ask why she hasn't paid them. They'll be begging for her business. The owner of the shop will be the one at the door with a rail full of the most beautiful dresses anyone ever saw excepting for Oscar night and they will be asking her to wear them for nothing because that's what happens to you when you become a star. No one is offering anything for nothing right now this minute even Tula can see that and you can't give back clothes once they've been worn. The shops don't want their clothes back even if Tula's mother was willing to give them. They want their money.

Tula doesn't want to be here. If she could choose a place she'd really want to be it would be Ponte City in Berea where she lived with her mother in a flat on the eighteenth floor but it was only after her mother had left that she realized how much it was she wanted this. When they first came, she was happy enough. She was happy when her mother's friend dropped them off at the gate. She liked to walk with her mother through the garden to the house. She likes the way her mother sways next to her with her pretty feet in their high-heel designer shoes.

'The most beautiful shoes in the world,' her mother says. 'They cost more than this "master" and "madam" give Koko for all the hard work she does in a month but you mustn't tell her that. She'll only get cross because she won't understand.'

Beautiful shoes make her mother happy. You would never believe how many pairs she has and Tula is allowed only to look, touch if invited and never, definitely never, to play 'dressing up' in them.

Tula's mother's shoes lie heel to toe in their boxes at the side of her bed and the boxes are six in a row and taller than Tula is.

Her mother says all the way, how pleased Koko will be to see her, how it won't be for long. Just until things work out and when she comes to fetch her she'll take her to Bruma Lake for a hamburger and Coke and she can wear neon pink hot-pants and sunglasses and her new hair-slides and maybe some nail polish too, all depending.

It's hot in the room and there's no place to play. At Ponte City there's a shute right down the middle of the building. It goes down so far there could even be some gold down the bottom but you'd never find it now because everyone throws their trash down there and who would want to look through so much rubbish just to find gold.

Then they all got kicked out and it wasn't just because of not paying the rent.

'To hell with them,' her mother says.

Her mother says they've called it a slum and were just about ready to close it right down but now they are going to tart it up for rich people to live in again. It didn't matter if people lived there right now and had a life and went about their business. Backwards, it seemed to her, is the way they were going because that is just like the old days.

She liked Ponte City anyway. Anything is better than a place like this. Here there are no pictures of stars like old friends on the wall and nothing very much for kids on TV because they only get SATV and not Satellite, choose any channel you want. On Saturday her Koko, her grandmother, puts on her grey Church Dress and her hat and her badge and goes to ZCC, Zion Church of Christ, and Tula has to go along with her.

She's ready to go at a moment's notice although it won't be to church. The things she'll need are in a pink plastic suitcase. It's hard to be patient but she can wait if she has to and that's what she'll do. That's why she sits so good and so quiet on the bed in Koko's room with the door open so the air can come in. She'll watch the silly, good-for-nothing Silkies high-step backwards and forwards in the little back garden and be in no one's way and not any trouble. She will sit there in her pedal-pusher pants and green neon shirt, with her hair in the plaits Koko made for her and pulled tight with the green bow hair-slides at the end of each one and wait even if it takes a very long time.

DOUGLAS' LOVER

Douglas' current lover, the one who lives above a Greek restaurant in Yeoville, is trying on Julia's life for size. She has driven past Douglas' house. He'd be furious if he knew but what difference can it make anyway? Even if his wife did drive out and right past her, she wouldn't know who she was. It wouldn't mean anything. All she'd see would be a young woman in a second-hand car who took a wrong turn by mistake and Douglas is in the telephone book after all, a listed number with an address.

You can't see much of the house. All you see are trees and one sign that says: 'This garden uses bore hole water' and another with a zigzag electric sign that says 'Protected by Flash Security Systems' and there's a spiked gate on rollers and an intercom. You could say it was a waste of time really but on the other hand, it isn't. She doesn't see very much but all the same, she gets a feel of the place and she likes it.

People who live in places like this don't drive small cars. These women drive Mercedes Benz sports cars that slide in and out of the driveways like fish. That's what she would like to have, with air-conditioning and a CD player and servants. She'd have breakfast in bed every morning and a personal trainer who comes to the house and a sun-bed to tan on without catching cancer. This is her idea of heaven and Douglas, if he cares to, if everything comes together in just the right way, can give it to her.

Douglas' house, Julia's house is, in fact, a co-owned property, which may prove a difficulty when the assets are reckoned and the liquidators come. A small stream runs past it. There are willow trees, there are palms and herons and frogs that go rivet-rivet when it rains and a small one-car-at-a-time bridge that crosses its span. There's an illusion of time slowing down, slow time, back to innocent time, for the pram-pushers, for the hard-hat, skate-board-carrying children and the snuffling dogs held in check on their leads.

The house where Douglas lived with Rosalie was nothing like this. That house was in Kensington, a turn of the century house but even so, right for that time when Rosalie lived there. It was quaint with a pleasant deep balcony going all the way round and big, airy rooms. The main room had a pressed metal ceiling and an elaborate cast-iron grate around a fireplace with a marble surround.

How quickly it all faded from Rosalie's memory and

became just a place where two silly young people once played at make-believe husbands and wives.

It was different for Douglas.

Long after Rosalie left, after she set up home with Michael Rosenberg in a house in Bez Valley, there were still some venomous lapses when Douglas enjoyed the idea of bringing some terrible punishment down on her head. He considered telling the security police about her. He was quite sure that if they only took the trouble to look they were bound to find something and of course in the end they did and they managed very well with no help from him.

He would like to have seen her bubble burst and herself destroyed. He would like to have seen her dragged from her jerrybuilt shack in Bez Valley and pushed into the back of a police van and in fact she was but that too she managed quite well by herself.

He imagined her pulling and pushing with all of her might, held back by rough hands with a stream of invective spewing like lava out of her mouth (because Rosalie and more especially Rosalie in this new incarnation would never go quietly).

All of this happened just as he'd wished it but once it was wished there was no way he could stop it. He couldn't simply wish it away again.

It would have been bad form to crow although there was a traitorous voice inside him that said he should go ahead and have the last laugh. If she'd stayed with him none of this would have happened.

He didn't want to crow. He didn't know quite what he wanted. He knew what he didn't want and that was one thing, quite surely, that was coming his way. It was the look he would get from his mother when she heard that because of him she still had attached to herself a recalcitrant daughter-in-law who had managed to land up in jail.

For people like Douglas the back of a police van is nothing more than an unknowable void into which those who make life uncomfortable for people like him conveniently disappear. When he thought about it before it actually happened he hoped it might smell of fear, of the sheer terror of everyone who's taken that ride before she does. He wished that upon her. He thought she deserved it but even so, he would rescue her. After all, she was still his wife. In the face of great opposition from his mother, his friends and on the advice of a Seventh Day Adventist who came to the door, who in desperation he invited inside, he denied her divorce.

He knew a great many people of influence. The Bannermans sprang to mind but he wouldn't ask them. Why should he? His family name was still good for something and he saw himself happy to offer it as security against her future good conduct, under his supervision, of course.

Douglas was twenty-five years old at that time and had no experience at all when it came to relinquishing things. He knew one thing for certain though. It would be no good at all looking to his family for help. They would no sooner allow him to proffer their name in this way, than they would ever again let into any of their houses a jailbird daughter-in-law who chose to cohabit adulterously with a Jew who, they were quite certain, was also, more than likely, a communist.

What's there to be said? Rosalie on her path of defection had managed faultlessly to touch every base and score a home run.

If she remembers correctly, and Julia is someone who never forgets detail, there was a pretty frieze of roses uncovered in the drawing room when Douglas began to renovate and original crystal handles on the door and Victorian mirrored plates above those. In the bathroom was an enormous bath with cast ostrich feet. The garden, she recalled, needed a strong hand and hard work.

She'd envied that house in those days and Douglas and Rosalie in it. It had all seemed idyllic to her. It occurs to her now that she may have done better staying just where she was, standing on the outside, and envying it all and knowing no better.

Perhaps there's something Douglas' girlfriend might usefully learn from this other experience, if only she knew.

Julia's house, this small piece of perfection she and Douglas have made, is very different.

By the steps to the riverbank there are big terracotta pots with bright spills of impatiens that need constant weeding. The grass must be cut. The bottom branches of the riverbank fringe of palms must be lopped off and here Julia concedes that, under her supervision, Gladstone can be of some help.

Julia and Gladstone, each locked in a world of their own, work happily together. There's no requirement that they should speak to each other and if they did, what is there they might usefully say?

Douglas is the one who's forever seeking conversation

with Gladstone, glad of his attention, over-generous with praise. Gladstone is Douglas' man, the foundation on which the once-thriving business of Merchant and Merriman was built in that long-ago time when Rosalie was the first Mrs Merchant.

Side by side, in silence, Gladstone and Julia set to work. Julia in her gardening gloves and hat, Gladstone in overalls, she pulling weeds, he trimming lawn edges with a quick clipping strimmer and the girl on the bridge, who appears to have time on her hands, may watch at her leisure 'madam' and manservant, working in harmony. After all, it costs nothing to look.

ROSALIE

Rosalie is losing time. It's hard to say exactly when this began. It was probably that night on the tube, after what happened, that her life became changed.

The things that were the milestones of her day have become unimportant. The unopened mail, the overflow of dishes in the sink, the unmade bed with the indentation of her head still on the pillow and the tangled sheets and bright blankets left exactly as they were when they were thrown back, are testimony to this. They are unimportant; there are other more pressing things now.

She knows where she lives. Brought with her from that old life along with the woman she once was, there's a card with her name on it, her address, a telephone number, fax and e-mail. She's stuck it on the inside of her front door. It's her talisman now. Each day, before she goes out, she runs her hand over it.

There's a card in her handbag, in her purse, in the canvas book bag (Barnes and Noble) she takes to the local library. There's a card inside her umbrella. You can't miss it. She attached it with string so it hangs down like an over-sized price tag in a poor man's shop. There's a card in one pocket of all of her coats, super-glued cards inside one of each pair of her shoes, she has quick-stitched one into a rainbow wool beanie she likes to wear in the cold.

It takes a long time to do this but it has to be done. She's quite certain of it. She woke up one morning, that morning after the tube ride, in her own bed, in her own flat under the thick bright blankets she loves with the sun, such as it is in this place, going scratch at the window to get her attention. She was wide awake at once. Something had cracked in the night and she knew with great certainty what had to be done.

It takes a very long time and a great deal of planning. She keeps thinking of other, important places where the cards must be planted. The satisfaction of thinking it all out and then doing it is immense and after that, as far as she can judge, everything is all right and exactly as it always is, for what seems like a long time.

What happened on the tube is this. Rosalie is travelling on her accustomed line. She no longer sees the names of the stations. They are part of her now. She can count them in screeches and wheel beats. She can feel the pull of them in the snaky way the carriages sway round the bends. The stops, the starts, the delays, the murky heat, the unnatural light and the vast waves of people coming and going is nothing more than the ocean in which she now swims.

She has to be careful. She has to be very careful indeed. She looks out for herself as the train rumbles into the dark in that moment when she waits for and finds the reflection of the dark-haired, dark-eyed woman who blends so well with the crowd she might be invisible.

Lately, she's been behaving badly. She'll push and shove against others, shove them hard in the ribs if she must, show no mercy at all in that scramble to secure a suitable seat where a glimpse of that reflection will be assured. It's a small enough thing. The sight of her self-contained self, pinned down on the glass, constant in her place is a comfort.

She has told no one this.

She has, in the past, been for trauma counselling. Her friends recommended it. One cannot go through what she has been through, imprisonment, house arrest (which is what she minded least), constant harassment, banishment, flight, loss, coming back damaged to this place that's no longer her own, and come out unscathed. She will need to talk to someone. This is what her friends here say and so she goes for trauma counselling but she doesn't wish to talk about herself. Instead, she tells the trauma therapist that other woman's story and they agree on how such a woman might pick up the pieces of her life and re-assimilate.

'You might find you've come to just the right place after all,' the therapist suggests and Rosalie agrees.

The therapist is thorough but more than happy with Rosalie, who is told after a given time that she may now make less frequent visits, who may if she wishes come only as and when she feels the need. Always forgetting that Rosalie, in her way, is thorough too and has been a deceiver in her day.

'Unless there's anything else you'd like to discuss?'

'But there isn't,' says Rosalie.

'Well, that's that then,' says the therapist. 'If you need me, telephone.'

Rosalie should have told about the mirror woman but she thought she was in control and safe. The mirror woman can always be summoned when needed. (She keeps an empty Marks & Spencer crème blusher compact, 'Bronze Shimmer', in her bag. It has a mirror in its lid, just a small rummage in her handbag away, ready for any time she needs it and Rosalie is secure.)

It's the early evening lovers that undo her. They come and go with the others in the drift. The doors of the train slide open (Mind the Gap), they slide closed and there they are and everywhere you look in London these days are South African young. She is nothing to them and they are nothing to her, except in snatches when their strange, hard accent beats too heavily against the shores of her past.

They seat themselves, neatly, unknowingly, opposite her so her face set on a dark-scarved neck, above black wool shoulders, floats between them on the black-backed plasticky glass and she is invisible to them.

'Do you know how much I love you?' he says. 'Have you any idea how much I love you?'

Here is a boy with a voice rough, like a chain saw, making love to a girl with his eyes, who unknowingly has drawn her straight into his heart along with the loved one. She had a lover once, whatever name he went by, and she loved him so well she must keep him away because there are things far more important than love or a personal life in these days.

'Will it make you more effective in the Struggle?' That is the question you're supposed to be asking yourself. Maximum effectivity is the only criterion.

Even so, sometimes he slides into her mind and she remembers how it was and no matter how roughly she pushes memory out of the way, her body betrays her and whether she wants it or not, her body remembers and grieves for her loss.

At the next station the lovers are gone and Rosalie with them into old times, down old roads that take her through summer days and hot nights, small rooms, large starlit gardens, brandy and ginger ale, bare legs, hard breathing and lies.

The dark is coming. She's quite sure of it and Michael is the one she will know in the dark. If he should come to look for her even at the darkest, furthermost end of the tunnel everything will be fine again. She may forget everyone else. She will always know him. She will know him by the feel of him, by his smell and the warm taste of his saliva.

After the first detention she writes him a letter. She is thirty-five miles away in Pretoria staying in a house with eight other people. There are rats in the house. There is a Catholic Communist from Mozambique who has strong feelings about toilet paper. He is an expert. The bourgeoisie use double ply, the lower-middle class goes single and the workers use newspaper.

In the lavatory, with some satisfaction, the people here find that the daily press that rates sport as highly as politics is more than sufficient to service their needs.

They eat Kupugani soya mince and white bread and drink chicory coffee.

She misses him.

She asks someone to take the letter for her. She can't telephone; the phone may be tapped. She can't trust a letter to the regular post. That too is unsafe. She's being taken care of. She should be grateful and do as she's told. There's useful work to be done. People look at her differently now. She's beginning to be known as a person that can be counted on. Because of what's happened, whether she was foolhardy or not, she commands some respect.

She's been told not to contact anyone. She's been told not to contact him. His behaviour since that night on the Pretoria Road has been out of step. His heart might be in the right place but it's becoming very clear that when the chips are down he hasn't really got what it takes.

You need that little bit extra. You need 'what it takes'. She badly wants to have 'what it takes' whatever that is but he's only thirty-five miles away, she is not yet the good 'soldier' she should be and she misses him.

She writes and says that if he sends her word she will come to him. This is not the only country in the world. There are other places. She's seen them. They could see them together but she has been apart from him for a long time. It feels like a long time. She no longer knows what's in his heart. She needs to be close to him to know what's in his heart. If he sends for her she will come.

Her comrades say he's a lightweight. He lost heart or perhaps he was never committed in the first place and that's no good to anyone. He may not know it yet but one day he will and that day will come soon. Her life is not with him. She's involved in far bigger issues now. If she means what she says then she knows that the commitment must be total. It's that or it's nothing. There's no room for a personal life in that place she's set out for.

She has a dream. Michael is walking down a road towards her. He's coming to her in bits and pieces, dark arms, short white shirtsleeves, shirts that are always too tight across his shoulders, which are much broader than other men's. The road is somewhere outside Johannesburg in that place where the veldt rolls in to lap at the walls of the city. It's a farm road. There's the dry smell of dust. He's shimmering towards her in a heat haze. It's very hot. She can feel it, so she knows that it's real. She knows by the feel of it just how long she has waited. Her heart is so full, she thinks it must burst. He's walking in that determined way he has as if he knows exactly where it is he's going. He's beginning to speak but she can't hear what he says. She may never hear. This is what makes her think it's a dream. Soon he'll walk past her, not seeing her waiting for him in her dream in the dust because if there's one thing that's sure, it's this. We never get that thing we want most. We may be shown it but it never becomes ours. Those who fought so hard for freedom can tell you. Even freedom when it comes is not that exact thing that they yearned for or anything like they imagined it to be.

This is what she knows. This is what she remembers even as she's dreaming, while the woman in the glass remains perfectly still, patiently waiting as the train clatters on towards Morden.

In the end she has to take a taxi back and it takes a long time and then she's not quite certain of her address and the mirror woman has to answer for her. It's late when she gets back. The taxi is costly but she doesn't care. She wants to empty her purse of all that is in it and give it to the cab driver she's so grateful to him but he won't take it. Perhaps he thinks she's been drinking. She's profusely grateful, too grateful. She can feel him withdraw. First his eyes, then his head which he turns into profile, then himself. Then the window slides up and her face is superimposed upon his. Then he's gone into the night. She stands on the pavement outside the house where she lives and watches until he rounds the corner and then she turns toward home.

Her hands are unsteady as she lets herself in. She has all the right keys but she isn't at all sure she can manage the lock. She might ring for the opera singer or her Senegalese lover. If she doesn't, she may have to stay on the street. She may go in quick and quiet so as not to disturb anyone, which is the way they prefer it here, and get to her flat and cover the mirrors as if someone has died.

She's tired. She would like to lie down beside the Senegalese lover and lay her hands on his bare skin and feel his smoothness and smell the sweet dark essence of him. The ground smell, rain smell, man smell and lie there until comforted and have it understood it is not desire she feels but simply clanship. She has had a strange day. Something is being wrenched out of her and her blood pulls towards Africa.

DOUGLAS

Douglas is having one of those meetings Julia doesn't approve of. He shouldn't be here but would it really be such a terrible thing if she knew that he was? All it would mean is a row, the same one there always is. That never changes and here he is anyway, cruising down Melville Main Street in the middle of the day, in work time, when he should be on site sorting out problems which at least he knows how to deal with. Instead he is here; feeling irritated, out of place and berating himself for being so easily conned into coming.

He feels uncomfortable with Melville. Something inside him makes him wish he could put his foot down flat on the accelerator of his silver Range Rover and plough his way through the casually jaywalking crowd. They're all so young, so arrogant, so sure of themselves, this 'now' generation the country got sold down the tubes for; but that would be manslaughter.

Instead he concentrates on the smooth flow of cold air through the air-vents and looks up at the poor condition of most of the buildings, all those things so obvious to the experienced eye, which couldn't matter less to the jeans and T-shirts below. All they care about is picking at their mobiles for SMS messages, cramming into Internet cafés, fishing through the old clothes that come through in containers from Eastern Europe looking for street chic, with not a care in the world. That's how they live now, these kids. Parading around with rings through their noses, having henna tattoos put all over themselves and not even turning to look as the Harley Davidsons roar past zigzagging through the traffic like the lords of the street.

You have to think twice about leaving a car like Douglas' in a neighbourhood like this. If you turn your back you could find it gone no matter how loudly the car alarm might yodel for help. Nobody cares. No one will do anything. You must have a guard. On principle he detests them, these informal workers, who watch your car for a few bob and let your tyres down if you say you won't pay. So Douglas will do what everyone else does. He'll scrabble around for small change and hand it over dutifully even though it always makes him boil inside.

'Something now on deposit and something more if it's still here and in one piece when I get back.'

'Yes, boss,' says the parking attendant but it's not the 'boss' as 'boss' was in the old days. That's gone for ever.

If Julia had her way Douglas wouldn't be here at all. Kimmy chose the place and it's her place not his.

'It's convenient,' she says when she phones to the office. 'You know your way to Melville. Where else could be better? I won't exactly fit in at the Country Club. I don't really feel I want to come to the house and Mum's made it pretty clear she feels the same way.'

Which is true but there's more to it than that.

In those days when she did come to the house, there was always the obligatory confrontation and Julia cried for days when she left. Just when he thought she'd managed to pull herself together she'd start crying again, saying she just cannot do this thing although she knows that she must.

After a visit from Kimmy, Julia cries in shopping malls, she cries when she sees fresh young girls on the street. She cries without making a sound in the bathrooms of other people's houses when they're invited out to have dinner. Julia's whole being becomes a minefield after a visit from Kimmy and Douglas is wary of her then. You never know what small thing might ignite the next outburst.

Julia is wrong about Kimmy. She still remembers the time when there were too many raves and 'chill outs', too many Lucky Strike parties (word of mouth only), the best parties in town with the coolest overseas bands. Where you can dance to Cyrus Hill if you're lucky and the cigarettes come for free so you can sample the brand and get a taste for the flavour. It's Bacardi Cooler and Tequila straight up.

'I can handle it,' is what Kimmy says to her mother.

'No, you can't,' Julia says.

What will it take to make Kimmy understand about

drugs and unforeseen overdoses that end with young people being dumped on the steps of Jo'burg General Emergency in the hope someone will find them and sort it all out?

Kimmy says she just wants to be 'normal' for a change, just like anyone else. She's had enough of the right schools and the right people. She wants to make her own friends and they should be people she likes, no matter who their parents are. She wants to dress her own way. She will not go out looking like a leftover from some out of the Ark late-night television Sandra Dee movie.

'It's disgusting,' says Julia. 'How can she go around wearing clothes God knows how many people have worn before?'

Julia has told Caroline how Kimmy cries out to be 'normal' but still takes all the luxuries as her due. This is what she hisses at Kimmy when the quarrels come as they inevitably must.

'Normal' children don't run up mobile phone bills so enormous that their mothers don't dare tell their fathers about them. Has she any idea exactly how privileged she is? 'Normal' children don't have parents who hand over mobile phones as if they're a right not a luxury. 'Normal' girls who have mobile phones don't come home any time they like or not come home at all but never once using that same mobile to say where they are or who they're with.

'Normal' for Julia is a mother who doesn't see as obligatory reading all those articles that say what to watch out for in case your child is a teen alcoholic or a gleaming-eyed coke-addict and there are other things too. Does the mother of a 'normal' girl have to worry about whether she might be a 'user', of 'dagga' or crack or anything else that's going, and goodness knows, as Julia has discovered, it's all easy enough to get hold of once you know where to go.

'Ease up,' says Douglas.

'I've seen it before,' Julia says. 'That's the trouble.'

'Then at least explain to Kimmy why you're so paranoid about it,' Douglas says. 'Because, in case you don't know it, that's what you are.'

'Really?' says Julia. 'Do you think I should tell her that her uncle was an alcoholic? Do you think I should say how I worry that maybe addiction runs in our family?'

'Why not?' says Douglas. 'It's not a disgrace.'

'I won't do it,' Julia says.

'Fine,' says Douglas. 'Let us by all means venerate the dead while we both stand by and watch you driving our daughter straight into disaster.'

'Thank you,' says Julia. 'It's my fault, of course. I don't know why I ever expected you to offer any support.'

'What place is there for support?' Douglas wants to know. 'No one's as good as you are at managing things. Everyone knows that. Who am I to deny you your full share of glory?'

What in Julia's life has prepared her for a perpetually parched all-night dancer who keeps going on Ecstasy, just fifty bucks a pop? Kimmy has tried all these things, rejected some, clung to others, been detoxed, re-habbed, run away, slid back, become rather too familiar with the Juvenile Court, who are, thank God, lenient, at least until the age of eighteen or so.

Julia blames herself. She blames the state of her marriage to Douglas. Kimmy has grown up in a house where Dad's constantly absent and the bickering never ends. First Mum's turn, then Dad's. Julia, who knew her own parents as Mummy and Daddy, who could never conjure them up as the lovers they must once have been, who never saw either of them unclothed, unless they were going swimming, suffers sorely in this bed she has made for herself. None of what's happening is what she'd dreamed of for Kimmy.

Melville's Main Street is a bright, vibrant place. A world away from anything Douglas might call familiar.

There are sushi bars here and outside cafés and far too much business, in Douglas' opinion, done out on the street.

There are candle shops that send a whiff of incense out through their doors and clothing shops with one-garment-only window displays. There are chic little hair salons with minimalist décor and at the fruit and vegetable vendor small sprightly bunches of still-growing herbs offered for sale in white plastic pots.

The people on the street seem stopped in time. They all seem to be at that age where they don't have a care in the world and all that lies ahead of them is going to be good. This is Kimmy's place now and Julia might stick to her guns and refuse to come and see for herself but there's been a big change in Kimmy and Douglas is glad of it.

'Kimmy has no idea of just how bad things are.' Julia has said this to Caroline in regard to the state of her marriage so many times it would be impossible to count.

'Of course Kimmy knows,' is what Caroline says. 'Children know far more than we think they do. Children know everything.'

Except for her Jimjam, of course.

'Kimmy doesn't know there was another wife before me,' Julia says. 'She doesn't know about Rosalie.'

'Why should she?' says Caroline.

'We wanted her to have a stable home,' Julia says. 'It's what both of us wanted. The past, after all, is none of her business.'

'Of course not,' says Caroline, except that the past, so generous in seeding the present with potential surprises, not all of them very nice, is not always willing to vanish quite so obligingly.

Douglas loves Kimmy. No matter what happens, that never stops. He calls her 'old girl' and 'my sweetheart'. He likes to have her around. With Kimmy he's the enchanter who still has a few tricks up his sleeve and Julia doesn't like it.

'He promises her things he can't possibly deliver,' Julia says. 'When I warn her about it, I'm the one she blames. "Leave us alone." That's what she says. "Us" if you don't mind. If it's really just "us" that's so awfully important, then where is it exactly I fit into the picture?'

As far as Julia's concerned Douglas is almost as much of a problem as Kimmy is. Whichever route she elects to take to get Kimmy back on the rails again, Douglas is there just waiting to undermine her.

Douglas, who minds so very much about money, never once complained about the cost of 'detox and re-hab' at that nice place in the country even though it cost him a fortune. He said not one single word. He just paid.

After the first 'trouble' she tells Douglas they should send Kimmy to boarding school, not any old school but a really good school in Natal where no one will know her. The kind Jimjam Bannerman went to. If they do that, maybe she can start all over again as if nothing has happened.

Douglas won't even consider it. He says not in this lifetime.

'She has a perfectly good home here. She doesn't know a soul in Natal. What the hell is she supposed to do there? Why should she be uprooted just when there's a problem and she needs her family the most?'

Johannesburg, these days, is not the place for a young girl to grow up. It's too fast, too free and too easy. It's far too unsafe. Everywhere Kimmy goes Julia goes too. Kimmy needs to be taken; she has to be fetched. Julia needs to know the places she goes to, the people she'll be with. Kimmy may not go anywhere if Julia is not satisfied that a parent or some other adult will be there to supervise. Kimmy may not walk the street, may not use public transport, such as it is, may not accept lifts from anyone or make any last-minute changes of plan.

'Don't you see?' says Julia. 'She's in a prison here and I'm her gaoler. That's what she's rebelling against. She's on a leash with me at the end of it and she resents me for that and I can't really blame her.'

There is much that can be said of Julia and her relationship with her daughter but it should be recorded that at least she understood this much about it.

'Kimmy isn't going anywhere,' Douglas says. 'This is

her home. This is where she belongs and this is where she'll stay.'

Kimmy knows her father has women. She's seen him with them. She saw him once picking up Kelly Davis' mother, who was supposed to be her mother's friend, and he saw her that time and told her afterwards that she wasn't to mention it. He was doing a favour, taking Mrs Davis out to look at a property, which Mum might not quite understand.

There are other times too, when he doesn't see her. Johannesburg is not such a big place for people like them and whatever she sees, she keeps to herself.

'We all live our own lives here,' screams her mother at her father. 'Please don't insult this mess by calling it a family. This isn't a family. It hasn't been a family for a very long time. You've seen to that. At least that's the one thing you've done a good job of.'

Dad is Dad. She knew that he'd come. He looks too big in this nice little coffee shop, where the cups are enormous and all tastes are catered for. Muffins, curry pies, roti, tea, coffee, cider or beer and if you like it cold and straight out of the bottle that's OK too.

Her father doesn't belong here, sitting at this table, with too much of the old world still inside him, shining out of his eyes, but he is who he is. He's not going to change.

'I just wanted to see you,' is all she says. 'To know how things are.'

She looks like her mother but Douglas is there too, in the lithe way her body moves and in her eyes. No matter what's happened between them, those things she knows about him and he knows about her, he feels as he always does when she's near. His load is made lighter just by looking at her.

'If you do what your mother asks, if you just put your pride in your pocket and make the first move we could all see each other any time we liked.'

'Come on, Dad,' she says. 'Get real. It's not going to happen.'

'Your room's still there.'

'Yes,' she says. 'I can just imagine.'

'Look, Kimmy,' says Douglas. 'I don't give a shit about all that bullshit your mother picked up at "Tough Love".'

'It's OK, Dad,' Kimmy says. 'I'm not like that any more. That was a long time ago. I know it was awful for you. It was awful for me too but I'm out of it now and it's over.'

How long can Julia go on blaming her, Douglas wonders? How long can she possibly keep it up? How long is a piece of string? That's his answer. It's the only answer he has.

'I'm not blaming you about the "Tough Love" thing,' Kimmy says. 'You might almost say it did some good in the end.'

'I didn't want it,' says Douglas.

There was a fight about that too but in the end, because both parents are required to show their commitment, at least at the outset, Douglas went too.

It's hard to keep faith with a child who has done the things Kimmy has done. Julia could understand the raves, the fun and the all-night parties. She neither liked nor approved it but if it comes to that, even the substance abuse can be taken on and be conquered, but in those days, before 'Tough Love', when she came to the house Kimmy borrowed money from Gladstone which she never repaid. She removed the DVD player that was bought for her use in her beautiful room most other girls can only dream about. She smashed up a car driving drunk.

'All she ever wanted was for you to get yourself together,' says Douglas.

'I am "together",' says Kimmy. 'I've never been more together in my life. I'm as together as I'll ever be and what's even worse, I'm actually happy. Now there's the one thing I don't suppose she'll ever forgive me for. Isn't that what this is actually about?'

She and her mother are more alike than they know. They can't even mention each other's names without there being some anger involved but even so, between them, they can't muster enough of the indifference it would take to cut themselves free.

'How is she?' says Kimmy.

'Same as always,' says Douglas. 'She misses you.'

'You could have fooled me.'

Kimmy drinks brand-name water out of a bottle. Douglas has Coca Cola.

'If you asked for a glass for that stuff, I'm sure they'd bring you one,' he says.

'Is that what's important?' says Kimmy.

'Is this?'

He means the café, the street and the very bright, very 'now' people who'd rather shout out to each other than talk, who carry their music with them and play it too loud. Kids who seem to touch each other too freely, who share 'take-away' with the informal parking attendants and laugh loudly as if life is a joke.

'It's "Tough Love" both sides, Dad,' says Kimmy. 'Parents can sometimes be hard to love too. I wonder if she's ever thought about that?'

'Why don't we just pack it in then?' says Douglas. 'Let's just give it another shot and do things our own way. We could put all that past nonsense behind us and start all over again and see where it gets us.'

'Because Mummy won't.'

It's a statement of fact and she's right. Julia, in search of the perfect life, the best husband, the golden girl daughter every other mother can't help but envy, has set a path and she won't easily turn back now. At least this way people know that even if Kimmy failed, Julia tried.

'How about money, Kim?' Douglas says.

'Don't need it,' says Kimmy. 'I'm fine. More than fine. I've got a job waitressing. In fact, things are going well with me.'

'Anything I ought to tell Mum?'

'Just that I'm happy. I'm good. My work's going really well and, by the way, I'm clean. She might like to tell her Tough Lovers that, not that she'll believe it, not that they will and, my God, if they did, where would she go every Tuesday? She might even have to take up bridge, God forbid.'

'That's all right, darling,' says Douglas. 'That's good.'

'I love you, Daddy,' says Kim and what can he say? He puts out his hand and she puts her hand in it and it's her baby hand, her little girl hand once so dependably trusting he sees. 'Catch me, Daddy, here I come!'

'I know that, sweetheart,' he says. 'I love you too.'

He reaches toward the back pocket of his trousers, looking for his wallet.

'No, Daddy,' she says. 'I'll get this.'

'I wasn't . . .'

'I know,' she says.

She's already scratching through a tapestry shoulder bag. It's an old bag bought off a street market. It looks as if it's been scratched through many times before and by any number of hands but Kimmy has her own style and in its way, in the richness of its colours, the bag is quite beautiful.

'I told you. I don't need your money. I'm just happy to see you. That's all.'

She takes out her purse and puts a note on the table. Kimmy's hair, like her mothers, is true, pale gold. He hasn't been the best husband, the best father. She hasn't been the best, the easiest daughter.

'If you ever need anything, sweetheart,' he says.

'I know, Daddy,' she says. 'I know.'

'Car still in one piece?' he says to the parking attendant (who, in a multi-coloured Rastafarian hat and small, round sunglasses covering his eyes, is very 'informal' indeed).

'Yes, boss,' he says and he gives him a five-Rand coin, which he wouldn't give normally, because suddenly the day is so fine and the street, this run-down old street, seems for no reason in particular to be shining with light.

ROSALIE

Tuesday morning in London, edging toward lunchtime and wherever you happen to be there's rain rolling across in leisurely waves with the same freedom the wind takes with the grass and all of the world is in monochrome. Water cascades down, soaking everything and then there's a quick snatch of brightness, great pearls of water shake free from umbrellas and they're folded away till they're needed again. All it takes is a small, uncertain glimpse of trepidatious blue sky but it won't be very long before the next roller comes in.

It's Celebrate South Africa in London and Rosalie, who was sent an invitation to the special reception for Nelson Mandela at South Africa House, has made herself conspicuous by not being there.

'Did you ring her?' someone in the High Commissioner's office wants to know from someone else.

They did ring. Someone rang in that check-up of those who had failed to respond, a follow-up which, in this case, takes no time at all because everyone wants to see Nelson Mandela and the closer they can get to him the more privileged they consider themselves.

'The number we have doesn't seem to be working any more. Either that or it's permanently engaged.'

No one bothers all that much about phones any more. Perhaps Rosalie, like everyone else, depends on her mobile but no one really knows her, except as a 'name', so no one can offer a mobile number, if she happens to have one.

She's one of the 'old guard', still important in this moment when the present will come together to celebrate with the past, but perhaps not for much longer.

'It'll make a nice change for some of that old lot to be inside the building this time, instead of standing outside in the rain in a picket line.'

It will be, but those days are past.

These days this old square that's seen so many things, taxis, tourists, picture-takers and touts, will celebrate South Africa's freedom and see something new. Young people with flags for faces, showing green entry bracelets, free for all, but still beyond price, will dance to the Corrs and to REM. Those who miss home and long for it will find it again in the thunder of the songs of Ladysmith Black Mambazo which is, after all, nothing more, nothing less than the call of their land.

Brixton welcomes Nelson Mandela. There's a T-shirt that says so. A man in a blue peaked cap is wearing it. Around his neck is a camera and on his face, for no reason that's clearly apparent, a smile which makes you forget that in the daily grind and grimace thousands of shoppers and commuters scowl and hustle their way along here. Here, in this very same place which is made different today on this drizzly Sunday by one grizzle-headed gentleman the entire world loves.

Everyone wants to see Nelson Mandela. Be careful of flashbulbs please. He has a problem with his eyes. All those years in the lime quarry on the Island have damaged the tear ducts. Bright light hurts him. They'll be careful. He may be in his eighties and joke that he's a hundred but everyone will be careful around Nelson Mandela who they know is invincible but even so, must be handled with care.

'Phone her again. Just once more to show that we tried.' This is the final word from the High Commissioner's office. Very soon, in the flurry of final countdown, someone, even someone like Rosalie, who has without doubt earned her place here, will be lost in the rush.

Was there ever a day like this one? Will there ever be again?

The stone-faced lions who have seen so many things will see something else when Atomic Kitten takes to the stage because these are the new days and everything's changed.

People climb the barriers around one of the fountains in the centre of the square. They climb to the top and sing and dance for freedom in this extraordinary place on top of the world. Until the security officials ask them politely, for their own safety, please to come back, to come down into the singing and dancing crowd and even reach up to offer them a hand.

What a day! What a turnaround! Life back home was never like this and Rosalie, most conspicuous by her absence, who, once upon a time, would most surely have been there, has missed every minute of it.

The girl from the High Commission is on her way to see Rosalie. Nelson Mandela has sent her. Not directly himself but in the aftermath of the concert the word has come down that the absence of Rosalie, expected, not there, was noted and remarked upon.

The general opinion is that she must have died. What other reason can there possibly be?

It's the girl's job to find out.

'Take an umbrella,' her supervisor says. 'Take the tube. Take your *A to Z*. I really don't know why people don't have voicemail. If you find her and there's anything wrong call back to the office.'

What happens if she really is dead?

'Phone Emergency Services,' says her supervisor. 'If she isn't dead find out what her problem is and make sure you tell her that Mr Mandela asked after her himself.'

Mr Mandela is like that. He's just like people say he is. A nice man, very quietly spoken, with time for everyone. Even her mother said in an e-mail how lucky she was to have this chance to meet him because even if you live in the same country you can go through a lifetime and never see more of him than what you see on TV or in the newspaper pictures.

People say Mr Mandela is a man who makes magic and now she has seen for herself how he can. When he's there the whole world is different. Twenty thousand people will stand happily in the rain and

114

wait just to see him. You don't see that every day of your life. One Nelson stands in stone on his column and no one really notices him any more except for the pigeons because the real Nelson, today's Nelson, is out on the balcony of South Africa House.

He just stands there, a man in a coat and a scarf, looking down into the cold and the rain and everyone's quiet and then he smiles and they start to cheer and call out for no special reason, except they can't help themselves.

There must be something wrong with the woman who said she'd be there and didn't turn up but she must have been someone because afterwards, when Mr Mandela asked to see the guest list just in case he'd missed anyone, he saw he'd missed her and asked what had happened to her and if she was well.

You have to be someone for Mr Mandela to ask about you because Mr Mandela asks very few things. You only have to watch him for five minutes moving through a crowd to see that. He always has a nice word to say but all the questions he asks have their own answers. 'This is very fine and what about all those people out there? They haven't come to see me? It's our music they like.' 'We should have some South African sunshine sent in. I see you've all worked hard and done a good job here. I suppose it wasn't possible to organize that.'

There was no sunshine so it was singing in the rain but even the rain stopped when Mr Mandela came out and you can say what you like, no matter who you are you can't help but feel the magic when a thing like that happens.

* * *

115

The girl from the High Commission comes out of the tube station in a break between downpours, out onto clogged pavements and taxis and private cars snarled in a traffic jam and gutters gurgling with water. Michelin people bulky in overcoats jostle each other but at least the umbrellas are folded away. Out on the street, the ice air in her face, she's only a few blocks away from the square and the crescent and the patchwork of elegant houses behind wrought-iron railings where Rosalie lives.

She doesn't see this place the way Rosalie does. She walks down the road, past a fig tree and the smell of fig is the smell of summer and home and walking along in shorts and a halter-top and eating pink-hearted figs hot from the tree and sticky fig milk on her fingers.

She walks round the square where a Japanese girl in a yellow anorak and pink Alice band is out for air with her sister who's wearing bright orange Wellington boots.

The cats today perch like tea-cosies on windowsills, safe behind glass, looking out with unsurprised eyes at the weather. The gap-tooth girl draped in an oilskin poncho is puddle dodging with her lover on her way to the organic produce shop to look for eggs, so there will be omelette for lunch today. A man in a fedora with a paisley scarf round his neck is walking along at a comfortable pace in the company of an amiable-looking Labrador dog.

The girl walks sure-footed now in the manner of the young, in this part of London that's new to her, but she isn't Rosalie and it isn't the calm of a still life she sees. She sees houses. She feels people moving inside them, working, calculating, reading and planning. Even away from its heart there are the sounds of the city. Computers hum, lights are switched on, kettles bubble, tea is made and children pinned in by the rain are rattling these houses nearly to pieces with boredom.

She can feel the Underground shudder through its tunnel beneath her. Ever since she's been here, three months now, the whole city seems always to be in a state of vibration.

It's meant to be spring. The chestnut trees are in leaf. There are blossoms like white candelabra and there's clematis too, pink and purple and grey, and the girl with barely a glance at the *A to Z Guide* has her direction by this time. It's what she might find when she gets there that worries her.

The High Commissioner's office has telephoned and got through at last. Rosalie doesn't want a visitor and doesn't know how to turn her away when she gets there.

'Yes,' she says. 'Yes.'

It was all a mistake. The phone came unplugged. She hadn't noticed it but that's fixed now. (Silvie, who brings a packet of coffee as a gift and a fresh list of complaints about those others they're compelled to share house-space with, has attended to that.)

'I was worried about you,' Silvie says. 'I don't like to intrude but when your phone wasn't working and I didn't see you going out, I thought I'd come up.'

She might have waited to be asked. Rosalie thinks this but she doesn't say so. It's so much easier to switch off. Rosalie can't deal with intrusion. She needs time, more and more of it these days, to prepare herself.

The invitation from the High Commissioner to celebrate South Africa's freedom lies on the table still in its envelope. The pile of post is growing and perhaps she'll get round to it and then again, maybe she won't. The bright blankets are pulled over the bed. She manages that but she eats food out of tins now. It's amazing what comes in tins these days and it's easy enough if you can just remember how the tin opener works. After that you can spoon it up if you want to and if that doesn't work your fingers will do. What does it matter? There's no one to see although it's rather alarming in those times in between to see the tins emptied and all those things left undone that must be quickly attended to.

Garbage put out, the washer put on, jerseys, underwear, tights, everything thrown in together and the shopping to do. It's important to be seen on the street. Just to be seen is enough. She feels like a marathon runner living out that small space readily recognizable as life, between the deluges that batter away at that space in between which is where she actually lives out most of her time in these days.

No one comes to her flat now except Silvie. It's easier that way, but the girl with a mission is persistent. She rings at the doorbell, then rings again. Then she bangs on the door so she has to be heard and Silvie lets her in and her Senegalese lover, irate, stands behind her, draped in a towel just in case after all that furore the door opens to trouble.

Silvie's the one who brings the girl up the stairs. She's the one who taps on the door, says sorry to disturb but this is something important. Silvie, in a dressing gown, her shoulders cloaked with an abundance of untended hair, seems enormous.

'You must please open,' she says. 'This young woman has come from South Africa House. She has a message from Nelson Mandela, especially for you.'

There, it is said and Silvie is glowing. She's smiling with certainty.

'If that doesn't get her out I'm quite sure there's nothing that will,' she says and she's right.

Rosalie is not what the girl's been expecting. This girl who hasn't been quite sure what she's expecting at all. What she finds is a thin, aloof, self-contained, grown-up kind of woman dressed entirely in black. Black skirt, black tights, black sweater and shoes and a vivid pink shawl thrown round her shoulders. The air inside the flat is colder than out, which is to say it is icy.

She doesn't say anything, this woman that Mr Mandela has known as a comrade and friend. She just stands there and looks and she has peculiar wide-apart eyes that seem to look into you and through you as if she knows you're there but you still stay invisible.

It makes the girl fumble and her umbrella, still dripping from the first furious wave of the last downpour, makes marks on the beautiful floor.

'I'm sorry to barge in. Without being expected, I mean. It's just that you said you'd be there and you weren't and so people were worried.'

For an instant Rosalie thinks the girl has found out. She thinks it's her life that she's talking about but she knows it can't be, she's been far too careful for that.

119

'You were expected,' Rosalie says. 'Someone telephoned to say so.'

'They got through, then?' says the girl. 'They phoned before but it seemed as if something was wrong with the line.'

'Nothing's wrong.'

The girl doesn't know what to say so she says in a blurt what she came for and who sent her and watches as Rosalie's face changes and thinks of those tight-packed paper flowers from China that burst into bloom when you float them on water.

While the girl talks Rosalie is making up her mind about things. It is such a nice thing that Nelson wants to see her, that he remembers still and asks after her. She would like to see him.

She never really considered it before. She considers it now, in that moment while the girl is there in the room with her holding everything stable and it's all very clear. The time has come. She would like to go back. That thought has strolled into her head and the feeling that comes in its wake is a comfort. It's the safe feeling of turning toward home, back to safety, before the light fades. It's a strange thought. It's exciting. She supposes it's been there, in her head, all the time, a resolve already made waiting among all those other things, short of nothing at all except being remembered.

'Mr Mandela specially asked after you,' the girl says. 'That's why they sent me.'

The girl says it confidently and hopes that it's true. She didn't hear it directly from Mr Mandela, of course, but no one would lie about something like that. He

120

must have asked about her, otherwise she herself would not have trekked half across London to be here this minute.

'Nelson knows how I am,' Rosalie says with great certainty. 'He always knows. It's amazing what he knows but that's because he cares about his people and always makes it his business to find out.'

'He would like to have seen you.'

'Would he?' says Rosalie. 'I would like to have seen him too.'

The flat is ice-cold as if someone decided that the time for central heating was past, switched it off and hadn't bothered to turn it on again.

She feels confident now with the girl Nelson sent. She thinks it might be nice to talk for a while. There are still things she remembers that might like to come out for an airing. There are things she might like to say.

If she switches the heating back on, in a little while the room will be warmer. She unwinds her shawl, that bright splash of pink, and sees herself without it, a thin woman in black. The same woman who stares out from the dark windows of the tube as it races toward the tunnel but she has no place here. Not right now, this minute. This nice young woman who has come all the way from the past with a message from Nelson has banished her. All the same it's best not to take chances. She takes up her shawl and drapes it over the mirror, tucking it in tight on all sides and the girl, politely, stands where she is, waits to be offered a seat and pretends she doesn't see, but is this not the way one banishes the dead?

CAROLINE

Caroline and Julia have been friends for a very long time. When Gus had his accident, on that terrible night nine months ago now, Julia was the first person Caroline called. Caroline told Julia what she herself had been told and asked if she would come and pick her up and drive her to the hospital. The news wasn't good. She knew from the first moment the call came that it wasn't going to be, which is why she wanted Julia with her and Julia, ashen-faced, came. She was the one who held Caroline's hand while they sat side by side in the hospital corridor waiting to hear.

Caroline's first thought was that Gus didn't belong in that hospital. It's the place he was brought to but it wasn't their kind of place and he didn't belong there. It had a good reputation for being competent and hard-working but it was a poor people's place. You could see it just wherever you looked and there was not very much either Caroline or Julia could do about it.

When you enter a nightmare, Caroline realized, your options shrink and become radically limited.

At the hospital she was just like everyone else. She counted for nothing at all. A 'relative' of the accident victim is what she was there and she must wait, locked in her own thoughts just the same way everyone else must wait, holding tight onto Julia's hand, waiting until it pleased someone to come along to tell her what her fate was to be.

Gus, on the N1 coming back from Pretoria, has been swiped from the road by a runaway truck. The policemen who tell them are lavish with detail. The truck, which was going south to Pretoria, for reasons not yet determined, went out of control, jumped a barrier and landed on the incoming freeway, the one coming north. Eyewitnesses say that, at one point, the truck appeared to be airborne, its wheels no longer in contact with any tarmac at all. It flew through the air just like so many pieces of metal welded together and when it came down it landed with a terrible crash on the freeway below, the one on which Gus was travelling, right in the path of the oncoming traffic.

Caroline, Julia can see, is totally tuned out as if this is someone else's story that has to be suffered through to the end out of politeness because, quite certainly, it can't be her own.

There were cars jack-knifing all over the place, the police say. Some were instant write-offs and there were injuries, some really quite bad but all the same, it's nothing less than a miracle that anyone who'd been there could have come out alive. Even if it is 'only just'.

They can't say exactly why it happened. Perhaps the truck driver lost concentration. Something might have distracted him. They'll never know now because he had no hope at all and aside from him Gus bore the brunt of it. His car was thrown up in the air, the seat belt held fast and the airbag inflated. The 'jaws of life' got him out and the ambulance came. They're sorry to have to be the ones to tell her, it's not a nice job but someone has to do it.

The car's a write-off. It's so badly damaged the people who came on the scene after it had come to a standstill couldn't tell for sure what make of car it had been. A good car though, says the policeman. If it had been one of those Japanese jobs, the kind guys like them drive around in, her husband would have had no chance at all.

Which is, presumably, meant to be of some comfort to her.

Before she knows the worst, just after the first phone call, while she's waiting for Julia to come and fetch her (she is shaking so much, driving herself is out of the question), she thinks all those things that have to be thought even in moments like this.

There's no question of Gus staying at Johannesburg General. He must have his own doctors, a private clinic and a room of his own. This goes without saying.

No point phoning Jimjam in London. That will come later. It has its own place in the grand scheme of things. 'Mummy's looking after it. Everything's going to be fine.' Fire, earthquake, volcano or flood. This is how things are between James and his mother, between Caroline and her son, because Caroline has made it this way.

There will be no dinner for Mr Bannerman at 'Stonehenge' this evening. The staff must be told.

There's been a phone call, an accident. Mr Bannerman is involved and no, she doesn't know how bad it is yet. Mrs Merchant is coming to fetch her, will be here shortly to take her to the hospital, if someone will just be good enough to let her in when she rings.

Caroline, in stirrup pants and a sweater, dressed for an evening at home, goes upstairs to her bedroom to fetch her handbag and a jacket and pulls from her cupboard a Hermes scarf for her neck. By the time she brushes her hair and has a quick check of her make-up Julia is there.

'How bad is it?' says Julia.

'They didn't say.'

They speak in that tone adults use when something unstoppable is happening that the children will have to be told about but perhaps not quite yet.

All over the country people drive like lunatics in over-full cars. Road carnage, they call it, and that's what it is, with all that comes with it. If the camera crew's quick enough, you can see it on television. The shocked, weeping victims, the gaping mouths of the onlookers and there are always onlookers and women crying out loud in their anguish, seeking lost children. Those blanket-covered bundles laid out neat by the roadside and the bizarre twists of metal that once was a car, a bus, a 'kombi', and always the sad scattering of bric-à-brac that was once someone's life.

But they are not those 'others'. You will find no hysteria here.

'Are you all right?' Julia says.

'I'm fine,' says Caroline.

Caroline, who is unable to drive, whose teeth are clenched so tight shut she can hardly get the words out, whose face is only kept together by the greatest effort of will, steps out of her house, allowing anxious, pale-faced Julia to close the door behind them.

She will get through this and Julia will help her. They'll take one step at a time and they'll get there and it's a strange feeling because she can feel herself behaving well in a bad situation and there's some comfort in that. Somewhere in there, inside herself, surely there must be something she can hold onto.

Cuckoo Bannerman, wherever she is in her white 'madam's' heaven, where the tea is Earl Grey, where there's always plenty of ice for the drinks and the table napkins are so heavily starched they can stand up by themselves, would be proud of her.

Since the accident, life at 'Stonehenge' revolves around Gus. It can be no other way.

'If I have to handle this, I will,' is what Caroline says. As though it's as simple as that.

She's his wife and she's made certain commitments directly to him even though the doctors say he can't hear her. What would they know? What is it about doctors that makes them think they know everything? She and Gus have always understood each other so perfectly well they can read one another without a word being said.

Caroline will take care of Gus now and Caroline will make him well. Caroline, brisk, in her element, has had a room fitted out to accommodate every possible need. There's not a hospital in the country, private or public, that has anything better.

There's a day bed in the dressing room for the use of the nurse and the nurses change in shifts of eight hours each. They have their own shower and a lavatory in this, their own part of the house. There are oxygen cylinders for those times they're needed and a steel table for needles and kidney dishes and a cupboard beneath where those other more intimate utensils are kept that need not be on view but that is as far as Caroline will go.

Life may have changed and robbed Gus of himself but Gus' life will not change. Caroline will make certain of that.

ROSALIE

Rosalie is preparing to travel. She's travelling already. She realizes now it's what she's been searching for as she speeds through the tube tunnel. The past is familiar and she knows she'll be safe there.

She hasn't told anyone, how could she, when there's no one to tell, but when things are bad and the world simply refuses to stand steady, she rests in the past. It's easy to do. She walks down a road in Bez Valley. The quality of the light deep-etches everything here. The red brick of the buildings is the deep dark colour of blood. The sky is azure. The people move slowly but here and there is a deep smudge of colour that glows like a jewel. A red sweater, a woman's yellow headscarf that seems to have deepened until it shines radiant as gold. The summer leaves on the trees are indolent. There's no wind to stir them but the air is light, it sighs into the lungs with a will of its own and fills your head up with light.

But what better place is there to be than Johannesburg, where unrest vibrates through the streets and the smell of things to come is hot on the air?

There's the politics. The night drives through the townships, the urgent bang at the back door in the middle of the night that isn't the police and certainly isn't a delivery 'boy'. In this new life there are voices in the dark that resonate with the kind of intensity you will hear nowhere else.

Douglas doesn't know why she left him. How could he not know?

Douglas is in the building business. He goes out each day in an open-back truck to load up casual labour. This is how he tells Rosalie it works. Gladstone was his boss boy. Douglas chose this name himself because, as he said, 'You have to have something you can get your tongue around and their own names are just too bloody difficult.' Gladstone appears at their house every morning; she has no idea where he comes from or how he gets there. When she gets up and goes into the kitchen, aching from the satisfactory assaults of marital love still in its bloom time, parched for tea, he's there, standing at the back door. Douglas says he comes from the township.

'How does he do that?' she wants to know, yawning in this strange air that seems to keep her these days in a state somewhere between bliss and a kind of perpetual irritation she finds hard to suppress.

'By bus, by tube, by taxi perhaps? Don't look at me like that, I'm only asking.'

'Is it important?' says Douglas. 'He gets to work. He makes his way here. That's all that matters.'

She asks if they shouldn't let him in. Even in summer it's cool outside at this hour, in winter it will be icy. Surely he can sit in the kitchen while he waits? Perhaps he would like a cup of coffee. Perhaps he would like something to eat. Douglas, who apparently knows such things and can answer for others, says he would not. He has his own food and drink with him. That's the arrangement. This is Johannesburg, South Africa, her new home, in case she hasn't noticed. It isn't England. The next thing she'll be inviting him in and offering bacon and eggs.

'And would that really be such a terrible thing?' she says and because there's nothing to be said about that and everyone knows how it works and because her sense of humour, being imported, must be different and more droll than his own, he laughs.

'This is the way it is,' he says. 'You'll get used to it in time.'

She's not so sure she will. In fact she's quite sure she won't.

Douglas has a story he likes to tell about a landlady in Brixton who was eaten by her tenants for no better reason than having the temerity to demand the money for her rent. It's the first recorded case of cannibalism in England for as long as anyone can remember. The tenants, of course, were not white people.

This is the way these people talk. As if some divine light shines on them and makes them somehow removed from those other lives that just happen to be carried along on the same tide as their own.

With Michael it's different. Now Rosalie may offer tea with condensed milk or a mug of coffee to a black man and carry it in from the kitchen with her bare feet on patchy linoleum wearing nothing but a petticoat or a faded cotton caftan that in these new days passes for a dressing gown.

She doesn't think her friends from her old life will speak to her now, in these days of her defection, but that doesn't matter. If she has to admit it, she will admit it only to herself but she feels like someone who's arrived at the place she was destined to be and has become, because of it, slightly superior to those others she's left so far behind her.

It is she, the outsider, who knows this place now in the way they never could and what she sees is a city imperfectly woven out of dust, gold and greed.

No matter how big it gets, how it sprawls outward or edges its pushy way up to the sky, the veldt is always there, lapping against its perimeters. It can't outrun that. It's a cocksure place but uncertain in its heart. Nothing here is sure. The dark rumble of uncertainty is everywhere; it's all around. The jumbo jets overhead, the occasional underground tremor from the emptied out mazes that once were the mines, the gold-dusted mine dumps that change colour with the light are a part of it.

You think you could wake up one morning and find it all gone in the night. Gone in that way dreams go at the moment of waking so that all that remains is a memory of some fabulous place once etched on the skyline that shimmered for a while in a dance with the sun and was gone.

She'd forgotten how wonderful it was. Now, she remembers.

The past is a strange place. She moves through it as a familiar. There is a house and a fence and a man and vegetables dying in the back yard because there's always something more important to do than to water them. The dying vegetables are her responsibility. She's been negligent but she's happy in this place. Her clothes hang on her lightly. She can feel the fabric of her skirt as her striding legs touch against it. She can feel the uneven pavement under her sandals. She's aware of her body under her dress and the bones beneath her skin that keeps it all together. She can feel her hair floating round her face, light, as if it's no longer rooted and as she gets closer, as her foot touches that same small eruption of root pushing up from under the pavement, she begins to yearn for the smell of him.

'You're in the newspaper,' Silvie says. 'That South African paper they give away at the tube station. Name, picture, everything. I suppose that girl who was here must have told them.'

Silvie is enormous. Each time she comes heavy-footed up the stairs, wearing the edges of carpet right down to the weave with her large slippered feet, she seems to get bigger. Rosalie is beginning to feel slightly intimidated. Soon, she suspects, Silvie will be too large for the flat and blot it out altogether.

'Have a look,' Silvie says.

She clears a space on the table top, scoops up the unopened post, puts it down on the sofa, moves aside books, exposes dust outlines on the wood and wipes them away with her hand.

'There you go,' she says. 'Take a look. It is you, isn't it?'

The paper makes a terrible noise. It crackles like fire.

132

Rosalie doesn't want Silvie in the room. She doesn't want the newspaper. Rosalie is happy in that other time, in those other places she goes to where Silvie has no place and nor does the newspaper.

'See what it says here,' says Silvie. 'Just look. It says the bells of St Martin-in-the-Fields nearly drowned out the music. Well, they would, wouldn't they? Someone should have thought about that beforehand but I don't suppose it made any difference. Tony Blair got a boo. No one wanted him. They can see him any day of the week, I suppose. It's Nelson Mandela they came out for.'

The paper is quiet. She's grateful for that. There are pictures. A band playing, people dancing. She always liked the freedom songs of the people pouring out, rolling out smooth and steady, unstoppably in harmony with the great world outside. They gave her comfort. She can quite clearly remember they did.

There's a list of highlights and observations.

'Here you are,' says Silvie. ' "Most Conspicuous by Her Absence". It just goes to show. I never knew how important you were. I hope our fellow inmates here see this. They'd just love it. Then they can tell everyone you live in the same house.'

There's a small, long-ago picture.

'Where did they get that?' Silvie wants to know.

It's cropped from a bigger picture, often reproduced because of the unlikeliness of the subjects, a motley assortment of student radicals, pacifists, revolutionaries, trades unionists, clerics, journalists, feminists and others. Seven young men and women and a King Charles' spaniel called Jefferson who might, on the street, have blended into invisibility the way she does

133

now. A politically incorrect group for that time, unremarkable now, shaded to monochrome by black and white Kodak film and the grainy reproduction of news-print.

They always considered themselves ordinary people doing the thing they thought was right. None of them were heroes although she once thought they were. They were far too imperfect for that. When you got to know them too well or found out too much about them you realized that they were all flawed. She went out looking for heroes and found nothing but people not unlike herself whose failings took them in different directions, just the same way their strengths did.

Even so she has no regrets about the choices the girl in the photograph made. Except one. If he'd ever acknowledged her letter, if he'd ever come for her, if she'd ever had the chance to tell him that his flaws were no worse than anyone else's, that everyone had moments when they were uncertain, afraid, deeply anxious, things might have been different.

Here is Rosalie in today's paper, between Martin McGuiness, 'Most Surprising Person Spotted in the Crowd', and the *T4* presenters, Margherita and Joy, who got 'Biggest Goof' for telling the crowd they couldn't wait to see Nelson Mandela on stage, when it was meant to have been a surprise.

'It says here you're going back on a visit,' says Silvie and Rosalie says yes, she is. That's what she told the girl. She doesn't know why. One minute it was new in her head, the next it came out of her mouth. It's what the girl told the young man who wrote the story. She told him over Castle Lager and vinegar chips under cover of the music booming out at the Springbok Bar. 'That's what she said. She told me so herself so I can't see why you shouldn't say so.'

'That's great. Good for you,' Silvie says. 'The break will do you good. I wouldn't mind going with you. One day of rain after another gets you down after a while although things seem to be looking up now. Have you been out? It's really quite warm outside. Shall I turn off the heating?'

'Yes,' says Rosalie. 'That would be nice.'

'She's a peculiar woman,' is what Silvie says to her lover.

'I suppose it must have got to her. All that stuff in South Africa.'

He speaks with his mouth full, looking down at his plate. He eats big pieces of white bread dipped in hummus. On the side of the plate are pink slices of smoked sausage. He likes his food and he likes to eat it like this with his fingers, black curved around white, neatly dipping the bread, everything disappearing through a sparkle of teeth into the pink cavern of his mouth.

'I don't think it's that,' Silvie says. 'Perhaps it is. I wouldn't know but she was always all right, quite nice really. It's just lately she's got so peculiar.'

'It isn't your business,' is her lover's opinion as he holds out his plate for more sausage, indicating the lack of it with a jab of his finger.

'Well, I can't have a woman going barmy right upstairs from me and not make it my business,' Silvie says as she heads for the fridge. 'I don't suppose you've noticed but she hardly ever goes out any more. She just stays up there in her place.'

'I see you've been doing your trick at the window again,' he says and 'thank you' for seconds.

'It's not that. I'm sorry for her. That's all. It's beginning to look like a tip up there. It doesn't bother her at all. It's as if her mind's somewhere else.'

'And what are you planning to do about it?'

'Nothing,' says Silvie. 'To tell you the truth, I'll be quite glad if she does go on this trip. I mean, she must still have friends over there and if there's anything wrong, they'll know what to do.'

Nothing is wrong. There was a time when Rosalie would sit in small rooms with her friends. In those days when she was out on the road, organizing protests, making sure people turned out for boycotts, passing the word along about impending mass meetings.

In those days she'd be led in the dark to those places where the meetings were set up, sit on upturned fruit boxes, use candles for lighting, have only those things around that could disappear in an instant in case of a raid.

What a life it's turned out to be, being part of this big turn of the tide, being swept along by it, taken out of yourself along with this fast-running current that you're told makes individual destiny unimportant.

The newspaper lies open where Silvie has left it. She's glad it's gone silent. She can't stand the noise of it. The small postage stamp face that looks out 'Most Conspicuous by Her Absence' is the face of a dead person. What can it possibly have to do with her as she sits very comfortably, tidily tucked up in her top-floor flat among the pretty houses, Mushroom, Nasturtium and Sage, drifting in and out of the past with her door locked safe against anyone who'd prevent her. She's no trouble to anyone these days and even staying quite still, she's moving just as far and as fast as she wants.

MICHAEL

Not everyone in Johannesburg reads all of the newspaper, not even on Sundays. Rhoda Rosenberg, whose son sees to her wellbeing and has her ensconced in a nice security block of flats in Rosebank, does. What else should one do on a Sunday morning, especially when the security guard brings the paper up, right to the door? First with the news, that's Rhoda.

Sunday, lunchtime, she goes out with Michael. He takes her to a nice, fancy restaurant for lunch. 'Quags', or 'Villamoura' or Zoo Lake. The staff in restaurants always remember Michael because he's a good tipper. In his mother's opinion he tips too much and she's said so to him and said it so the waiter can hear. So, these days, he settles the credit card so she can't see it and gives her that look that says it's his money and he should do what he wants with it.

Sometimes it's just the two of them. Sometimes the

children are with them. Mandy and Tracey, such names for children these days but that's all right too. He could have found a decent girl and had a few more. He could have called them anything he cared to, that would have been fine. He's a good son, no mother could ask for more and as a father, no one can fault him. He would be a wonderful husband to someone but what man can you trust to find the right woman?

People won't say it to her but she knows just the same that as far as looks are concerned he has over all these years been growing into himself. What can be plain at eighteen or nineteen or twenty can be very distinguished as a man moves through the fifties into his prime which is a very nice thing and she's glad for him.

Michael has done well but then his mother never doubted he would.

On Friday night then and now, just as long as they're in the same country, Michael eats at his mother's house. It's always been like that, it always will be just as long, please God, as she's spared. Not even the revolution if/when it came could have been powerful enough ever to stop that.

'You want to see a revolution?' his mother would say. 'Let me look at your place at the table and see you not in it, then you'll find out what a revolution is all about.'

There are certain problems attached to being the son of a capable woman who'd prepared herself for a life blessed with many more children. On Friday night, or so it seems to her son, she cooks for them all, the one she depends on to be there and those others who will never arrive.

'What does he know?' says his father.

It's what his father always says. For a great many years now his mother has spoken for his father. If there was a time when it was different, he can't remember it.

'You're wasting your talents,' his mother says. 'Your father had plans for you. It's a tragic thing for him you're not interested but I won't say it. If it makes you happy it should be good enough for me but if you should ask me, which I know you're not going to, I still say you should give it all up and come into the business where you belong.'

'I'll think about it, Ma,' he says. 'I can't give you an answer right now this minute but I'll think about it. I promise I will.'

He has given up arguing, which would come as a surprise to the people who know him and know his political views but it's a wise man, even in the heat of the Struggle, who knows when the best path is the path of least resistance.

Michael loves his mother's food. His table manners are not always what they should be but when he sits at his mother's table he's in a hurry to eat and he's a big man and the food is delicious.

'Eat,' says his mother.

'He knows nothing,' says his father. 'Kids these days think they know it all. He should ask me. I could tell him.'

'Thank you, Manny,' his mother says. 'But what you know a man doesn't learn in five minutes. It takes a lifetime. He'll find out. He'll come to his senses.'

This is Michael, not as Rosalie sees him or his fellows in the liberation movement, but show me a young man who is ever a hero or even a potential hero to his own mother.

'He's going to end up in jail or worse,' is his father's opinion stated categorically over the brisket.

'He's not going to end up in jail,' says his mother. 'Why do you say such a thing? To say such a thing is to wish such a thing. What kind of father would wish such a thing on his own son?'

'You show me another father whose son wants to change the world. Show him to me. Bring him here so I can see him.'

'Your food's getting cold,' says his mother. 'Do you think it's a pleasure to me to stand all afternoon in a hot kitchen just so I can sit here and watch while you sit around waiting for your food to get cold? Eat.'

'Now, I hear that on top of everything else, he's also a non-believer these days,' says his father. 'All of a sudden he knows it all. What does he care about the cost that got him where he is today and I'm not just talking you and me, Rhoda, you know what I'm talking about.'

'Calm down, Manny,' his mother says. 'You know what the doctor says.'

He looks at his father and wonders how he can sit in his place in a comfortable home at an overfull table, patiently filling his mouth with food, which he eats with no pleasure, and not listen himself to one word he has said.

'No politics at the table,' says his mother. 'You may not agree but you should have a little respect. You know it only upsets your father.'

His parents are who they are. Over the years he's asked his questions and their lives have taught them that least resistance is best as long as it keeps you inconspicuous and out of trouble. That is their answer but it's not good enough for him.

'Is it such a bad life?' his mother asks him after his father has given up, got up from the table, left them, despaired, gone to sit in the quiet of the stoep or into the living room where he sits hunched up right on top of the radio.

What is there to say?

Michael loves his mother and when they're alone has been known to say so.

'Why do you do this to me?' she says in the softer voice she keeps especially for him. 'Sleepless nights I have, because of you, and I'm not so young any more, I can do with my rest.'

'You shouldn't worry so much,' he says. 'All I do for the movement is routine work. A little bit here and a little bit there. I like to help where I can. It does no harm. I'm not looking to be a hero, believe me.'

'I shouldn't worry?' says his mother. 'And since when are you the one to tell me when I should worry and when I shouldn't?'

Is this the same Michael who, hot with desire, lies each night beside Rosalie and speaks only of honesty and never of love? If she saw him now, would she know this boy, who every Friday takes all his life, his hopes and his insecurities and offers them up to his mother in her modest house in Cyrildene?

That's life for you and why should he be so different? The love of a woman, spoken or unspoken, is a nice thing to have. The love of a mother is another thing altogether.

'Stop worrying,' he says. 'It'll only make you old before your time.'

'I am old,' says his mother.

'It'll give you grey hair.'

'What do you think this is?' she says. 'Or maybe I'm the only woman in Johannesburg who goes to have her hair dyed grey just to make her son see she's old enough to know what she's talking about.'

'I love you, Ma,' he says as if it needs saying.

'Thank you,' she says. 'For that, I suppose I have to be grateful.'

How has Michael ever come to be where he is today? There's no 'Midas touch'. There are no spectacular bribes and no secret deals with stakeholders who prefer to remain faceless. All these things have been said about him. None of them is true. At the bottom of it all he is just a small-town boy who happens to be in 'synch' with this city. When the time came for 'cluster' housing he anticipated the trend. When entire villages were required, built behind high walls, discreetly laced with electrified fencing, he can do that and if he thinks of Theresienstadt perhaps he can be forgiven because he is a man who had dreams once and they have turned upside down. There are still people who want apartness but they want it differently now and are prepared to pay for the stage-set ghettos where they live out their lives.

The demand is for residential estates, walled, gated precincts like Fourways Gardens where each curving street is planted with a different indigenous tree whose name it bears: Wild Pear Crescent, Paperbark Street, and Soetdoring Way. There are cobbled crossings, an immaculate park along a watercourse and a nature reserve stocked with small buck, birds and a breeding zebra couple.

Fourways Gardens is the bushveld in suburbia and the ex-patriates doing their African stint love it. The Americans in particular have taken it straight to their hearts and the Americans, their culture so well defined it needs no re-definition, are always anxious to share.

Here the Fourth of July is celebrated with Elvis lookalikes, Cadillacs and hot dogs laid on by the homeowners' association. Hallowe'en and Thanksgiving are bigger than Youth or Freedom Day and estate flags are flown at half-mast on September 11.

Michael has after all played his part in changing the world, but not in the way he intended. His wider dream was of a place where people planted things in the earth and stayed around long enough to watch them grow, but this is a mining town after all. Here some people live out of sight in appalling conditions while others stake their claim, just as they always did, take what wealth there is to be had and move on.

He has taken his father's business and made something of it. He has replaced the city of his youth with sanitized lifestyle packages protected by closed circuit television cameras and parking basements hidden under the cobbles.

Those who know the city as he does can even find here the mixed-use suburban high street they used to know long ago when people still lived above where they worked. Here there are coffee shops and hairdressers and delicatessens and people greet each other in a neighbourly way as they go to work.

Here you may find Parkview as it once was, or Greenside or Yeoville and it's all uncomfortably, unashamedly fake although the site architect disagrees. 'A public bus route runs through this development,' he says in defence. 'Should the security situation change, we will pull down the perimeter fence and connect back into the surrounding fabric.'

Which will be encouraging news for those buildings outside with boarded up windows, cracking pavements and poor people who lie around on the street.

These days in Johannesburg if you look hard enough you can find all of Buenos Aires packed in one over-detailed building or even catch a glimpse of Berlin's reconstructed Potsdamer Platz.

Everywhere there are places that look as if they've been plucked out of some other country and put down here, in this place, fresh, readymade, with no dubious past to account for and it's these places that are changing the skyline. So, in that way at least, he has played his part in changing the world and he wonders if that is something he did that would at last have pleased his father.

If his life hadn't changed the way it did and he'd gone Rosalie's way life might have been very different. Spells in security police detention, extended periods on the run from the police during the various states of emergency tended to turn the people he knew into hardened activists. That never happened to him.

If it had it could have been his face on television and a place in the Government now. He could have sat on the grandstand at the Union Buildings when the

145

change of government happened, along with the rest, and watched the jets flying over.

He might have been offered a big job in London, or Geneva or Paris as a 'thank you' for services faithfully, unquestioningly rendered. Or he could have been dead in an unmarked grave somewhere along with so many others.

Maybe it started off well but he just wasn't cut out for the job.

His mother's right. It's history. If you look for it now you can go to the Apartheid Museum. It stands behind a ten-metre-high stone wall close by Gold Reef City Casino, Johannesburg's own Coney Island between Nando's and a Chicken Licken 'fly-through'. There's the rumble of roller coasters and a big wheel and the brass springboks of the Gold Reef City Casino flank it on either side and in the townships it's known as 'Alcatraz'.

Some people like its rough concrete and face brick and the cavernous spaces beneath that shape the memory of apartheid's history, traumatic, shocking, bewildering and absurd. Others think it trivializes the past, situated as it is with little to see on the outside but a mound of earth planted with Highveld grass and the muted silhouette of the city draped across the horizon.

He has not seen it himself. He got as far as the entrance and then he turned back. He has a history of his own written on his heart but it's history of a more personal kind. There's no point looking back or even talking about it now but even after all this long time that old trickster, memory, will catch him with his guard down and give a sly display that serves to remind him just how potent those old powers once were.

He remembers well enough then and those things that come back to him, those same things that never really left him at all, still have the power to prick at his heart.

There's a big meeting in a house on the Pretoria Road. It's dangerous to have so many big names in one house at one time but sometimes the risk has to be taken because strategic decisions must happen. Everything has been checked and re-checked dozens of times. Michael will drive someone. He won't know who it is until the night and Rosalie will drive too. She insists on it. She says she's already proved her mettle and it will be safer for her than the others because she is white, a woman and English.

She wants to do it and she will. The biggest fish won't be in her car, he'll be put in the care of older hands than hers but someone is assigned to her and she'll have her day.

'Pick up and drop off,' she says like a child repeating a well-rehearsed school lesson. 'How difficult can that be?'

If everything goes well they can both be home by ten. Their instructions are the same. Don't linger. Don't go into the house. Don't hang around waiting to see who'll be there. It'll be dangerous even to know that. Pick up, drop off and leave. How difficult can that be?

Sometimes he wondered if she wanted to get caught. He decided she didn't. She wasn't by nature self-sacrificial. Get away and get them back another day. That was far more her line of thinking.

When he got together with the others afterwards what they talked about was who had betrayed them because the trap was too neat not to have been based on really good information. When they got to tally up the damage they agreed she'd been foolish. She'd stayed too long. She could have got away but she'd acted like the amateur she was. She stayed and she'd been caught.

Had she, they wondered, been waiting to warn someone, the one who might come next? It wasn't her job. She didn't have to know the whole plan to know there'd be a backup and there was. There was someone on the road to give the tipoff.

He knows because it happened to him. He was stopped on the road and told to turn back and he did as he was told and after the stomach-churning fear receded what he felt was relief. He felt light-headed with relief, more grateful than he could say to a person with no name who took his own risks by flagging him down and sending him back.

'Take the old road,' no name said. 'There's probably no roadblock. That would be too much of a giveaway. They want surprise. But don't take any chances. You can never be sure.'

Everyone knows what has to be done. No one should swim straight for the net the way she did.

In these days of defiance, when one half of the city has no idea what the other half's doing, these things happen and she is, in the grand scheme of things, not all that important (although she will be in time).

You take what comes your way and some people get

long lazy days with iced drinks under the purple pomp of jacaranda and others, like Rosalie, get ninety days' detention without trial, renewable at the pleasure of the State.

It is Friday night. Michael goes to his mother's house. Don't think it's as easy as that. It isn't. 'Carry on as normal.' That is the word. 'Do the same things you always do.' 'Trust no one.' 'If they come asking questions you know nothing.' 'She was a woman you knew. She lived her own life. You know nothing.'

If it comes to that, look right in their faces and lie. They'll know you're lying and you'll know they know but what can they do about it? You were nowhere near the Pretoria Road that night. They can check. They're going to have to spend a lot of time checking. You're not the only one. There are any one of a dozen places you might have been and people to vouch you were there. Trust in the plan. The plan is in place in case just such a thing happens and the plan will work. It has to. So much depends on it.

Don't go looking for her. Don't ask after her. You're out of it now. We'll get our own people involved. Don't try and get word to her. It's not a good idea. In fact, it's a very bad idea. When we have something for you we'll let you know.

Her absence is a great calm. He lies alone at the centre of their bed, not on his side, or on hers, in a dark, deep stillness that might be the eye of the hurricane. It's a calm night and beautiful. If he were Superman, which he's finding out daily he's not, he would see through the ceiling and the corrugated iron roof that strides it. He would look down and find

149

himself there in his proper place, in a place no more than a pinprick on the face of a great wasteland of a continent that's long since forgotten what it once might have been.

He has come to the divide and he knows it.

He has come down a poor street, past the chop shop where the cars mutate, past the greengrocer and the vendor making barbecue curry kebabs with lamb of dubious provenance, where on the corner grimy-foot children are having soap-box derbies, playing at Le Mans.

How sad to come to a house of such emptiness, filled with so many things left unsaid.

If ever she walks down this road again, in her confident, catch-me-if-you-can kind of way, it can't be the same. If he reaches for her in the night, which he knows he never will because that too is over, it will not be the same because she was the one who waited to warn him and he was the one who turned back to be safe.

'And so?' says his mother. 'You're not looking so good. I'm not going to say what you know I'm going to say. You know what I'm thinking.'

'Your mother doesn't sleep,' his father says. 'She doesn't like what she reads in the newspaper. And you know what she worries about? She worries about you, our son the big shot.'

'Not such a big shot,' he says.

'Leave it, Manny,' says his mother.

To him she says, whatever it is, this thing she can read in his face, it will pass. How does she know? She knows because that's the way it works. How could any of us go on if it wasn't like that?

*　*　*

When she's released from detention and comes out of prison she doesn't come back. It wouldn't be wise. They've had a close call and they're already too exposed. Already things have moved on and there's no point looking for trouble.

There's no contact. She doesn't telephone him. She sends no word. He hears from others that she's doing good work in the Women's Movement. She's detained again for taking part in an unlawful protest. He's no good on the street any more. There's probably a mark on him and he doesn't mind that. He's lost the belly for it. He thinks maybe it was never for him in the first place but he imagines they know that.

He hears she's placed under house arrest, is freed and detained again but no word comes from her and he expects none. He looks at it and it's passed and she is on her trajectory, flying high in her dangerous game and he has that place that is his life to get on with. He puts behind him his boy's dream of glory and gets on with that very ordinary business we call being a man.

GLADSTONE

Gladstone stays in his daughter's house on Kututsa Street, Dube, Soweto. He has a wooden Wendy house of his own. There's a bed in it, a table and chair and a rail where he can hang his things. The suit he goes to work in, his shoes and his shirts neatly pressed. He cleans his room himself. He insists. He lived alone for a very long time. He's used to taking care of his own needs. He makes his bed. He folds his towel away neatly. There's a card for electricity, Eskom power, paid for in advance.

Gladstone has his own light but even if he hadn't, there's nothing he couldn't find in the dark. He's a man who likes order. Life has taught him this is the best way. There is no Gladstone here in Kututsa Street. Here there is only Pappa or 'ntatemkgulu', grandfather, or Mr Malipile when he walks down the street.

This is his place now. His daughter says so. He has

taken care of her all her life, now it's her pleasure to take care of him. She doesn't know why he goes into town, into work every day. There's no need for it. It's not safe on the train and the taxis aren't much better. No one has any respect for the elderly any more. He can sit back now and watch his grandchildren play. He can sit with his family in the evening and talk about the day and watch Tula's mother on television. He can eat the food his daughter prepares for him. There's no need for him to go into town to do odd jobs in a northern suburb garden. Those days of hard work are over.

'You gave that man his start in life,' his daughter says. 'And what did you get for it? An "old age" job and a watch and you're supposed to be grateful and you still go in to do odd jobs for him. It wouldn't happen today.'

Today things are different. He knows it. He can see for himself, he can feel it in the air but his daughter was not there in the old days. If you weren't there and a part of it, as his daughter was not a part of it, then it is a matter of the heart and a feeling in the bones and there's no one that can tell you exactly what it was like.

'These days you would have ended up being the boss. You could have given Mr Merchant a job if you thought he was good enough and you would have had a proper pension fund to look after you.'

His daughter has a job in a bank and her husband works in the accounts department at Pick 'n' Pay. They were the children of the future everyone had such plans for and now the future is here. They can look after him now. They have told him so often enough but he goes to work anyway.

He listens to Mr M talk about the old days. He remembers them too but not in the same way Mr M does. Jo'burg is different too. It's Gauteng now but people still call it Jo'burg or Jozies. It doesn't matter to him. It's his daughter's place and his grandchildren's. It's not what he wanted, it's not what he planned but it's not always up to you to choose the place where your seed takes root and as long as it's strong and healthy you must be grateful for that.

He is grateful but that doesn't make Jo'burg his place. He walks slow motion through the streets in his suit and his hat, with his shiny shoes on the pavement and the young in their bright clothes move past him with their loud talk and their music that seems to be everywhere.

He feels like a stone in the middle of the river, knowing that river in all of its moods, so that he knows that even after rain the current will never be strong enough to dislodge him and let him move free.

Even so, he's going somewhere. He has a yearning to go to Makhado, which was once Louis Trichardt, back where he came from. His daughter, if she knew, would shake her head and say what for? He'll say it's because he's old and this is not his place and when you're old and your strength has begun to leave you, you hunger for those places you knew as a boy.

He would like to build himself a house and he has a piece of land he can build on. He knows the exact place and although he hasn't seen it for many years, he knows that no matter how many things may have changed, this will not change.

He would like to take time to talk about things with

people of his own, who know the same life he knows. He would like to see cattle graze. He would like a mielie field that is not just a patch but a field big enough for a man to walk through. He would like a few chickens, good-for-something chickens, like giving eggs and for eating, not like the Silkies he showed Tula who high-step in Mr M's yard.

He knows other men from that district and they have gone back. Every year at holiday time they get on a bus and they go and their families are there waiting for them in that same place they left them twelve months before but they have to come back to Johannesburg because this place is where the money is.

As for him, he never went back even though his wife lies in that place and his mother and his father. He thought that place was no good for him but then he remembered that it spared him his daughter and his thoughts began to turn again to those times when the people he loved were still with him.

He has walked down a dark tunnel, a boy, a man, a hard man, a man who has sometimes turned his face even deeper toward the dark to get to this place but it is done now even though the road has not been an easy one.

Very soon he will tell his daughter how tired he is and how his heart longs toward Makhado where his people are buried. He will tell her that he has chosen a place there to build a house of his own where he can sit outside and rest his eyes on the field and hills of that part of the land that he knows. He will tell her how he will wait there for peace to enter his heart.

He may not have a pension fund the way his daughter says he should but he has money. He gives some to his daughter each month and keeps a little for himself and his savings he keeps locked up in a cash-box in the room in the back of Mr M's house. In that place between the mattress and the bed in the room Mr M says is his room whenever he wants it.

'You can tell him you don't need that room,' his daughter says. 'You're not a servant. You never have been all your life. You're not starting now.'

His daughter would be cross if she knew he kept money there but he likes cash money. He likes his money paid out into his hand, counted over again to be sure, put in the cash-box, safe, where he can look at it any time he likes and where can it be safer than where it is now?

If someone comes in the night, it'll be the TV, the sound system, cash and jewellery they'll want. It's not the staff quarters the people who come in the night are interested in. That's the last place they care about. Which is not a thing you can sit down and talk about, especially not with a daughter who works in a bank.

His daughter has a way of her own. Sometimes, at the end of the day, when they're sitting by the table, she'll call her children away from their schoolbooks, away from the TV and say they must ask him to show them his hands but he doesn't want to show them.

They are just working man's hands. What is there to see about that?

That's nonsense, she says.

'No matter what anyone may tell you that says different it is these hands and hands like them built this city.'

This is what she tells her children and she wants them to look long and hard at his hands and remember. There are some things they will find in their schoolbooks but this is not one of them.

'Look closely,' she says. 'One day when people ask you what Jo'burg's all about, you can say it's the city your ntatemkgulu made and if they ask you how you know, you can say you saw it written on his hands.'

They're good children. He is old. It's nice to make your mother happy when she has something to say but it's hard to be as grateful as she expects when you're their age, especially when you aren't quite sure what exactly it is you're supposed to be grateful for.

Was the world not always like this? How could it not have been?

'You need a pass book, a "dompas", to go where I have come from,' Ntatemkgulu says.

It's all right if they don't understand because they are the new world and they have ideas of their own. They have eaten Kentucky Fried Chicken. They can go to Rosebank Mall whenever they want. Even so, there is one thing he asks of them and one thing they do for their ntatemkgulu. They're smart children, these Gauteng grandchildren of his. That's what he tells them. That's why he's given them this job. They are the ones who check his Lotto card when the numbers are shown on TV on a Saturday night.

His eyes are tired these days. He thinks perhaps they have seen too many things and the brightness of television bothers them so his grandchildren check the numbers for him.

'It's time, Ntatemkgulu,' they call out.

'You keep your eyes open,' he says.

It's the grandchildren who watch the balls spin, nine o'clock on TV, and work out his Lotto 'Ta'ta ma chance, Ta'ta ma millions' ticket for him. One day, they say, it will be Ntatemkgulu's turn to win millions and who knows, maybe it will.

Who would wish them a 'dompas' to go back in time and look at that place? It wouldn't be him because he has been there and he knows.

JULIA

Not everyone in Johannesburg reads all of the Sunday newspaper. Douglas doesn't. A Celebrate Freedom concert in Trafalgar Square is the last thing that interests him.

'Taxpayers' money,' he says. 'As if the Rand isn't bad enough. They can throw a few more away and have a good time. After all, it's only our money they're talking about.'

Just hearing about it is more than enough to put him in a bad mood for the rest of the day. By mid-morning he and Julia will have managed to pick a quarrel about something. It's easy enough. The list of combustible subjects is lengthy and growing by the day. It's easy to settle on any one at random but these days the quarrel is a red herring, no more. He already knows perfectly well where he's going. He has his day planned. Sometimes he'll say he has work to do at the office.

'Of course you do,' she says.

It's what wives like Julia always say and the words are worn down with long usage and have a bitter bite to them.

'I might take a drive out and check on that site. The one I told you about. The one we're tendering for.'

He has told her nothing at all.

'In any case. I don't how long I'll be.'

As long as it takes is what Julia expects.

Sometimes he says nothing at all. All she hears is the furious snatch of his car keys from the hall table and the bang of the front door. Forty-three seconds before the sound of the car pulling out of the garage onto the driveway. Julia's timed it and a little while longer till she can get the furious choking feeling out of her throat and the house settles down into order again.

They used to entertain but they don't any more.

'Because you always make excuses and leave,' she says. 'You leave me with our friends and we have to carry on without you. People aren't stupid. It happens so often, they want to know why.'

'Can I help it if I have a business to run? It's my booze they're drinking, my food they're eating. You're in heaven with everyone saying how wonderful you are. What more could you want?'

She could want those things she once thought she had in that time she believed they were happy together but perhaps she's forgotten and that wasn't true either. Perhaps it was just some story she made up to comfort herself with.

On Sundays Julia has her house to herself. She reads the newspaper with great care and attention. She has

160

something small and delicious for lunch, a nice gin and tonic, tangy with lemon, to kick off with and a really nice bottle of wine with the meal. Douglas' 'best', the kind whose absence he'll notice and comment on. First class on the *Titanic* is Julia's view. If it's her turn to be burgled, molested, held personally accountable for collective sins past, now is the time. Any Sunday will do.

Things look very much better on Sundays. Douglas is accounted for. She may have Thai chicken salad. She may have smoked salmon sandwiches. Those fresh Friday flowers, the enormous bunches she likes to see the house filled with, are in their full glory by Sunday. The backyard is quiet. Gladstone has gone back wherever he came from. Adelaide goes to the township to be with her friends. Sunday's a good day. Julia's gold bracelets jingle as she moves the glass to her lips. The fountain has a pretty splash. No wind stirs the trees. You hear such terrible stories but if one really has to, a Johannesburg Sunday is a nice kind of day to become just another statistic in a police dossier.

MICHAEL

On Sunday, if he's up early enough and the weather is fine, Michael drives around Johannesburg. In the week you can't move in the city centre because of the traffic through the main city arteries, the people and vendors, but on Sunday with the people drained out of it the city is a quiet place. It's a ghost town and the sound of a single car going down Commissioner Street is an intrusion.

He likes the quiet of it. He likes to drive slowly past the façade of the Rand Club in Loveday Street. Past the Post Office with its round-faced clock and the spring-boks leaping through cascades of water in the Oppenheimer Fountain below, past the classical pillars of the old City Hall and the Library and Africana Museum that stands at the heart of the town. As he drives he sees all around him the bones of the city that once stood in this place, that city that could never quite hide its humble beginnings under its hastily acquired veneer of European respectability. He does not wish it back. There are not bronze fountains or statues or deep-foundation buildings enough to ever quite manage to keep Africa at bay because that is the way it is here. People come, people go and given time, Africa always comes back seeking its own.

After his drive through the silent city or on those other Sundays when he has his girls with him, Michael drives to the News Café in Rivonia for coffee, for croissants, for fruit salad and fruit juice. He likes these drives with his girls cheerfully squabbling about whose turn it is to sit in the front with him.

'One seat belt, two young ladies. You sort it out.'

He has not been a man accustomed to having women vie for his favours in this way that comes with no price-tag attached. He's glad he has daughters, who have women's ways without having their guile. He wishes he could keep them this age for ever.

On Sundays at the News Café people read the Sunday papers, they eat bacon baguettes and watch the black-gear Harley riders rev up the Fatboys, roar around, throw 'wheelies', and screech backwards and forwards. They're here every Sunday making a sideshow for the designer people from the north side of town before they set off on their rally.

It's a buzz. The girls love it, the diners love it and Michael likes it too.

'You could take them to Sandton Square,' Liane says. 'They're getting to be bigger girls now. The boys are beginning to look. If they come home dragging someone with a tattoo along with them, you may not like it but you shouldn't ask why.'

What she's saying is that when the 'looking' starts in earnest, it's the Sandton Square boys that should be looking at their girls, not the biker boys from the News Café, but he thinks it's far too early to think about things like that yet. He'll know when it's time. Fathers always know this. They keep right on knowing till it's far too late and they find it's grown women they're looking out for. Women who look back at them and know every time Dad looks at them, no matter how old they are, it's still Daddy's little girl he wants to see.

The Rosenberg girls are safe for today. They sit at a table outside, chattering on, gossiping on and every now and then asking Dad for his opinion. It's a good life and a fine day, clear, as if someone got up very early to polish it up, in the way these late summer days are up here on the Highveld.

Michael, in slacks and docksiders and a Lacoste T-shirt, is at one with the world. The air is filled with a scent of coffee and wellbeing. The bad times are past. You can see it just by looking at the waitrons, kids in all shapes and sizes and colours playing the new game in town in which it's every person for themselves because destiny, when they write it these days, will be written in economic and not political terms.

Their waitress likes Michael. He's a good tipper and he's nice to his girls, those two little girls who always have all of their father's attention and don't know how lucky they are.

If she asked Michael he'd tell her how much children change you. How they have a habit of turning the world upside down and then re-arranging it with themselves at its heart. Until you have children you don't know about love. Where is it you find enough love to give them when there's never enough?

'You want to go out and watch the bikes get started? Give Dad ten minutes alone with the paper.'

The bikers will go off in a crescendo of noise that shakes the more hesitant leaves from the trees. There'll be wheel spins and maximum revs and there's always a small crowd of kids, neat kids, like his, waving and egging them on and why not? They're good kids. There's nothing in this world they can't have. He looks around him as he goes through the motions of picking up the paper and opening it out and he wonders. Does it really matter how they got here, all these lightly scented women and designer-shirt men? Here they are, safe and wrapped in wellbeing. The fruit they eat is organic. The coffee's Blue Mountain. There's unsalted butter. The 'confiture' is hand made, lightly sugared. It still has the fresh taste of real fruit in its heart. There are eight different kinds of tea and probably more if you cared to ask. He's counted. He knows.

He settles back in the chatter and opens the paper, magazine section first, because you need at least the sweetness of jam with the main news these days and the first face he sees is Rosalie's.

CAROLINE

On Sunday Caroline has a business appointment. A man is coming to talk about the house.

'Not the main house, Mrs Bannerman,' he says. 'Unless of course you'd consider including that in the deal. It's the property surrounding it we're interested in but if you've looked at our proposal, you'll see there's no reason at all why the main house shouldn't stay just as it is.'

Caroline would have preferred to meet him at her solicitor's office. She wants to wait until Jimjam flies out for the summer but Jimjam doesn't spend all that much time at home any more. Not even when he's out on a visit, referred to as a visit 'home' when all that means is little more than a courtesy fly-past.

'They're your friends, not mine,' he says of the parties she organizes for him. 'And honestly, I wish you wouldn't. I just don't know what to say to them.'

Dinner with Dinosaurs is how she imagines it seems to him.

As far as the property is concerned, he says she should sell it.

'I wish you would, Mum. Really, I do. I mean, what's the point? What are you holding onto it for? Don't say for me. You know how I feel about that.'

She doesn't want to think too much about it. It's too big a thing to deal with on top of everything else. She knows she has to think about it some time and sometimes she does. She lets it sit in her mind for a while and when it starts aching, which never takes very long, she pushes it aside and turns her thoughts to other things more easily dealt with.

Jimjam, or James as he likes to be called, is happy in London. He has a good job there. The bank who 'head hunted' him have done wonders with residence permits and he's not coming back. At least, not in a hurry. For holidays, yes, for a while, but the world's a big place, there's so much to do and annual leave is not very long.

'You want my advice?' he says on the telephone. 'If you get a good offer, take it. Get a smaller, safer place for yourself. Pension the staff off. You don't need all those people. Change, Mum. It's all change. You've got to hook onto it.'

It isn't that easy. There's something else too. Something they talked about on the last visit, not to be spoken of again. Not by James, not by Philip Stevens, a good friend, Gus' doctor who still comes by once a week on his way home and stops for a drink, not by Father Oliver, the new young priest down at St George's, not by Julia, not by anyone at all.

'Face it, Mum,' James says. 'Things with Dad are not going to change. He isn't ever going to be his old self again. He isn't even going to improve all that much. He just isn't. He hasn't actually been "here" for a very long time. He's not going to be "here" again.'

It may be so but even so, she doesn't want to hear it, especially not in her own home, with Gus lying upstairs in his cool, airy room in that part of the house that revolves around him.

'You ought to listen, Caroline,' Philip Stevens says. 'What he says is good sense and I can recommend an excellent care facility.'

Gus owes his life to Caroline. This is Philip Stevens' professional opinion. She's the one who oversees his meticulous care and ensures that the money, the energy and expertise that keep him breathing in, breathing out is always available.

'Gus was a person who never gave up,' Caroline says. 'If things had been the other way around he would never have given up on me. I don't intend to give up on him either.'

To the priest, who is not much older than Jimjam, the answer is simple. Whatever is meant to happen will happen, in God's own good time.

'You should listen to what James and Philip say to you,' Julia says. It's all she says because Julia knows the whole story and if anyone asked her, which they don't, she would have to say what Caroline knows, which is that 'God's own good time' is a very long time coming.

Before he married Caroline, Gus was not exactly a saint. Everyone knew it. There was a previous wife who died young. No one said it out loud but there was the smallest sliver of accusation about Gus being indirectly responsible. The greatest nonsense is how Cuckoo Bannerman dismissed it. You don't go into the bush without taking Daraclor. Everyone knows this. Her late daughter-in-law was a grown-up woman. Surely no one could have expected Gus to spoon-feed her anti-malaria pills to her.

No one did. What people expected was for Gus to be a little less adventurous. The general opinion is that people with money, like Gus, tend to think the world has been set in its place just for them to do as they please in. As far as the bush is concerned, the advice of the Parks Board doesn't apply to them. When they feel like a bush break they don't concern themselves with any of those small irritating details like the rest of us do; like making themselves known at patrol points to show they have permits, say who they are and where they'll be going.

News about local conditions holds no interest for people like them. That is for local people. They are Johannesburg people. That's plain to see and it sets them apart.

They 'know' the bush. That's what they say. What they seem always to overlook is that the bush knows them too. It was there long before they came along and discovered it. It will be there long after they're gone. It's always there, ready for them, waiting for them to get just a little bit too sure of themselves so it can put them right back in that small place where they belong.

'She died of cerebral malaria,' says Caroline, referring to her predecessor. 'How on earth can anyone blame Gus for that? You didn't just pop a Lariam in those days or smear yourself all over with Jungle Juice. The poor man was devastated.'

'Sticking to the beaten track might have been a better idea,' is Julia's mother's opinion. 'What is all this nonsense anyway? Why do these men always want to go "where no white man's been before"? If no white man's ever been there before, there's probably a good reason why. They ought to take that into account.'

People talk about it for a while and then forget. Gus comes back on the market, with his bravado intact, as eligible as ever, maybe more so and, properly managed, the loss of his first wife may be Caroline's gain. This is Cuckoo Bannerman's opinion. There's nothing wrong with a reasonable age gap in a marriage, particularly if the woman is younger. Caroline is a pretty girl and no trouble at all. She still has her reputation intact, which is more than you can say about most young women in Johannesburg and there's something alluring about her. Perhaps it's her innocence. She could, Cuckoo tells Alice Merchant who has after all a son of her own, 'keep Gus fully occupied' but even so, Gus gives them a run for their money.

There's one thing, no longer spoken of, that Gus Bannerman raised from the status of courtesy to that of an art form, and that is the farewell gift. 'He gives a great kiss-off,' as one woman put it.

At one time, when there was a run on, it was hard to say which was more desirable, being courted by Gus, which was not without its pleasurable side, or being dumped by him for the next one, which was not without its reward.

He did it so charmingly, with such genuine regret, that it was almost worth getting into it just to get out.

Kitty Kavanagh got yellow diamond stud earrings although nobody liked to ask what she did for them. Tish Bailey got a very pretty serpent bracelet with emeralds and rubies that snakes up her arm to this day and if Caroline knows where it came from she doesn't mention it.

JULIA

Life changes, none of us lives for ever, none of us knows what lies round the next corner. If we want to do something, now is the best time. It might be the only time we have.

Gus is Caroline's responsibility but Julia thinks of him more often than anyone knows because in a way they are both a burden to somebody else which makes their positions not all that dissimilar. Caroline has never given up on Gus. Julia's guess is that Douglas wrote her off a long time ago. As far as he's concerned she might be as Gus is, living and breathing, using up her allocated space in the house, there for just as long as it takes and not one minute longer and then it will be over.

But she is not Gus.

Douglas thinks she has run out of surprises but he's wrong. If Douglas only knew his wife he would know that Julia is filled to the brim with surprises. She hasn't had the inclination to spring any of them on him just yet. That's all.

'If Rosalie really does come out, I'm thinking of giving a party for her.'

It's the Monday after the Sunday papers and this is what Julia says to Caroline.

'You saw it in the paper then?' Caroline says. 'I saw it too but I thought I wouldn't mention it, not unless you did first.'

'Why ever not?' says Julia.

'I thought you might not want to talk about it.'

'Why shouldn't I want to talk about it?' Julia says. 'I think it would make the perfect finish, for Douglas, for me, perhaps even for Rosalie and after all, aren't we reaching the age when we're supposed to seek closure?'

That is something Caroline has been thinking about too lately. She thinks about it as she sits beside her husband, half an hour each morning, half an hour each evening, watching the ventilator breathe in and breathe out and people think she doesn't know or overlooks them but she thinks about the diamond earrings too and the snakes. Those snakes of gold with emeralds and rubies for eyes that may slither up and down where they please now and rope themselves around arms no longer as young as they once were. It cannot make any difference to Gus now.

This is what Caroline thinks about when she thinks about 'closure' and it's a very different kind of 'closure' she and Julia seek.

'Douglas doesn't know about this, does he?' she says.

'Why should he?' says Julia.

'You're not going to tell him?'

'Why should I? When he needs to know, I'll tell him everything and that's time enough. Douglas of all people should understand that. It's been his way for years.'

'It's a rather nasty surprise, don't you think?' says Caroline.

Yes,' says Julia. 'It is rather, isn't it?'

ROSALIE

Silvie is worried about Rosalie who appears to be becoming more peculiar by the day. What she's worried about is that she might end up getting landed with her. She already has two nutcases to deal with. The osteoporotic psychoanalyst has started chanting in the night, an eerie, atonal sound that goes on far too long. In the communal hallway she's as icy as ever, filled with accusations of unspoken outrages she offers up to Silvie with her eyes.

The lapsed priest's boy's Piaggio has been staying overnight, shackled to a railing with a businesslike Chinese padlock that seems to speak more of fore-thought and planning than a spur-of-the-moment passion too strong to resist.

A phone, which ought to have had its service suspended, receives calls loud and long across time zones and finds voice at all kinds of inconvenient hours in the locked and barred basement flat that belongs to the Spanish woman.

It is how people live now and Rosalie, last seen coming round the Crescent toward the road, wrapped in her usual black with a mauve hat on her head, dragging a heavily laden basket-work shopping trolley behind her, seems to be behaving more oddly with each day that passes.

If she didn't know better Silvie might think she was harbouring a convict or a lunatic on the run, which would be more easily explained than her other thought, which is that Rosalie, out of loneliness, has bought a large dog. If a world was ever destined for destruction, a dog on the premises is all it would take to seal this one's fate.

No single woman needs so much tinned food. Rosalie has to take it up the stairs a load at a time because of the weight of it.

'Especially if she's planning to go away. It doesn't make sense.'

'She isn't going anywhere,' says the Senegalese lover, who likes to eat mango. He is eating mango now and the smell, so supremely out of place, is exotic and delicious with a faintly erotic undertone to it.

'There's something wrong with her,' Silvie says. 'It's not natural. I think maybe she's sick or something.'

'She looks all right to me,' says the Senegalese lover.

'I'm not so sure,' says Silvie. 'You can't always tell by looking. Don't look at me that way. I'm only saying. But with some things you can't.'

JULIA

Julia has telephoned External Affairs, not named for Douglas but it occurs to her while she listens to Vivaldi and waits for a voice human and not electronic, that it very well might be.

It mattered once. It doesn't matter now. Now she can find a number for South Africa House. She can make an international call. No, she doesn't mind holding, the meter's running and the sound of her husband's money being consumed with the kind of gluttony that would make a slot machine proud, is not entirely unpleasant to her.

If South Africa House can find Rosalie once, to come to their great Freedom party and have it splashed all over the Johannesburg Sunday papers, then they can find her again and Julia has waited a very long time. She can wait just a little bit longer. She will 'hold' all day if she has to, all the way across continents, until

she finds some person who can string two words
of sense together and give her the information she
wants.

CAROLINE

When Caroline paces the house, walks alone through the garden, she walks through time past. Where are those friends that once danced here? Where are the swimming parties, the tennis, those days Cuckoo opened the garden for the 'needy' and cadged once-worn designer dresses from her friends to put up on sale?

Where is Jimjam with his Nanny? Where are his friends? The Marcs, Nics, Pauls, Davids. Home for the holidays. 'Can I bring friends, Mum?' Where is it they all went to, she wonders?

She pauses on the lower terrace and looks back at the house, at the way the light brings out the sweet hues of autumn buried deep in the stone. What a day it was when Julia married and the guests danced under a float of white muslin to Dan Hill and his orchestra.

All of it wonderful until the hail came down and ended the day.

What a pity to spoil such a beautiful day. Her first party all to herself as the new Mrs Bannerman with Cuckoo on best behaviour, definitely not to interfere, supposed to be strictly sequestered in her own part of the house.

Cuckoo and Caroline, the two Mrs Bannermans, are a formidable pair. Everyone says so. Julia's wedding party will be an event. Julia, who has waited so long for this day, with the shadow of Rosalie not yet dispelled, deserves this. There will be an arch of flowers and a service in the garden. Julia will have Mendelssohn to float in on and walk back down the specially laid carpet to Purcell, with her prize on her arm as other brides before her have done.

The service will be tasteful and simple. There will be no surprises. As a favour to Cuckoo, Mimi Coertse, out on a visit from Vienna, will sing 'O, Perfect Love'.

'Oh, dear,' says Julia's mother. 'Surely not? Must she really?'

'We can't ask her to change to something else now,' says Julia. 'It's all been decided.'

'Can't we?' says her mother who is privately of the opinion that while there are people living who are prepared to trump their partner's ace you can do practically anything you please. 'Well, I suppose we must have it then.'

After the service there will be champagne in the garden. Black waiters in black coats will glide through the crowd offering Krug Grand Cuvée, Cuckoo Bannerman's gift.

What price on a house sold along with its memories?

Does the value go up or does it decrease? Houses are, after all, like those racy ladies Gus so enjoyed in his heyday. They're beautiful enough, to be sure, but their past is not to everyone's taste.

No one uses the swimming pool any more. Caroline has never cared much for swimming and so she avoids it. You can't help but see it though. It is situated where it is for precisely that reason. At night it's underlit and the water, egged on by the pulse of the vacuum cleaner that slow-dances over the bottom, makes restless patterns through the light as it goes. Sometimes Caroline can stare out at it for a very long time and sometimes she can't look at it at all.

On the day Julia married all she had to do was glance out of the window of the room set aside as her dressing room and she could have seen it as well. What she would have seen is Caroline's surprise. A sea of hydrangeas cut fresh that morning afloat like a cloud, pink and blue and every shade of purple you can think of.

'Quite heavenly,' says Caroline. 'I knew we simply had to do it.'

Julia's mother is not quite so certain. The house is already so full of flowers there's barely room left for a buttonhole.

'Looks like a funeral,' says Julia's mother, which as it turns out is not the most fortunate remark.

The rose bedroom has been opened up for Julia to dress in. She will walk into it an attractive enough young woman with all the options in the world hers for the asking and come out a bride, a new person altogether, with this new creature, a husband, to consider and a lifetime she's promised, cross her heart, she will share.

The room has a pair of brass beds and a fine Japanese lacquered screen not completely in harmony with the overblown flora in the wallpaper.

'They might have chosen a more cheerful painting,' says Julia's mother.

'It's Millais,' says Julia. 'It's called *The Mistletoe Cutter.*'

'I don't care what it's called,' her mother says. 'That poor girl looks as if she's going to burst into tears any minute.'

Julia's mother in turquoise brocade and a view-blocking hat does not care for weddings.

There's a photograph in her house of her own wartime wedding. When it's her turn to play 'host' to the bridge ladies she arranges the tables and places herself with her back to it. To be near the kitchen, she says. To order in tea when they have their break.

When people remark, as they've been known to, on how striking the couple are, Julia's mother concentrates on getting more important bridge matters in hand. She has long since disassociated herself from the glaze-eyed twosome looking into the lens with about as much good sense between them as a pair of rabbits with myxomatosis staring into the lights of an oncoming car.

She does though occasionally voice an opinion in that brisk, dry way she's learned over the years. War, she says, does women a dreadful disservice. Men tend to look misleadingly better when packaged in uniform.

* * *

Hydrangeas in the swimming pool are the fashion for parties that summer and they may as well enjoy it because the fashion won't last. The garden is strung with lights small as fireflies. You can't see them in the day but as the light fades someone will see to it they're turned on and the effect will be dazzling. The garden will be a fairyland spangled with minuscule stars. Those beautiful ladies in their long drifts of chiffon, of lace, of organdy, some of it sewn with beads and with sequins that glitter in the dark, will 'ooh' and will 'aah' and everything will be perfect, just as long as the rain keeps at bay.

The staff in the Bannerman house is accustomed to parties, except for the new maid called Regina who is still on probation. This is Cuckoo Bannerman's policy. All new staff have to come recommended. Even so, they come on three months' probation. If there's anything you need to know, anything left conveniently unsaid because a person happens to be in need of the work, Mrs Bannerman will know in less than three minutes. Three months is a more than safe margin to guard against any mistake.

There will be no husbands or boyfriends who are troublesome and want to come in and out in the night. There will be only a reasonable amount of time given off to attend funerals. Surely everyone has a finite number of antecedents? You wouldn't think so if you listened to the stories the white 'madams' tell. Good, clean, hardworking girls are what they want, preferably with no past, especially if bed and board is to be included.

* * *

Regina's an odd one. She doesn't fit in very well. 'She's there but she isn't there,' is what Cuckoo tells Alice. 'We'll just have to watch her and see how she goes.'

Regina comes recommended by the Fordyces' maid. She's a 'cousin'.

'But of course they're always related,' Cuckoo says. 'One expects that.'

Regina knows the rules. Cuckoo always takes a newcomer into the study and explains things herself so there can't be any 'I didn't know' afterwards.

There will be one day a week off. Thursday is that day. On Thursday the family look after themselves and her Sunday will be the last Sunday of each month. There will be no exchanging days off. Laxity here can only lead to chaos. If there were some extraordinary circumstance in which any variation at all to the schedule might be considered this must be discussed with Mrs Bannerman, but it should be noted at the outset that the circumstances will have to be very extraordinary indeed. In the case of anything less than what Mrs Bannerman considers 'extremely extraordinary' such requests will be looked upon with disfavour as being simply another device to waste time.

There are to be no men at all hanging around, not for any reason whatever. She isn't interested in husbands, boyfriends or babies. If there's anything like that going on it must stay in the township where it belongs, she doesn't even want to know about it.

There will be no borrowing money against wages. There will be no borrowing money at all. This must be understood and understood clearly. No family member is ever to be approached for financial aid. If there's a long story to tell with a price-tag attached to the end of it, and in Cuckoo's experience there usually is, that is Regina's own business. No one here wants to know about it and that includes other members of staff.

If you are Regina, invisibility is an asset. In a place like this it's the only asset she has, for which her cousin says she must be grateful because she's in that worst of all positions, in which she has to be grateful for just about everything.

When she goes back to Alex, to the township, she can put on her red dress. She can walk down the street in high heels. She can feel her bum move side to side, nice and smooth as she walks and if that gets a whistle that's all right too. She's still a young woman.

'It's work,' says her mother. 'No one's going to come after you. Not in a place like that.'

On her first Thursday 'off', afternoon after two o'clock only, she sits in the small hot square that's her mother's house and wishes 'they' would come. Let them come. She would welcome it.

'It's just till I find something else. Just till Habs comes to fetch me.'

Habbakuk, Habs, is her man. He will come. He'll come for her but even if he's found someone else, even if he doesn't come for her, he'll come for their daughter Lindiwe and when he does come, what they'll do is go back with him, wherever it is. She doesn't care. Any place is better than the place she is now.

She knows he's in training camp but what does it matter? She can like Cuba. The sun shines there too. She can like any place if Habs is there, if her daughter is there, if she can walk down the street showing her bum, letting her breasts point in any direction they like, laughing her laugh just as loud as she likes. People can look if they want to. They can look all the way past her teeth right down her throat to her stomach if they like. She has plenty to laugh about. She has to do all the laughing in the township now but that won't last. When Habs gets back, when they stamp out their self-appointed masters once and for all and they will, that will be the day they all laugh together.

If you believe this and she does, then you can still laugh because there's still something to laugh about. The day you doubt it, she refuses to think of that day except as a day on which all the laughter in the world will have died.

She can go around Mrs Bannerman's house, she can dust, she can make beds and clean and she will be what they call her, odd Regina with her last laugh, the one they don't know about, locked deep inside her.

'I'd rather work in a shebeen. I'd rather walk streets.' She says this but it's big talk, despair talk and it isn't the truth. Habs' friends say she's safe where she is. The police are everywhere. In the streets, in the townships, you don't know who'll inform and where they might turn up next but they'll never come looking for her at the big house on the ridge.

Soldiers do as they're ordered. She is a soldier despite her headscarf and overall, arrived from nowhere, with no outside life of her own just the way Mrs Bannerman likes it and if the other servants are wary of her, who can blame them? They have their jobs and she has connections, suspected by all of them, spoken by none.

Mr Douglas, when he comes to the house, looks at Regina. A man is a man after all. The headscarf and overall may satisfy Mrs Bannerman but a man can see past that and Douglas, so close to making Julia his bride, is a man who knows women but there's something in Regina that's too strong for him so that even he turns away.

Regina can wait. She can be alone if she has to. She can sit in her small room in the compound. She can wait for her turn in the shower room. She can grow used to the familiarity of the other workers, the way they talk to each other, the sounds of their voices, their coughs and their snores. She can listen to her radio, keep it turned low on the shortwave and listen to Radio Zambia to hear how things are going out there, in the struggle for freedom.

There are other people sitting alone in the dark waiting. She is safer than they are. She, who must do as she's told, who never asked to be safe. People who start early go to bed early and it's quiet here behind the big house on the ridge although you can hear the city humming below.

She would like to be down below in the hum. She would like to be borne up on it. She would like to lie in the hot dark and drink beer and maybe make another baby and why not? She's not old and she's strong, she likes the feel of life taking root in her womb. If she could be mother of all of the new world she would do it. But she can't do it like this. She can't do it here.

The city looks beautiful from up here. A city spun from lights that rests in the dark of your eye for an instant and then floats away and is gone in a blink.

She has had no letters and she misses her man. Letters are dangerous. She misses her daughter, blood of their blood, who doesn't yet know her father. She fears sometimes that she will lose that woman she was. It must be some other woman who walks through the night garden up on the ridge and feels the cool prick of night on the soft dark of her skin and something else coming, while the white house sleeps.

There are things she feels in her womb, in her breasts, in the soft hollow of her neck and the tender places behind her knees that tell her something bad and terrible is coming her way.

There is no laughter in her in the night. That other woman of the red dress has been borne away to that other place where she may be at this moment, wrapping men in her laughter, keeping fear at bay with her certainty. She is afraid for her daughter. She wants to keep her with her. She wants them to sleep in one bed. She wants the certainty of her body and the feel of her sturdy heart beating. She wants to hold her close and smell the child smell of her hair and the smell of her man, that man who made this child with her, that lingers in her skin.

She wants to be somewhere other than this place which is not a good place for her. She wants the world to turn around again toward morning and things to fall back and settle this time each into a proper place they may claim as their own.

* * *

Lindiwe is not allowed to be there but her mother insists. Everyone has to work extra time to help with the wedding. No Sunday off for anyone this week and no Thursday either. Everyone in the big house is busy with the wedding and if a woman must live for one Sunday a month and that Sunday is taken away, then surely she can take back for herself these hours, these minutes that are the cloth from which her daughter's childhood is made. She deserves that. Any mother deserves at least that. If she were not invisible, if she were given her voice back, she would demand it not just for herself but for all of her sisters.

Those others in the rooms at the back of the big house steer clear of her because no matter what their years are, they're old and this is the only life they know. This is what she tells herself. Even if they were given change in their lifetime, this change that is coming, she wonders if they would know what to do with it.

When she goes to the back gate to let in her daughter they know what she's doing but they won't tell anyone. They may be unsure about her but some things stay certain. In this matter she can do as she pleases and if anyone betrays her it will not be these people.

It is the day of the wedding. The florist has delivered Julia's flowers. A modest blush of pink rosebuds that go straight into the fridge. It's these chilly flowers she will carry down the hastily constructed aisle in the Bannermans' garden.

Her dress is a froth hanging down from a padded satin hanger against the door of a mahogany cupboard. The wedding shoes stand beneath it. Insubstantial

189

shoes made of satin with pink and green ribbons and a stub of a heel, suitable for dancing but not for much else. Her veil, trimmed with pearls, with baby's breath and more roses that must take their chances in the heat, is perched on a wigstand. All that's needed now is the bride.

Julia's mother is missing Roley. She's said nothing to Julia but Julia knows. Roley has been a great trial to them both. There is nothing in heaven or on earth that can keep Roley from having an absolute bloody final drink at the golf club but heaven and earth are not going to help and perhaps his sister's wedding will do in their place. Men look their best in evening dress and Roley Merriman is no exception and it's important. Douglas and Roley are partners too now, in a nicely growing building business. Merchant and Merriman, guaranteed the support of their friends and all those connections those two names will assure them. Merchant and Merriman, all in the family on every possible front and just the way Johannesburg prefers things to be.

The wedding party is Caroline's event and Caroline, in floral chiffon, is up to the occasion. She has that ability of mustering staff, of attending to even the least conspicuous detail. Caroline keeps her composure even in the face of inadequate facilities to keep the minerals properly chilled and a pianist guaranteed totally adept at all the intricacies that come with the Mendelssohn, who hasn't turned up.

No one is going to notice a small girl in the staff quarters but even so, she shouldn't be there.

'I'll come and be with you later,' Regina says. 'Here's

190

a picture book to look at and all kinds of chalk and a slate to draw on.'

This is just the beginning. The promises are for later.

Later she will fetch her and take her outside and from against the back wall she will show her a garden of lights. They'll have a party. Regina was not there for her birthday. It was not her day off, but Regina is not like the other mothers. Regina can make things possible where other mothers have been reduced to weeping for their failure. Her black dress and apron white on black, trimmed with *broderie Anglaise*, specially supplied for the wedding, should not fool her daughter. People are not always as they appear to be and Regina is more powerful than any other woman around in this place. She can make Lindiwe a new day on which to eat cake and drink Coca-Cola with ice cubes from a big glass. She can have pink pudding with cream and with ice cream, as much as she likes and sweets too, pink and white sugar sweets with almond nuts deep inside them that brides have for good luck.

'Was it our fault?' Caroline says afterwards.

How could it have been? No one knew she was there. What an irresponsible mother to have a child that age uninvited, left alone without supervision. What can happen but tragedy?

'It's no one's fault,' Cuckoo Bannerman says. 'The mother's if anyone's. These girls and their children, when do they ever learn that having a baby is easy enough, it's being able to take proper care of them that counts.'

The big thing is that no one should know. Why spoil the day?

'For goodness' sake, don't tell Julia.'

Caroline was wrong about one thing. In those years that came after she would see on television those endless sight-bytes of tragedy, of assassination, drive-by shootings, road deaths and the terrible soundtrack of mothers keening for their young, or so it seemed to Caroline but perhaps it was only after that day.

'Switch it off,' Gus always said. 'That's the trouble with them. They have no restraint.'

The weeping, the wailing, all the ululating in the world, a river of the bitterest tears can't bring someone back. That was then. This is now and there are nights now when Caroline sits for a while in a room with her husband in her big house alone watching the ventilator breathe in and breathe out and wishes she could go out in the garden and howl like a dog to the moon.

She can't recall that Regina cried on that day but then, she was a peculiar girl. There was great consternation in the kitchen. She remembers that. She remembers her young self being called, going fast from the outside and the air full of pleasantries and the guests and the women so pretty, talking in time to the old-fashioned love songs the tuxedo-band played.

She expected a carton of caterer's crystal broken, a cat that had licked its way across sides of Norwegian salmon freshly flown in. She was geared for catastrophe. A chef attacking a waiter with a carving knife. These things have been known to happen but not the thing that happened that day.

A child has drowned in the swimming pool, in among the hydrangeas. One minute she was safe in the staff quarters, the next she was in the pool in among the flowers that always look so attractive, so many shades of blue upon blue, being nudged around gently by the current from the filter pump.

It's a tragedy. No one's to blame. If anyone is to blame it must be the mother. What lunacy to sneak a child in here, on this day of all days and all the other staff gone blind, gone deaf. They are all responsible. If they'd only spoken up none of this need have happened.

'No one need know about this,' Cuckoo Bannerman says. 'Philip Stevens is here and so is David Pollard. They're both medical men. Send them down. They'll know what to do.'

Can you have a wedding party while a child's body lies on the deep-pile towels on the floor of the pool house? Cuckoo Bannerman can.

'Don't look at me like that,' she says to Caroline. 'What do you expect me to do? I hardly think an announcement's appropriate.'

All the same, Caroline's shaken. The music floats in from the garden. The light is beginning to purple. The house seems, at its core, to be vibrating to some discordant music of its own. Everyone is quite still in the way a person should be when a soul passes by.

Caroline has never seen a dead person. There's no need to see one now.

'Josephine,' Cuckoo Bannerman says with the point of a neat-lacquered forefinger. 'You go down to Regina. Ezra, you go with her. You wait there till the ambulance comes.'

Caroline thinks she should speak to Gus. He'll know what to do.

'For God's sake, don't have the ambulance come

down the front drive,' says Cuckoo Bannerman. 'It's too late for any help. Let's just keep it discreet.'

Caroline didn't tell Julia for a very long time and then one day she decided she must. She told her about it and it sounded strange, the way it came out, like a genie released from a bottle and it was good to say it out loud because she'd thought about it and it worried her.

She knew Julia would understand. She didn't mind telling her. It was just that she thought there was something else that should be remembered that was more important than the hailstorm that wiped everything out.

They gave money, of course, and sent condolences and a wreath, which might have lain fresh on the grave for five minutes, if the mother chose to put it there, before the flowers shrivelled in the sun.

They gave all the servants the day off to go to the funeral and there was cold meat and salad for supper and as there was no question of Regina coming back she went her own way.

'It's a tragedy and it's done with,' says Gus. 'A bloody stupid thing that should never have happened.'

'I can't stop thinking about it,' Caroline says.

'Put it out of your mind,' says Gus.

It's not so easy to do because there's something Gus doesn't know. Despite what Gus says with such certainty about 'them' she knows for a fact that Regina sat holding the body of her daughter and didn't shed a tear. What she learnt that day is that there is a place far beyond tears and its borders are open to everyone, even to someone like Caroline Bannerman.

Caroline slips away from Julia's wedding, nothing more than a soft float of floral through the garden. There's a thickening in the air and the smell of thunder. The last thing they need now, on top of everything else, would be rain.

It's a pretty time, this time when day keeps its rendezvous with night. Tonight it is beautiful. The light in the pool house is on. It makes small puddles as it spills through the window. Caroline has never seen a dead person. There is no need for her to see one now.

She takes off her shoes and walks barefoot on the grass, onto warm paving, right up to the pool house window. Philip Stevens is there and so is David Pollard. They're both in evening clothes, standing in that awkward way people stand when they wait and David Pollard is smoking. The smoke spirals up blue in the air. Josephine and Ezra, in their special order wedding uniforms, are kneeling on the ground and the girl, Regina, is holding her child, in a splash of yellow child's dress, and the child doesn't look dead at all. She looks as if she's sleeping.

Caroline is an intruder in that place among those people knitted together in that moment, waiting for the ambulance to come and the details of death to be attended to.

She should leave but she doesn't. She is that most awful of creatures, a fascinated onlooker at the scene of an accident and she should look away but she can't.

Regina knows someone is looking at her. She holds her child's dead body cleaving to hers, wishing her warmth into it; willing her life into it. Wishing with all of her being and a desire so great there are no words to describe it and into that place where she is, that terrible place of affliction, comes Caroline, who has never seen a dead person before.

'I believe that after that day nothing was ever really the same again,' is what Caroline tells Julia.

'You may think so,' says Julia. 'I don't think it's true.'

'I think it jinxed us.'

'What nonsense,' says Julia. 'You, of all people, know better than that.'

She doesn't know better. She knows what she saw. On the day of Julia's wedding, she stood barefoot on the grass, in a place she should not have been, with dance music floating down from the terrace and saw a mother nursing her child.

Is this death, then, she thought? How natural it looks and how peaceful. How comfortable that child must feel held close to the mother like that. It is what she thought, standing barefoot on the grass with her rhinestone evening sandals dangling from her fingers and then she saw it was not so.

'I looked into that woman's face, into her eyes and knew something terrible was going to happen to me,' is what she tells Julia.

It was at that moment she reached the place of unreason, where no comfort is possible and all that came after was already there in that dank place that always smelled of chlorine and antiseptic and mould, no matter how hard you tried to get rid of it.

DOUGLAS

Johannesburg comes to life very early in the morning. It seems to Douglas that no matter how early you set out, someone is there before you, no matter how many alternative routes you explore, through the twists and turns, the stop streets and the small traffic-slowing roundabouts of the suburban back roads, it all ends up the same. When you eventually find a place in a filter lane that will take you to the freeway, the whole of Johannesburg is there ahead of you, nudging its way stop-start towards work with Highveld Stereo belting its way into the day.

In the old days Douglas liked to start the week by going straight out to a site before he went into the office. It was his own time; his planning time and he liked the long drives. When he's past the 'This is a Hijacking Hotspot' road sign (National Roads Agency, At Work for You) and out on the freeway with a long road ahead of him, Douglas likes to listen to opera. He likes to turn it up loud on the sound system so the music rolls over him blotting everything else out.

Julia ignores it. On the odd occasion when they're compelled to drive in the same car the minute the engine is turned on a great blast of music blares forth.

'I do wish you'd remember to turn it off before you turn off the ignition,' Julia says.

What she doesn't say is that when Douglas turns off the ignition for the final time on any given day he's usually unacceptably late and in a hurry to clock in at home.

On Mondays, when he drives out of the city, with his hard hat lying on the passenger seat next to him, when there is no ice-maiden profile, no hands folded tightly together and none of the fresh expensive scent that is Julia, Douglas likes to unwind to his music.

He likes Puccini and Bizet. He's more than happy to let Rossini wash over him or give himself over entirely to Mozart but there's no site work these days, so Douglas must tackle the traffic like everyone else and start his week at the office.

On Mondays Douglas' secretary brings in the newspapers with the first cup of coffee of the day. The dailies, English, Afrikaans and the Sowetan and the Sundays as well, the *Sunday Times* and the *Independent*.

Douglas' secretary is a sensible woman of a certain age with a husband made newly unemployed by a bank that went 'under', and this bringing of the papers, which she has gone through herself before he ever gets sight of them, is a new thing.

People are fearful for their jobs now. In an economy where a bank as large as the one her husband was in gets into trouble and not even the police can draw their pay, who is safe? The building business is not what it used to be and Douglas' secretary, who has a lot of time for her boss, and would like to help if only she could, is privy to all his travails.

Douglas' newspapers come to him still crisp, neatly refolded with all matters relating to the building industry highlighted in marker pen with neat neon stars at each corner to single them out so Douglas can't miss them.

Her husband, a once gregarious man, in his days in the 'customer service' section of the bank, on the way to becoming a 'personal banker', always used to say that to stay alive in business, especially in these cut-throat days, one had to stay ahead of the game.

It is not Douglas' secretary who brings him the story of Rosalie, 'Most Conspicuous by her Absence' (picked up off the wire, reprinted with all proper acknowledgements). Douglas' secretary knows nothing of Rosalie. He finds her for himself.

Douglas' office is panelled in African mahogany. On one wall is a gallery of framed architectural drawings of some of Johannesburg's landmark buildings of the past. Douglas was a sometime collector and a practised eye would see that he chose with discernment, but there's no time for that any more.

There's a neat display of certificates and awards, modestly framed, for safety, for excellence, for being the best of the bunch.

There are photographs too of the projects of the past

he's helped bring to fruition. On the steel struts of big buildings, beneath cranes that tower above them, stand small groups of hard-hatted men in the throes of doing big business and he is among them. Those buildings he helped create out of nothing stand there still. He can drive out and look at them any time he likes. Each has a history and no one knows that history better than he does but even so sometimes he goes back to the pictures to seek himself out and make quite sure he is that same man who was actually there.

In Douglas' office is a black leather sofa with a black-buttoned back rest, two chairs that match it and a glass-top coffee table with current copies of *Specifier*, *Architectural Digest* and *Architect and Builder* set out in low stacks.

Underneath is a home industry rug made of rough weave, handspun wool the dull peculiar colour of precious stones the way you first see them before they're cut and polished and end up in jewellery shop windows.

There's a rack for hard hats that over the years has become a trophy case. It's the custom, in this business, when a cornerstone is laid and a new project set on its way with champagne on site for the white-collar workers, the architects, the quantity surveyors, the building contractor and commissioning client, to hand out special name-of-the-project hard hats to celebrate.

Douglas has come a long way since he loaded up 'boys' in his open-back truck and talked his way 'in' anywhere work was on offer, but then it isn't where or how we begin that's important; it's where we end up. Julia may think Douglas never once stops to consider this but he does. He considers it more often and with a great deal more sadness than she can possibly imagine.

On his desk is a picture of Julia, of Kimmy, of Douglas himself taken on the boat at Loch Vaal. Julia is wearing shorts and a sweater that shows off her rather fine breasts. He's in a swimsuit, brown from the sun. He has just come in from water skiing. His hair gleams wet with dam water and so does his body. It feels so good after skiing to be at the dam, to drink ice-cold beer with his friends. It's nice to have so many pretty young women around showing brown arms and long legs, unselfconscious in shorts. There are always unlimited quantities of children, each with a different degree of demand, and Douglas likes to see them with their mothers. It fills him with a sense of wellbeing. It puts him in a place he knows he belongs. It's his life, this good life of long summer days, and it's scented with the smell of sizzling chop fat and sausage sending delicious fragrances up in the wood-smoke, scenting the air.

There are other pictures too but he likes that one. If you could stop life in a freeze frame (and after all, can we know for sure that this isn't exactly the way that it will stop?) he might have stopped it that day because that day he was happy.

Douglas comes upon Rosalie without any help. Here she is in the newspaper. He remembers those dark eyes that could see out and single out exactly those things they wanted to see and close down at will and not allow you to look in. She wasn't exactly a 'looker' but she had something and it was a long time ago and the world has moved on and a great deal has happened since then.

In the same section back to back with Rosalie and the face-painted new generation dancing to REM is something far more interesting, more important, to Douglas. Pictures of Nelson Mandela obligingly smiling his polite gentle smile are pretty much an everyday thing. For all of his young life you weren't allowed to see Nelson Mandela at all. Some or other Department put a stop to all that as if it was dangerous just to look at his face, but things have changed now. Everyone who knows how to point a camera, how to press a button is making up for lost time. Now you can see Nelson Mandela any day of the week with any language text of your choice without even looking too hard.

Here he stands, muffled up with only the grizzled grey of his famous head visible and the top half of his face and his eyes that weep involuntary tears because of the damage done to them in the lime quarry. On the following page, neatly marked out with marker-pen stars that seep pinkly through to the concert, is an artist's impression of a proposed new casino development in the Johannesburg area. This is where the next major building project will be and far more important to Douglas and closer to his heart than any concert in any square in the world.

You can visit the world in Johannesburg these days. You can even time travel if that's what you want. At Montecasino you can have Tuscany with its authentically fake ornamental landscape where regularly changed underwear flies from washing lines in the street and the flags draped in the Piazza del Duomo follow the fortunes of the teams in the Italian soccer leagues.

In Sandton there's a piazza to rival Siena's. There's ancient Rome with all its excesses if you care to visit at Caesar's and Xanadu at Sun City which is only a plane flip away if you find yourself not inclined for a car ride. You can have a fake beach with real sea sand and electronic waves you can surf on and pawprints embellishing the bed covers and your laundry, cellophane sealed, brought to you in a basket carried on the turbanned head of a generous-hipped, sloe-eyed laundress with skin the colour of cinnamon. You can throw your money away in dark rooms where there's no day and no night and no clocks and no time at all except 'now' but if you're in the building business as Douglas is, this is where the money is.

Is it wrong that this titillates his interest far more than Rosalie does? Douglas has other things on his mind. The present is rattling hard at his order with far more persistence than the long-ago past has ever managed to muster. There are bills to be paid. There are the people who work for him who have begun to look at him wide-eyed with doubt when the end of each month comes around. He is no longer invited to the once-a-month cocktail party the bank always gives so clients they value can get together with each other and maybe strike up some synergy that could be of benefit to them all.

In the boom days Douglas used to talk to Julia about the business. They used to go out to celebrate a new contract, a new victory, yet another advance on their path to success. There were times they sent Kimmy to the Bannermans and 'lost' whole weekends together, at the coast, in the Berg, at the Maharani Hotel in Durban or Granny Mouse's in Balgowan but those days are past. Douglas can't talk to Julia about anything any more.

He would like to speak to her about his bid for the new Casino contract. He could have showed her the article. They could have talked about it. After all, it's important to both of them. It's more than important. Their future depends on it. He'd like to be able to say this out loud to someone he feels safe with, who he can trust, who he knows will be listening to him.

It's harder these days to keep the self-assured jut to his chin and walk in the way younger men walk, as if they know where they're going.

Douglas has had too many near misses lately. He's losing that edge he once had. He can feel it slipping away. He feels like a man whose fingers involuntarily begin to uncurl themselves from a lifeboat and panic is somewhere not far behind and it's not a good feeling.

First thing in the morning Douglas plunges into the dark-bottomed pool at his house and swims a few lengths, then he showers. Sometimes, if it's hot, if he's been on site, he goes to the gym and showers in the middle of the day. On those nights he goes to his girlfriend in her box flat in Yeoville he showers before he leaves.

'To get the smell of me off you,' she says and she's right and he showers again when he gets home just to be certain. There's something he's become convinced of lately and it troubles him. He thinks people can scent failure on a man with quite as much certainty as a wife can snuffle out the scent of another woman.

He doesn't want this to happen to him and now he has to go to Michael Rosenberg for work although not directly to him of course. He has people he works with, and a penthouse suite of offices in a building he owns, but if what one hears about him is true, the final decision is always his own.

All of this he would like to tell Julia. He would like the relief of it.

He wants to talk about Rosenberg so Julia can see that his name, the idea of him, has none of the potency it had in the old days. It isn't important now. In the old days Jews gave their business to Jews. This is what his father always said and he said to avoid doing business with 'them', but his father lived in a different world and he remembers that too although it would certainly be more comfortable to forget.

Douglas believes he is in with a chance for this job. He can do it. He knows he can, just as he's always done it before. You don't need a token smattering of black names on your letterhead to show what you're capable of. His past work can speak for him and as for the new legislation, people can turn a blind eye if they want to and they do. They've done so in the recent past because the philosophy of the recent past was always that there was no black business or white business, there was only 'business', although he's not at all sure Michael Rosenberg will feel this way.

He would like to have Julia back as she was in the old days of his confidence before she became this woman who weeps in other people's bathrooms for the loss of her daughter. He would like to look at her without being reminded by her, with every word, every look that if ever a man failed to live up to his youthful promise, then he is that man.

MICHAEL

Tracey Rosenberg, aged twelve, will tell anyone who cares to listen that her father hardly ever goes into his office. His office is for the people who work for him. He does his business on the telephone. Everyone who has been with him for more than ten minutes will tell you this. He has two mobiles and a landline telephone with extensions all over the house. She and her sister have their own phone and phone number at his house and at their mother's house and their own mobiles.

'Which you keep with you at all times,' their father says. 'When I dial that number I want to hear your voice at the other end of the line.'

'Tell your father too much time on the mobile causes brain damage,' says their mother. 'Just because he's attached to the telephone like it's a hospital drip and a lifeline doesn't mean you have to be.'

'She should know,' says their father. 'What did she have for breakfast today?'

'Green tea, multivitamins and glucosamine tablets,' says Mandy, the younger. 'She's detoxing.'

'Thank you,' says their father. 'The only brain damage you have to worry about is what comes through the genes and not from my side, I can promise you that.'

'We can't have our mobiles in school,' says Mandy. 'It's not allowed.'

'I don't care what the school allows or what the school doesn't allow. I'm your father. I'm more important than school. I'll speak to the school about it, in a nice way. You don't have to worry. I'll speak in a nice way and they'll understand.'

'Your father is paranoid,' says their mother pointing her finger at her temple and twirling it around to show a scramble upstairs. 'You can tell him I said so.'

'She should know,' says their father. 'How much does she weigh today by the way?'

'Forty-eight kilos,' says Mandy. 'She says one kilo more up and she's going back to the fat farm.'

'Not the fat farm,' says her sister. 'It's the Hydro, you know that.'

'Good,' says their father. 'Then you can come and stay here. We don't have to wait for the holidays and tell me by the way, who loves his daughters more than anyone else in the world?'

'You do, Daddy,' they say.

'Who are the only women in this old man's life?'

'We are,' they say. His two little duplicates, the centre of his world. When he looks at them, he sees himself made over again and this time, in this new incarnation, made perfect.

* * *

There have been days when Michael's gone looking for Rosalie. She's in his computer and sometimes, for a long time, in stormy times in his marriages, in those soul-searching times when he feels the old shame for turning away from the Struggle and being disempowered by the bravery of others, he looks for her there.

All it takes is a search engine and her name and he can call her up and walk through her life, sometimes with photographs, sometimes without. This virtual world is a wonderful thing where a man may stalk a woman he once knew in the darkened privacy of his own quiet corner of a house, a continent away, a lifetime later, but it's unsatisfactory. It's unsatisfactory in the way facts standing up alone, all by themselves, open for scrutiny, always are. Reported facts do only what they're required to do, then they come to an end and life goes on and they can never quite keep up with it.

He would like, for a moment only, to be that young man that he was in those days. That man of the early days would know what to say to her and he thinks, even now, there are things that might still be said but then again, he's not even sure of that.

There's been nothing new about Rosalie for a very long time. Life has swallowed her up. Even if she does come out on a visit it can make no difference. He doesn't think that if she found him now, she would know him. She would know his face. At least she would know that. His is a face not easy to forget but she would not know his heart and he would not care to show it to her. So it is perhaps, after all, better this way.

JULIA

Douglas has taken Julia's mobile away.

'Confiscated it,' is what she tells Caroline.

She doesn't protest. What she does is go to the hall table, pick up the mobile and slam it down in Douglas' waiting palm and Adelaide who sees it all forms her lips into the amazed circle of an 'O' that matches her eyes. Then she raises her hand to her mouth to cover it.

'We're going to have to make cuts all round,' Douglas says. 'We have to start somewhere.'

The common wisdom is that a mobile is an essential safety precaution, not a fashion necessity.

'You could have fooled me,' Douglas says.

No white woman in Johannesburg goes out without her mobile stuck to her ear. There are stories about Sandton ladies who ring the reception desk of the restaurant they're sitting in to summon a waiter if the service is too slow. Even the rest of the country shakes its head. 'The Gauteng earring,' they call it. There were so many visiting 'earrings' on bikini beach Clifton, Cape Town, one summer holiday, all calling back to Johannesburg at once that they brought the whole system down.

No woman worth her salt can be seen dead without one.

'If you're assaulted between here and Sandton City or the hairdresser or any shopping mall within five kilometres of this house, all for the want of a mobile, I'll be happy to take responsibility,' Douglas says. 'The fact of the matter is we simply can't afford it.'

This is the bad time. The time when the tenders are in and the long wait for the formal notification of nominated contractors is made. When there are two or three or even just one other job going at the same time it isn't so bad. When all your hopes ride on landing just one new job, it's a very different story altogether.

'It's not only you and the cost of keeping all this going,' Douglas says. 'We're doing cut-backs at the office as well.'

Douglas has drawn no profits for a very long time now, far longer than Julia knows. Every cent he takes adds to the overdraft and the interest on overdrafts is fifteen per cent.

'Forget it. Just forget it,' says Douglas looking at Julia. 'It's no good expecting you to understand any-thing.'

When he goes the mobile goes with him. It is in that moment that Julia makes her decision and picks up the telephone. Wafted along by electronic Vivaldi, passed from one person to another at South Africa House, cajoling, imploring and in the end lying she eventually comes to the newcomer, a nice young woman, anxious to please, who says yes, she knows Rosalie and yes, she can help her.

All she needs after that is to dial the international code, try the number and find out for herself if, at the end of the line, she will find Rosalie.

ROSALIE

Rosalie remembers Julia. The others play tennis. Julia doesn't. Her mother, the bridge player, has put her off all games for life. Rosalie doesn't play either. She can't see the point of these sportmad people. She will not take up golf, will not swim, do exercise at a gym, cycle or jog. She will not support Caroline's project to take tennis to the townships to 'give the youngsters a chance'.

'A chance of what?' she wants to know.

'They play soccer, don't they?' says Caroline defensively. 'Tennis is a far more interesting game.'

Rosalie and Julia might have been friends but Julia avoids her.

'You mustn't mind,' Caroline says. 'It's because of "you know".'

Rosalie doesn't 'know'.

'It's because of you and Douglas. Before you came

along everyone, I mean, we all thought Douglas might end up with Julia but it didn't happen that way and well, here you are.'

Here she is indeed and Julia's hopes are in shreds and the plan, set so neatly in place by these people so overly concerned with each other's comings and goings, has gone all awry.

'Should you have married her?' Rosalie asks Douglas.

'No,' he says. 'I should have married you and I did.'

Julia has hair like gold and a brother who loses at tennis on purpose so he can go into the house to ask for the drinks to be sent out. Julia is forever apologizing for him. She's his partner in the doubles and she plays like a demon, then says it's her fault they lost, she must work on her serve. In those days of Julia, she remembers her with her brother as if they were attached to each other like Siamese twins.

She fills up his gin glass with ice and with tonic when she thinks no one can see her. She goes into the house and asks the Bannermans' 'boy' not to give Mr Roley any more drinks. She's the one who says it's time to go home.

'You've had enough,' she whispers to him very soft, in lover-like tones, her hand on his shoulder, her lips close to his ear.

'Never enough,' he booms back so that everyone hears. 'Just one more but only one, only to keep you happy though, Jules. One ABF, absolute, bloody final. One for the road.'

Julia has pale skin. She's a blusher and the others pretend not to notice.

'It's all right, Jules,' says Gus Bannerman. 'We're all

213

old friends here. Let him enjoy himself. You can always drive back.'

When Julia's voice on the telephone calls her back to her place in Rosalie's mind she arrives there perfectly formed and with absolute clarity. If she closes her eyes she can see her, in white cotton trousers and shirt, in a pudding bowl hat made of straw, her eyes hidden behind sunglasses. She remembers her always smelling of Nivea Sun Creme and the nervous way she keeps reaching into her basket for Vaseline Lip Ice with which she coats and re-coats her mouth.

She's going to Julia's house. Julia has invited her. Of all unlikely people Julia has been the one to summon her back and the relief is indescribable.

There's the tomcat with a red collar that sidled up to her on the street the other day. She saw him from the window. When she was down on the street pushing through the blur pulling her ridiculous wheeled shopping cart behind her he preened himself beside her in that familiar way cats have as if she should know him and she feels that she should but she doesn't.

It's a feeling she has these days. She feels that in some part of her mind the cat does have a place and that his right to reside there is unquestionable. She thinks she ought to make some effort to seek him out but she won't because she knows that even if she tries very hard he will continue to elude her.

She knows Julia though. Her telephone rings, screaming like a demanding child insistent for food in that way she can't stand. She would like to rip it from the wall but she's afraid it will bring the woman from downstairs up to bang at her door. She comes up on her enormous feet. She floats up like a balloon. Rosalie doesn't want to let her into the flat in case she blots out everything else but when she answers the phone it is only Julia Merriman phoning from the past to ask her to a party.

'When are you coming over then?' Julia says. 'Perhaps we can settle on a day right now.'

'Now,' Rosalie says carefully, repeating what she's just heard in case she gets it wrong. 'I would like to come now.'

There's a black man living downstairs. He always seems to be eating something. The enormous woman keeps him locked up there. She feeds him on mango, avocado and litchi. She's seen her at the greengrocer buying these things, rumbling with laughter along with the greengrocer, carrying her trophies home in brown paper bags, two enormous coffee-coloured babies, one on each hip.

'So soon?' says Julia. 'Then I'm lucky to have caught you. I suppose you already have plans?'

Julia is speaking in the tight-throated way of a woman who knows what she's doing is wrong but Rosalie who hears only the voice of the past can know nothing of that.

'I'm coming to see Nelson,' Rosalie says and in the face of that name her footing's more certain, her direction is clear. 'He has asked to see me.'

What is there Julia can say to that?

'But I would like to come to your house,' Rosalie says, afraid it is all a mistake, that she is talking into silence, summoning Julia back.

Julia is her lifeline now. Julia can help her and she

can find Julia. Sometimes she forgets things but she can remember exactly where Julia lives.

Julia lives with her mother and brother in an old house in Hazeldene. It has a beautiful garden and a card room where her mother plays bridge. Julia and her brother are very much alike to look at. They go everywhere together. People say what a handsome pair they are but they are used to that by now and she spends a lot of time whispering to him.

'I want to go home.' 'You never said they'd be here. How do you expect me to face them?' 'Please, Roley, don't have any more. You promised. Remember?'

Julia wants to get out of that house. You can tell just by looking at her.

'Saturday next then?' Julia says. 'Will that fit in with your plans? If not, I could change it to suit you. I thought lunch might be nice.'

'Yes,' says Rosalie carefully, following Julia's words so she can stay in their echo where it's safe. 'Lunch might be nice.'

She's had lunch at Julia's house before. Lunch at Julia's house is always the same. Douglas says so. Avocado with shrimp smothered in shocking pink mayonnaise, 'Coronation' chicken that skulks under tinned apricots, lumpy cheesecake to follow. Julia's mother doesn't care about food. Even the bridge ladies say so. Sponge cake and cold tea slopped all over the place and then she wants to get on with the game.

Julia wants to escape. She has to.

'Put your money on Julia,' is what Douglas says. 'She'll get out all right. She'll get hold of some bloke and if you ask me it won't take very long and she'll be grateful as hell, no trouble at all and make a bloody good wife.'

Rosalie, who can't bear the idea of anyone bought, sold or abused, not destined ever to be a 'bloody good wife', feels kinship with Julia. She remembers she did. She feels it now. She is so filled with gratitude to Julia for taking the trouble to turn back and find her she could weep. She wonders if she came all this way by tube. She must have come through the tunnel.

'Where will you stay when you get here?' Julia says. 'The Westcliffe, I suppose? Is it all sorted out?'

'Yes,' says Rosalie. She doesn't know what the Westcliffe is but she doesn't want to say so, in case Julia gets angry with her and says she can't come any more. She imagined Julia would know she would be in her own house in Bez Valley. Where else would she go? That is, after all, her home.

'It's all set then,' says Julia. 'I'll go ahead and organize everything. I'm just so glad that you'll come.'

Julia says she will confirm everything by e-mail or by fax as that is the way things seem to be done in these days. Rosalie says yes, e-mail or fax, that is the way things are done these days.

Next to the telephone stuck down on the desk by the woman in black who sometimes still lives in this house, crammed together with all those other ghosts of the past, is that other woman's card and all her particulars. They will do as well as anything else provided that today the letters lie quite still in their places so that Rosalie can read them and they do and she does.

CAROLINE

Someone has been stealing the plants out of Caroline's garden. In the grand scheme of things it should not be important and yet it's become the most important thing of all.

The cycads went first but then they're protected and therefore desirable and one might expect that. She woke up one morning, looked out of her window and they were gone. They'd been there for as long as she could remember, a part of the landscape, taken for granted. Then they were gone and nothing left but raw earth to show where they'd been.

Then went the pretty yellow blaze of the marguerites and the pink and blue salvia, gone together in one night like a pair of lovers fled away from a place that had lost its enchantment for them.

She speaks of this to the gardeners when they come round on garden days but what can they say? They're here to work and move on. They have no opinion. This is a new generation. The days of Jonas and Elias and Josiah are gone. The new generation come from a service company and come as a team with the name of the company emblazoned on the backs of their overalls. They come and they go. The security button is pressed in the kitchen when they ring at the front gate and say who they are. When they go the gate closes automatically behind them. When they leave here they go on to the next garden and then to the next until their quota of gardens for the day is done and then they go home. The comings and goings in Caroline's night garden are no concern of theirs but it worries Caroline.

Someone slips in through the security cordon that's supposed to be fail-safe and while she sleeps in her bed, in her large sleeping house, they steal her plants as if to remind her they're out there and may come and go as they please because they know what she's done.

The 'Just Joey' roses went. The yellow ones that look golden like butter and smell so sweetly. They are dug up neatly enough and removed very tidily. They will die at whatever roadside stall they may find themselves even if they're sold very quickly. They cannot survive such mishandling. Caroline knows this and it worries her.

She thinks her house is turning against her but she can't tell anyone. She can't put the cruising security services on alert for the loss of a black-hearted daisy. She'd be too embarrassed. She can't even tell Julia.

One night she wakes up and thinks she hears digging. There's the distinctive sound of a spade in soft soil but it's a still night and unnatural sounds carry. They carry into her dreams. They carry her away and make her restless. She dreams of a small grave being dug and far too many flowers being sent to put on it, the kind of guilty, nonsensical tribute the rich pay to the poor.

'I know of no florist who'll deliver to the township,' Cuckoo Bannerman says. 'They say it's too dangerous and they simply won't do it. I should imagine the family would far rather have money but even so, we'll send flowers. Ezra can take them.'

Caroline, undisputed mistress of the house, may do as she pleases. She was surprised to find after Cuckoo died, after Gus had his accident, that she had any power at all but she sees now how it works. As long as she offers food and shelter, fair conditions of employment and work that is not too onerous she may be a woman and not old quite yet but her power is almost unlimited. It's not what she wanted.

Downstairs, her house smells of maize porridge, of beans and of the cheap cuts of meat the staff like so much. The staff's quarters still stand at the back of the property and she goes down once a month 'on inspection' so that anything that needs attention can be pointed out to her and attended to.

She's the one who is handed the mail each morning in just the same way it was once handed to Gus. She's the one who sorts everything out, who deals with the bankers and brokers and handles the bills. She's the one who gets the Council notices shoved through the letterbox. Electricity 'on', electricity 'off' and please note the 'off' period to avoid inconvenience. This is Caroline's job.

'For heaven's sake, Mum,' says Jimjam-James on the phone. 'Pension all the old hands off. Sell the place. Put Dad in a private nursing home and get on with your life. Think about coming over to England next summer.'

The Queen is celebrating her Jubilee. There will be street parties everywhere. The entire nation has been instructed at an arranged time to sing 'All you need is Love'. All Caroline can think about is old Alice Merriman who, in her day, once told Rosalie that even in this age of jet travel we are still 'a very long way away from England' and Alice, as usual, was right.

He doesn't even sound like her Jimjam any more but all the kids change when they leave, like little chameleons taking on the shadings of those new places they find themselves, modifying so they can blend in, blending in till they're finally absorbed.

Jimjam is not coming 'home' for Easter. A group of his friends are hiring a villa in Tuscany and he's going with them.

'Wonderful, darling,' Caroline says. 'No problem at all. You'll have a marvellous time. I'm sure you will. Perhaps sometime later this year?'

Caroline, who sits in the big chair in Gus' room for an hour each day, divided into two half-hour sessions, morning and evening, has stopped telling him these things. She's disappointed about Jimjam of course but it's no good passing news on to Gus now. Bad news or good, it can make no difference to him in that place where he is.

Mrs Bannerman is a remarkable woman and always the same. This is the nurse's opinion. Her life runs like a railway timetable and nothing seems to upset her.

She never raises her voice. She's always beautifully dressed. She never has a hair out of place. She's never seen outside her bedroom without her face being lightly made up and she walks very quietly. Mrs Bannerman would make a very good ghost. If you couldn't set your watch by her, you'd have to be on your toes to keep one step ahead so you can be ready when she comes into a room.

The doctor comes once a week and the visit is always the same. He has a few words with Caroline, then goes up to see Gus. He takes his pulse, casts his eye over all the paraphernalia it takes just to keep him still breathing. He has a few words with whichever nurse happens to be on duty and then he comes down again to the Summer Hall and to Caroline.

Caroline has a whisky ready for him. It's his favoured drink and he likes it poured with a light hand just the way Caroline pours it. Then he stays for a while and talks and it's pleasant once a week for Caroline to sit alone with a man. She entertains fantasies, essentially modest but guilt about Gus always comes close behind and she puts them out of her mind, quickly, conspicuously, like a schoolgirl caught out.

She's not unhappy. There's no point in that. She just finds she doesn't like her life very much. Nothing has turned out the way she expected. She isn't 'poor Caroline' any more. She isn't a widow. She is no longer what the man on the street might call actually 'married' but even so, she is still the best wife she can be in the circumstances.

Gus is kept pristine. Today he was manicured. His hair is cropped close to his head and she has a barber come in each day to keep it that way and to shave him.

She shops for him in the same places she always shops where nothing for Mrs Bannerman could possibly be too much trouble.

Gus' pyjamas are imported and made out of silk. There is nothing in this world that Gus could possibly need that he doesn't have and yet, there's a baby-face peacefulness about him, this creation of hers, that offends her because it belies the man he once was and he deserves better than that.

She's been angry, resentful, then riddled with guilt and abject in her apologies to God for whatever it is she did wrong that has brought such a fate down upon her. She still takes a 'boy' down to St George's; a 'cousin' of Ezra's, 'Looking for part time work, "madam",' to help her do her volunteer stint in the garden. She prays while she works and there are a great many things that she prays about.

She would like Gus well again; she would like him back. She can accept God's will whatever it is but hasn't Gus, between life and whatever comes next, suffered enough and who is she to say what God's time is but it's occurred to her, she must say it even in prayer, that perhaps God's time might be now.

The one thing she has never said and will never say is that she would like to change places. Wives sometimes say that. She has heard parents say it often enough after a child has died. 'If only it were me.' Other people may say it but you won't hear this from Caroline. Gus is the one who was damaged. Caroline is alive and Caroline doesn't always behave quite as perfectly as people think she does because in her heart Caroline is quite happy to be the one who remained living. She wants to live still.

* * *

Philip Stevens wants to put her on Prozac but she doesn't see the need.

'What on earth for?' she says. 'I eat sensibly. I walk. I garden. I'm always out with the dogs. I would say I was in supremely good shape for a woman my age.'

'What's so wrong with your age?' Philip says in the avuncular way medical people have when they cross the bridge that separates doctors from friends. 'Many people would call it the prime.'

'Then, that's what it must be then,' says Caroline. 'And I still say, for a woman in her prime I'm not doing all that badly.'

'You know what I'm talking about,' he says.

She hates it. She will always hate this slight fall in tone to a hush when Gus is mentioned. It is, after all, such bad taste to talk about a man who lies upstairs in a bed, still living and breathing in his own house, as if he is not to be spoken of, as if he has ceased to exist. Especially if that man is a man like the man she remembers.

'I'm managing perfectly,' Caroline says and she is. If she asked him he'd tell her she's managing rather too well.

'You're not made of steel, Caroline,' he says.

'I know that,' she says. 'And you know if there's one thing you can depend on it's that if I needed help I would ask for it. I'll always be sensible. You should know that by now.'

'That's all right then,' he says and that's done.

'Something more to drink? Do you have time for another or are you in a rush?'

She has his favourite whisky, toasted almonds in a

224

small glass bowl and a fresh bucket of ice set out on a tray.

He doesn't know what she's made of. He wouldn't even venture to guess. Whatever it is, she's holding up remarkably well. Either that, or she's the best illusionist he's ever seen.

ROSALIE

Something peculiar has happened to Rosalie. There seem to be some strange woman's clothes in her cupboard. She wants no trouble. She's happy to leave them there. What she was looking for when she discovered this was something to wear to Julia's house and she seems to have none of the clothes that she came with.

She had a white dress made of handkerchief linen. She bought it at a street market. You can see right through it when the sun shines from behind but she doesn't mind. She has denims and skirts and short-sleeve blouses and sandals.

Julia has cupboards filled with clothes. Caroline Bannerman has a dressing room that looks like a shop. Rosalie doesn't need fancy clothes. She doesn't think he even looks at her clothes. All he's interested in is that she looks like a woman and is willing to shed

226

everything she's wearing just as fast as she can when he wants her. She can't go to Julia dressed in black like a widow. Julia will not let her in. Widows belong in the township. They have no place in Julia's house. She feels like crying. She's afraid if she cries someone will hear her. She wants to go to Julia's house because she's hungry.

It doesn't matter if she's hungry. She tells herself this. There are people in prison on hunger strike that are much hungrier than she'll ever be. The Bible is full of people who are hungry. They hunger and thirst after righteousness but it's perfectly all right, Nelson will see they are filled. She wouldn't mind a drink of water though. White people can have water whenever they want. They can even swim in it if they like. In the township you need to go out with a plastic bucket and see what you can find and in the rural areas it's even worse. Sometimes there's no water at all. In the summer when the rivers are full they're full of bilharzia and in the winter they're nothing but undrinkable puddles of mud.

She will not embarrass Julia but she is so thirsty she thinks that if she can find a puddle of mud, she might go down on all fours and drink from it. The idea of it makes her laugh. Is it her laughter? It comes out shrill and hard as a hag's cackle. Is that the sound of her laughter these days? All the same, she can't help laughing. She can see Julia's face and Julia is so particular. There are slivers of lemon in the glasses of water Julia offers and ice. If she can hold herself together and wait until she gets to Julia's house, she thinks that Julia will most certainly offer her water.

MICHAEL

Michael can't get enough of his daughters. He has countless photographs of them taken at every possible stage of their development. There are photographs of them at every important moment of their lives from birth onwards. Sometimes, especially when their time together surpasses those times they've already had, he follows them around with a digital video camera.

'Please, Dad,' they shout in embarrassment. 'Not again.'

They tell him that one day in the future when these pictures are looked at again people will think they were orphans and he was only a figment of their imagination. There must be thousands of pictures of them all over his house by now and thousands more at their grandmother's. His wallet has about as many photographs of them in it as it has credit cards and he's not in any of them.

'I'm old,' he says. 'I'm your father. Indulge me.'

Michael has a habit. Every time he picks up new pictures from the Kodak shop in the Mall he slides one or two of them into a book. Any book will do. He has floor to ceiling bookshelves filled with books. He's always been like this. Even in those long-ago days, the house in Bez Valley was filled with books. They stood on the kitchen table. They stood in piles on the floor. There were books in the bathroom and the windowsills were filled with them. To leave Michael alone in a bookshop is like giving free rein to an alcoholic in a bottle store. Michael's daughters say that if he keeps on like this he will have to find another, even bigger house, just for his books, or they'll all drown in them. He says books are the best investment anyone can ever make and if anyone asks them they can say that he said so.

He couldn't say when he first started sliding photographs into books, as early as his schooldays he thinks and certainly by the time he got to university, and not just photographs. There are other mementos too. Airline boarding passes, business cards from restaurants where a meal has been memorable, little notes his daughters leave round the house for him. 'School Concert, Friday. See you there. Love you.' 'New tennis racquet, you promised. Don't forget.' 'Friends forever. We love you Dad.'

These are his treasures and he keeps them between the pages of books. He slides them into the book he's reading, uses them as bookmarks then files them away and puts the book away on the shelf and in time when the sweetness of the moment has long since been overtaken by something even sweeter, he forgets about them.

He's been doing it for years and given time his little

habit yields up its treasures. He'll pick a book from the shelf and re-read it and sometimes, not always, he'll thumb through the pages looking for some favourite passage and something of his past life rich with memories he's almost forgotten will be exposed or fall out.

Somewhere in one of those books is a letter from Rosalie. It was brought to his house a long time ago. Not to this house, where he's 'Mr Rosenberg' and the guard salutes him as he goes through the gates. It was brought to his house in Bez Valley. He doesn't know who brought it. It was just there pushed under the door when he got home.

He has just been at his mother's house. When he comes back he walks down the street seeing nothing. His father's heartflutter has confined him to bed and the doctor says it could be something more serious than he originally thought.

'I'll take the pill,' Manny grunts from the bed and they all turn around because his eyes were closed and nobody thought he was listening.

'Let the doctor finish what he has to tell you,' Michael's mother says. 'He knows what he's talking about.'

'I know what I'm talking about,' Manny says. 'In a situation like this you take the pill. The other option's the box. The pill will do nicely, thank you.'

'And so?' Michael's mother says to her son, out of earshot of his father, after the doctor has left. 'What do we do now? What do you think we should do?'

Which is why he sees nothing as he walks down his street in this poor part of town with his future already upon him hounding him from behind. He opens the door, half thinking to shut it out to keep it at bay for

230

just a little while longer and there lies the past, in a neatly addressed envelope waiting to greet him.

It's possible he's never felt such relief in his life. He thinks he might step out of Coventry and go back but time has moved on and moved him on with it and it isn't as easy as that.

He hasn't seen Rosalie for what seems like a very long time. To see her handwriting is enough though to remember her. The script that flows from Rosalie's hand is so unlike Rosalie. It's so neat, so precise, its strokes so certain and unwavering they might have been penned by a nun.

He remembers the slow thick beating of his heart, the slowing down of time, the envelope in his hand and the terrible, gnawing uncertainty. He wants more than anything to open it; he wants, more than anything, not to.

The letter, folded small, tucked inside this cheap envelope, is very slight. The paper inside it so light you'd think someone had sent it off in a hurry, with nothing inside it at all but he's held it to the light and it may be feather light but it's there. You can see those firm, self-assured strokes inverted, in black ink, unreadable on a twice-folded page.

The letter is only paper and will burn, but he will not burn it. He could tear it in pieces and throw it away. He cannot trust himself to do this either. The image he has of himself, salvaging soiled pieces of paper from among the rubbish and trying to piece them together again, mortifies him. She deserves better than that. He would wish it away if he could but in that way it's like Rosalie. All things around it may be in turmoil but it will remain as if its business is to be there and be disconcerting.

Is what he feels for Rosalie love or is he simply enamoured?

If everything had gone on unchanged how long would it have been until she used him up, moved on, saw him as he really was. Of all unlikely things in this place, he thinks of his father eating forkfuls of brisket, sliding them into his mouth with no pleasure at all.

'Who does he think he is? Is he Superman these days? Well, you can tell him from me, Superman is fine in the comic books but comic books aren't real life. To be a Superman in real life, you've got to be something.'

He hopes he is 'something' but he isn't Superman. He knows that better than anyone else does. Rosalie is not for him. Her letter, pregnant with so many possibilities that could change his life once again, lies in his hand. If he reads it the construct that is his world now that she's gone will come tumbling down and he will have to start over.

He looks at the time they had together and sees that he's looking backward because for him, that time is passed.

He found a place for the letter in W.H. Auden: *Collected Works*. It has its place on the windowsill supported by other bulkier books and perhaps, one day, he will decide the time has come for him to seek it out, slide it out and read it and perhaps he will never read it at all.

What is there to be said? It's ended. Something has been broken that can never be put together again.

She was his lodestar and he the uncertain traveller who could not even be trusted to follow.

LALLY AND ALBERT

Lally and Albert call Rosalie their friend. There was a time, in the bitter run-up to change in South Africa, when she was far more widely known than she is today, when they were very friendly indeed. In her early days as an exile they had a holiday together in a cottage near St Ives. A conspicuously successful holiday, as Lally told everyone, but they haven't seen Rosalie for a very long time.

Lally has made up her mind though. Today she has nudged Albert into action. They are on their way to Rosalie's house and all that is going to change.

'We've all been so busy, that's the trouble.'

This is what Lally will say to Rosalie when they meet and Rosalie will say that's understood and welcome them in and offer them coffee and demand to know everything that's happened to them since the last time they were together.

Rosalie's like that. They know this although it would not be true to say they spend too much time these days thinking about Rosalie whose moment, they sense, has come and has gone.

'I still think you ought to have telephoned,' Albert says. 'I don't think it's right simply to descend like this.'

'I did telephone,' says Lally. 'No good I'm afraid. She's probably on a mobile and I don't have her number.'

'Bit of a waste of time if she's not there,' Albert says.

'Not at all,' says Lally. 'We'll find a nice place and have something to eat and then we'll come home again and at least we'll have tried.'

Lally would like to have been at the Freedom Day concert. Albert would not. If you ask him he'll tell you that his days of placard bearing in inclement weather are long past. Nelson Mandela on television is quite enough to satisfy all Albert's needs. Preferably on television in his own home with the heating turned up and a glass of sherry in his hand. You can drink South African sherry now, without having a lecture from Lally, thank the Lord. The price suits him admirably and it's far better than the watery Cypriot stuff.

'I would like to have been there,' Lally says. 'Rosalie would have seen to it we were invited. She could have introduced us to him.'

'She didn't even go herself,' Albert says.

'She'd have gone if we were here,' Lally says. 'I'd have chivvied her into it. That's probably all that she needed.'

Albert's quite sure she would have. Lally is zealous in matters like this. Over the years Albert has come to wish she were less so.

He knows Lally with this look on her face and Lally can do many things but she can't yet read minds. So he starts to think the kind of thing he's wanted to think for quite a long time now. 'Fuck bloody Exmoor.' The bumper sticker on a Piaggio, clamped with a large Chinese lock to the iron railing, spurs him into it and after all, you have to start somewhere.

'And what is it that amuses you so very much?' straight-lipped, fast-walking Lally wants to know. 'Is it something you'd like to share?'

'No,' Albert says firmly. 'I was thinking, that's all.'

Rosalie doesn't hear Lally's ring at the downstairs door. She's looking for a white dress, the one she'll be wearing to Julia's party. She thinks the other woman is keeping it from her. Perhaps because she's jealous of Nelson's special attention. If she would show herself Rosalie would tell her she never asked to be singled out by him. She knows what a small role she played and it isn't her fault he remembered and asked after her. He's a kind man. That's all it is. She has no complaint about those other clothes in the cupboard. She's hardly touched them at all, just moved them aside to find her own things and all she would like is her dress back please.

At least she isn't thirsty any more. There's water in the toilet bowl and she's eaten some cake left over from Christmas. Other people have been hungrier and thirstier than she's ever been and it's quiet in her part of the house and she can lie on her bed and hold tight to the bright blankets that hang down its sides as it speeds very fast toward the tunnel.

* * *

'Let's pack it in,' Albert says. 'She's clearly not here. I won't say "I told you so" but I did. As you may remember.'

'I'm not leaving it like this,' Lally says. 'We've come all this way. The least we can do is let her know we've been here.'

'Leave a note,' Albert says, thinking of a good pub he knows close by, round the corner, needing a lavatory, wanting rotund little Lally to shut up and give everyone just a small bit of peace for a change.

'I'm going to try again,' Lally says.

'For God's sake,' says Albert. 'Give it a break.'

Which is nothing more than a waste of breath because Lally is not that kind of woman.

'Go on then,' says the Senegalese lover. 'You know you're just longing to.'

'Well, I will,' says Silvie defiantly. 'I know it's not my business.'

'It isn't,' he says.

'But she hasn't been out in days . . .'

'You would know.'

'. . . and someone has to do something and I've got my own life. I don't want this landed on me.'

The Senegalese lover is eating a blood orange. It's beautiful to see. Orange, red, spongy white pith against the blue-black of his skin and the white of his perfectly symmetrical teeth. The room smells of citrus, of orchards in bloom, of zest, of summer.

'I'm going to let them in,' Silvie says. 'I'm going to tell them everything. Then I'm going to take them upstairs to see for themselves. They're her friends. I'm sure they'll be able to talk to her, to sort something out.'

'Suit yourself,' says her lover, licking juice from his lip, moving away from her to throw a bright spiral of rind in the bin.

'Have you any better ideas?' Silvie says. 'What else should I do?'

'I've already told you. You must do just as you please.'

JULIA

Julia, with a notebook in her hand, is at her desk attending to all the small details that will make up the day.

Her useless mobile number printed out in bold letters, laminated for protection, is stuck up on a bulletin board rubbing shoulders with the other bits and pieces of her life as home manager. The Flying Squad, the Security Alarm Company, the 'Useful addresses' booklet given free in *Fair Lady*, the locksmith, electrician, pizza delivery and the bill from the Plant Emporium that Douglas refuses to pay.

The garden is not at its best but it will have to do. She's considered having the Plant Emporium in, if she can sweet-talk them into coming, to pad out the less lavish patches with plants brought in fully in flower, but Douglas will notice and a woman, even a woman dancing on the rim of a volcano, must draw the line somewhere. She will, she thinks, order water lilies to float in the pool. The chlorine will kill them but they'll look good for a day and she writes 'water lilies' down on the list.

Adelaide can sulk as much as she likes. The silver must be cleaned and if it isn't perfect in exactly that way Mrs Bannerman or old Mrs Merchant would consider quite perfect then she reserves the right to give it back to Adelaide to do over. She may, if she likes, tell Adelaide, sulk or no sulk, to start all over again and this time and if it's not asking too much to get it just right. After all Adelaide works for her, not the other way round and it's high time she realized it.

The grandchild is still there, sitting on the step of the back room waiting, it would seem, for something to happen although not perhaps that happy something she expects.

Gladstone doesn't know it but Julia has things she will insist on today and no arguments. One of them is that 'his' room is made available to the waiters brought in by the caterer. She's already opened it up for the advance team to look at.

This room, as far as she's concerned, is a spare room. The waiters will need somewhere to put their things and his room will do. They need toilet facilities and the outside toilet, despite the bulldog-face sulks she expects from both Gladstone and Adelaide, will be quite sufficient for them. The days of separate facilities are over. They will have to realize this just the same as everyone else does.

She doesn't think any of the house bathrooms with their puffy white towels, Crabtree & Evelyn soap or small glass bowls of flowers can be of any interest at all to the helpers. The waiters' jobs are outside, serving drinks on the terrace, carrying plates out to the riverbank. They have no place inside the house except in the kitchen and she expects them to confine themselves to those places they're needed. She would like the guests, not the staff, to be the people to have a last look at her pretty collections of things.

You can't allow just anyone to stroll through your house any more. Not if it's a house like Julia's is. You couldn't even open up such a house as a 'Show House' if you'd decided to sell and the estate agency insisted. Not unless you stripped it almost bare and hired a posse of security people to walk through the rooms with potential purchasers or charged an admission fee to pass on to charity to keep petty thieves out.

If Caroline intends to sell 'Stonehenge' as she says she may, she'll be walking straight into a nightmare except that 'Stonehenge' is not like other houses and even in its last days only selected people will ever be invited inside and they will come 'by appointment only'.

You can't be too careful these days and Julia wonders if Dr da Costa's secretary knew this and that's why she stayed at her house on the day of the auction while total strangers all around her bid for her things.

'Do you really think Rosalie will come?' Caroline asks her.

'Of course she will,' says Julia. 'She said she would, didn't she?'

In these days before the party there's no 'good' time for Julia. There's too much to do. If Julia is to be damned for seeking perfection then she will be perfect.

For a party of the kind Julia plans you don't just pick up the telephone or sit down at the computer and whip off a 'round robin' to your newsgroup, not for a party like this.

For a party like this the invitations are printed and hand delivered by a nice young man who rides for 'The Mounties' and weaves through the Johannesburg traffic on his red motor cycle. Documents of any real importance can't be trusted to the postal system these days. Hand delivery is not a growing business without a good reason. It really is the only way.

'Now I know for sure you're stark raving mad,' Douglas says. 'And this, like everything else, comes at a price, I suppose?'

'Quite genteel, really,' is Caroline's opinion. 'Before we know it, we'll be back to quill pens and sealing wax. It's very Jane Austen. I quite like it, I think.'

The caterer is secured. The case of Krug Grand Cuvée chilling in the back-up fridge in the pantry has been spotted by Douglas who erupts like a volcano in a fire-burst of rage.

'Send it back,' Douglas says. 'It's absolutely, totally out of the question.'

'It's a present from Caroline,' Julia says. 'I can't send it back. That would be rather rude, don't you think?'

She's in her element, brisk and busy with lists, with her filofax, with reminders stuck on the fridge door with small coloured magnets; she's in some place where Douglas deserves no attention at all and might just as well not exist.

Douglas has come close to apoplexy since the party was first mentioned to him as a *fait accompli* and there have been the most terrible scenes but Julia will not be moved. Only one of them will be allowed to carry the day and on this day it will not be him. Julia has made up her mind about that.

To show his displeasure Douglas storms around in a fury, his face puffed with displeasure. It's a sad thing to see a grown man reduced to the lip-jutting, inarticulate fury of a child, but that's what it's come to.

Julia, who could put matters right if she cared to, watches him stalking the house red-faced with anger, about to explode, doing his best to make everyone miserable, but her mind is made up. There was a time she might have helped him. She might have done something to put him out of his misery but now he may rant just as much as he cares to because that time is past.

'I want you to get on the phone and tell whoever you've invited that this goddam thing is off and if you won't do it, then I bloody well will.'

'No, you won't,' Julia says and she's right.

Julia, who grew up here, married here, lives here, is grafted on here so tight, knows better than anyone else how this place works.

Douglas will rage. He will swear and berate her. He will go purple with anger and call her all kinds of idiot, bitch and imbecile but what difference can that make to her now? He may do and say exactly what pleases him just as he's always done, here in the confines of his own home, but he will never admit to his friends that he can't afford to pick up the bill for a lunch party.

'Just think of the phone calls it'll save,' this new Julia, the she-devil, says. 'That'll cheer you up I'm sure, even if nothing else does.'

Julia, in these new days, is far beyond Douglas' power and she's made a decision. She's been to see Dr da Costa just for a talk and a preparatory consultation. She's stood naked to the waist in front of a floor to ceiling mirror and bemoaned to a man the abysmal state of her breasts.

They're not what they once were. She's examined them herself from every possible angle in the multiple mirrors in her dressing room. They seem to her old and sad, depleted, sucked totally dry, used up. They reflect more clearly than she'd like what people would see if they could look past her beautifully maintained face right into her heart and she's ready for a great many things but she's not quite yet ready for that.

He doesn't need to hear it but even so, she has told all this to Dr da Costa. She would never have thought the day would arrive when she'd have this much courage, or such complete lack of self-respect. Caroline, she knows, would rather be seen travelling economy class on an airline than admit, even in the privacy of a doctor's consulting room, that her breasts are not what they once were and how much she would like, if at all possible, to have them restored to her.

None of which is anything new to Dr da Costa, who stands a pace behind and looks over her shoulder with a doctor's disinterest and manages to be both clinical and yet empathetic. She sees his perfect face in the mirror and feels the same surge of confidence in him that he always engenders and knows he will help her.

Something must be done. She's sure he can see that. This is what Rosalie used to think in her day. It's certainly what Julia thinks now. It must and it will. She's made up her mind even further. She will make one last sordid little journey to her saviour in the shop by the railway station. 'Lady' he calls her. 'Hello, Lady.' She doesn't like it but she doesn't mind it as much as she used to. It's better that way. She will sell her wedding ring and her engagement ring too. What use will they be to her now? The money can go to Dr da Costa. What does she care?

For all she knows her life might be doing more than simply turning a corner. It might be nearing a cul-de-sac. After all, what is there left that she's fit to do?

She's been everything life ever equipped her for, daughter, sister, wife and mother. What else is there left?

If anyone asked her she'd say that she's done her best, that she's used herself up and the sad thing really is that when she looks around her now she sees what a very inadequate best it has been.

What choice does she have now but to face up to the fact that that's all right too; it's all right because it has to be. It's all right because there's no way of going back now and doing it all over again and maybe doing things differently and hopefully doing them better. She's seen as much of life as she wants to see. If there are any more surprises left she really doesn't want to know what they are.

She has at least learnt enough to keep at bay any curiosity she might once have had about what's coming next.

Walking away from twenty-five years is no easy thing. Her husband used up by her, her daughter defecting is nothing to be very proud about. The only thing left to do is try and get out with dignity.

One day people will almost certainly say that for

someone who prided herself on persevering until things were as close to perfection as they could possibly be Julia Merchant didn't make a very good job of things and it would be true.

What she hopes for now is that when that time comes they will also say that in the end, when her story was done, she was the one who called it a day. She took her reverses with good grace and went out with dignity and no small measure of style.

DOUGLAS

'I've told you,' says Douglas. 'I can't stay too long. I have to get home early this evening.'

'Tell me again,' says his girlfriend, who knows that his wife is giving an 'old Jo'burg' party, the kind to which she would not be invited. 'Tell me again and then let me see if there's anything I can do to make you change your mind.'

Her flat is a young person's flat, small, hot, on the wrong side of the building. He used to think it was charming, a place where the world went on 'hold' and if it chose to revolve it revolved around him for a while and everything was permitted but he's tired and he sees it differently now.

There was a time when the succulent smells from the kitchen below entered his dreams, wafted through them carrying him along with them to that other place so different from his house and Julia's. What a happy land of lamb and lemon and those illicit meetings where a man can be truly free in this place where no one knows anything about him at all and he falls short of no one's expectations.

On reconsideration, in a more sober frame of mind, it occurs to him that someone more adult would have complained to the health department about the inadequacy of ventilation in the Greek restaurant below a long time ago.

It seems to Douglas that the entire apartment block and half the street on either side of it is steeped in the smell of lamb fat and oregano and grills over open wood fires that aren't cleaned as often as they should be.

It's an unsavoury neighbourhood. If you open the triangular-pane windows too wide or try opening the door onto the balcony to let in fresh air, the food smell is there ahead of it blocking its way. If that isn't enough, mixed in with it is the smell of hot tar, of exhaust fumes and then there are the street sounds. The joshing, the laughter and that talking in so many tongues that it's impossible to separate any one voice from any one of its ten companions.

In the old days when there were fewer people out on the streets and none of them black unless they had legitimate business and could prove it, the talk was about nothing but politics.

Kids don't care about politics these days. They walk on the street unencumbered by the past. All they care about is making it and preferably making it big time. The world is theirs now and there's no one among them on any side of the colour spectrum willing to pay obeisance to those people of the past who consider themselves benefactors. These kids are focused on the future, not interested in the past. They look forward optimistically, not backwards in anger. Nelson Mandela is great; politicians in general are boring. Clubs, games and concerts are more fun to be at than national days of mourning or celebration. They're people of the city. Rural pieties are irrelevant and can be embarrassing (can you imagine a country cousin who doesn't know what an escalator is) and the foreigners from other parts of Africa who make it good here are admired and not wished away.

Today's young want opportunities, not problems and as for the 'rainbow nation' it's a boring cliché.

The noise of the city seems to catch hold inside Douglas' head, and like an unwelcome squatter it simply refuses to leave. In the flat below there's a mobile insistently tinkling out 'Jingle Bells'. Then someone puts it out of its misery by accepting the call. There's the toot of car hooters, tapped out in that little salute people give when they leave someone's house after a good evening out, that one that always so irritates the neighbours.

'You'll change your mind. You know you will,' says Douglas' girlfriend.

'Not today,' says Douglas.

'Oh, really?' she says. 'I'm not quite so sure about that. You know if I want to, I can always find some way that will make you change your mind.'

It's a touching concept. It might have been true once. It's not true any more.

'Why do you want to leave anyway?' she says. 'Then on top of it tell me you can't come tomorrow. I thought

Saturday was my day. You know how much I look forward to it.'

She wants him to mention his wife but he won't. Here at least, whether she knows it or not, Julia is offered protection.

He looks past this girl and through her and thinks about Julia.

'No excuses acceptable this time,' Julia says. 'I expect you back early tonight and to be there to-morrow and I expect you to stay to the end and you better make very sure you do.'

'You should be so bloody lucky,' he says. 'Just tell me one thing. Is this party of yours some idea of a joke? Tell me what I've ever done to you to make you turn on me in this way?'

'My life is what you've done to me,' Julia says and he's tired right down to his bones. He doesn't have the energy for a full-on fight.

His girlfriend drones on. He would block her out too if he could. He would put his hands over his ears the way Kimmy used to when she was a child hating to hear what she heard in their house. He would like to blot this girl out with Mozart and *Così fan tutte* played at full blast very early on a Monday morning on his way to a site meeting with the veldt rushing past.

Nothing really changes. When you get down to it, they are indeed 'all the same'.

He's been spending his days closeted with his accountants who may or may not be compensated for their last-ditch advice. He has come a long way from the VIP list for the bank's once-a-month client cocktail party. No obliging 'personal banker' waits in his reception area and says he doesn't mind waiting because

busy people run late. When he rings for an appointment with his banker these days he is put on 'hold',
speaks to a secretary. While he waits he gets gratuitous
advertising telling him how 'quicker, better, smarter'
this particular bank is and he waits for a slot in the
queue.

He's reached for the phone more than once to speak
to Michael Rosenberg. He wants to explain to him the
difficulties of finding qualified black people.
'Employment Equity' is not quite as easy as it sounds.
He comes from a time when there was no fast track to
quality. It came with experience. Even if he scoured
the recruitment agencies now, even if they had some
suitable candidate to send in for an interview it would
still be too late.

He's afraid that when it comes to considering his
tender, the 'whiteness' of his company will count
against him.

He wants to point out the impossibility of placing
political priorities above proper training. He's willing,
more than willing, to do what he can, if that's what it
takes but it's early days yet. The engineering faculties
and the business schools are only just beginning to
offer their products. There's hardly been time for them
to test their wings yet and he can't be expected to do
the impossible and do it in five minutes flat.

He's got as far as asking his secretary to 'get
Rosenberg on the line' and his secretary, perpetually
anxious these days as her husband's job-hunting turns
into a saga with no happy ending, has got almost that
far before he cancels the call.

He has, in the quiet of his office, practised the kinds
of thing he might say to Michael Rosenberg if a

connection were made. All of it bounces back at him on a false note that sounds hollow even to him. There's nothing he can say now and no way he can say it in words that don't have about them the all too evident note of despair and he's learning, has learnt very rapidly, that there's nothing the world of business is more attuned to than that.

If he could weep, he would.

Here lies Douglas flat on his back on a queen-size bed far too small for him staring up at the ceiling, while the nubbles of a worn-out blanket scratch at his bare back. The walls of the room are very close to the bed. A young woman's teddy-bear collection, luggage brought along for the ride from a still younger past, lie shoulder to shoulder, willy-nilly on a chair, pushed out of their place to make space for him.

Douglas aches all over with the worry of it all. The smell of Greek food, once so seductive, slightly sickens him now and he yearns with all of his being to be allowed to go home.

There is something else that worries him too. He loses his breath. It's quite literally snatched from him and it usually happens just when he's most in need of it. He asks for water to be set out for meetings now and gets furious if it isn't there when he looks for it. It always used to be but lately, just when he needs efficiency most, his secretary who has a livid mark on her arm is becoming forgetful.

Pausing for water seems to help him.

'Excuse me,' he says. It's easy to stop in this way, to make a fuss of pouring and fiddling with the jug while you're trying to breathe. The fish at Kariba, at Sodwana, at the Loch gasp out their lives in the bottom of the boat. Their eyes bulge, their gills gape. He doesn't want anyone to see him like this but over the last little while even the short flight of steps from his own building, in 'hock' to the hilt to the bank, has defeated him. He thinks he may be about to have a heart attack. He's certainly a candidate for it but he can't afford even that. The premium on the 'Dread Diseases' policy has not been paid up to date.

'Why do you have to leave early?' his girlfriend says. 'Why can't you come tomorrow? It means I have nothing to do but hang around for most of the day. If you can't come, if you've found something better to do, you really should say in advance. It's only fair.'

He imagines in her way she's quite right but then who said life was fair? It's a question she'll soon have to answer for herself when he leaves her. It will happen. It always has. He'll stop phoning. He'll accept no calls from her, his secretary, who says nothing, will make sure of that. E-mail will be flushed from the screen, letters consigned to the bin. It will happen and it will be very soon, sooner than she can possibly imagine, although not right then, not that very minute.

He will not speak of Julia to this girl. He will say nothing that has the words 'my wife' in its content. He never has and never will. Julia lives in a different part of his life. They've had a life together. It's gone its own way but it has no place here.

Julia's brother died of a heart attack. People said it was a heart attack just waiting to happen, although they didn't say so to Julia. Roley didn't look after himself, never had and there was the drink of course. It was getting beyond a joke and everyone knew it.

252

Julia's brother dropped dead on the squash court. There was a doctor playing that day who got called off the court to help if he could but he couldn't. Massive heart attack, he said. He wouldn't even know what had hit him.

'Not such a bad way to go,' Douglas says to Julia. 'Not that I wished him dead. All I'm saying is what the doctor said. He wouldn't even have known what happened to him. Come on, Jules, there are far worse ways to go than that and we both know it.'

Douglas had been disenchanted with Julia's brother for a very long time and Julia, especially when their marriage had ceased to be young, bore the brunt of it.

'He is never, but never bloody sober,' Douglas says.

'I'll speak to him,' says Julia.

'And what good do you think that'll do?' Douglas says. 'Whatever Roley does is fine by you and there's always your mother egging you on.'

'That isn't true,' Julia says.

She has talked with Roley, reasoned with him and begged him. She made a call to a private doctor who specializes in 'such things', booked him into a clinic, and hounded him with support, advice, and entreaties.

Julia has talked to anyone who might possibly be of any help, been to seminars, read every single article, become specialist in her knowledge about all 'such things' in much the same way she was to do later with Kimmy when that time came.

'He's an embarrassment in front of the clients,' Douglas says. 'I don't know how he can draw a salary each month with no shame at all. Mind you, I'd pay him every bloody cent just to keep him away from the business.'

'He does try,' says Julia.

'He doesn't try hard enough,' Douglas says. 'He's unemployable anywhere else and you bloody know it and so does your mother. That bit of capital he put in at the start was the best investment he ever made. It bought him his meal ticket.'

All that came to an end on the squash court.

What, Douglas wonders, does it feel like to have a massive heart attack gathering the momentum of a meteor inside one? Will it end in a headburst of thousands of stars and the hard thud of squash balls thundering against the walls of the courts all around you, gradually growing softer, fading down and away into nothing?

If the room closes in on him even one centimetre more he won't be able to breathe.

'Get me a glass of water,' he says and his girlfriend's face brightens but not for very long.

He's been taking Viagra. He has never been able to take pills without water and is constantly amazed by people who can. There's always a bottle of water in his Range Rover for long trips. When he leaves direct from his house he takes a water bottle from the fridge. When he leaves from the office his secretary gives him, along with his briefcase and hard hat, a plastic bottle of cold water from the office fridge 'for the road', but not lately. Lately his secretary is not the woman she once was. She comes in earlier than ever, sometimes it seems to him that she would sleep at her desk if she could. She makes much of her work and seems to manage less. She's become careless. She has a bruised eye. She says her mind was elsewhere and she walked into a door and even though she can't help it, it doesn't look good on display at the front desk in the reception area of Merchant and Merriman, an old-fashioned firm with a reputation to maintain. He's had to ask her if she'd mind very much sitting out of the way in the boardroom. Could she do her work there, just until it heals? He's quite sure she understands his position. She says she will and she's sorry, it won't happen again, she quite understands. She has no wish to be an embarrassment to anybody.

Sometimes, if he's in a hurry, Douglas takes his Viagra tablet in the car before he goes up to the flat and looks at his watch so he's ready for the exact time it will be most effective. Sometimes, when he's really tired and not quite sure which way he wants the evening to go, he slides one into his mouth surreptitiously and not without a certain coyness at the very last minute but he still has to ask the girl to fetch him some water.

There are so many jokes about it. He makes them himself but he's not taking chances and after all, isn't that what it's there for, this wonder of science? An insurance policy of the kind Douglas can no longer afford to maintain. A small blue hedge with which to forestall any possible embarrassment.

Douglas, these days, has no complaint with the perpetual twilight in this girl's bedroom. A firm-rooted old gum tree outside, left free to spread its branches where it pleases with no interference from Water Affairs and Forestry, blocks out the light and the light on this south-facing side of the building does not linger.

Douglas likes the curtains drawn, closing them in, making them anonymous. He has his ways with women and although Julia would not believe it and more than likely laugh out loud at the idea, he is, inherently, a modest man. He undresses carefully. Shoes first, then his shirt, socks, trousers. There's nothing more unsightly than a man his age standing in a room he should not be in with a woman not his wife dressed only in socks and a shirt.

'You're funny,' this girl says.

Her experience with men, it would seem, has led her at least this far and what can he say, except that he probably does seem 'funny' to her but as a matter of fact, he prefers it this way.

It's a strange thing to Douglas on this day before Julia's party to be here by arrangement, in the half dark, lying on a bed far too small for him. He cannot bring himself to look at the quartet of tired-looking teddy bears, staring beady-eyed at him from the chair where they've been so unceremoniously dumped.

He can feel his heart beating. He expects it to stop. It's a peculiar feeling to be greedy for air. The air in Johannesburg, thinned down by the altitude, is the easiest air in the world to inhale. It floats in and out of the lungs with no effort at all but not any more.

He doesn't want to die here. He would like to tell the girl this but she's too young, she wouldn't understand. He doesn't want to be here in this place. He would like to sit outside in the open air and tell someone he trusts that there's no possibility that any one of the banks he has accounts with will release even one cent to pay for Julia's party.

He would like to tell how his accounts are frozen, except for withdrawal of staff salaries, until the results of the tender are known and then if, despite

256

everything, things happen to go his way how hard it will be to get the business up and running strongly again.

He would like to go further than that. He would like to tell Julia how sorry he was about Roley who may have been pretty useless but had a good heart just the same (in every sense but the strictly mechanical one). He would like to say bugger 'Tough Love'. These days Kimmy is happier and more content than the two of them put together.

Forgive and forget. That's what people say. He thinks of himself and Julia. He thinks about Kimmy and the life they gave her, that wonderful life Julia kept telling her she should be eternally grateful for.

He wonders about Kimmy and all those things she must have seen, must surely have heard. He wonders about the thoughts she keeps locked inside herself and out of some residual love for them both is too kind to express.

Who is it, he wonders, that should be seeking forgiveness? Who is it that must try to forget?

He wants Kimmy back. He wants her coming in and out of their house again because it's her home, she belongs there, they both love her and they know it.

He doesn't want to die in this place, in the bed of a girl-woman who seems increasingly to look to him for deliverance, a ready-made passport to some kind of dream life that doesn't exist.

JULIA

Dr da Costa's hands wandering over Julia's breasts have a light, knowing touch. The texture of the soft skin of his hands, the tender skin of her breasts, his body temperature and hers seem to work together in harmony so it is not an unpleasant experience to lie here, face upward and wait till he finishes. After all, what is she to him? To him hers is just one woman's body among many women's bodies. She has nothing to show that can be of any particular interest to him. She is safe to lie here with her mind detached, free to think about other, more pressing things while Dr da Costa, who very probably has his mind on other more pleasant, more interesting things of his own, kneads and nudges and pummels at her breasts.

'That's fine, Julia,' he says. 'Get dressed. Take your time. Then come through for a word.'

She breast-fed Kimmy. Her breasts swelled up like

rugby balls. She thought they would burst. They ached all the time and wept milk in embarrassingly large quantities just when it was most inconvenient. She hated it but she persevered.

'For heaven's sake give the poor child a bottle,' Douglas said. 'No one's asking you to be a martyr. You go around snapping at everyone because you bloody hate it and the baby hates it too. I think she gets it from you.'

Kimmy does hate it. She screams like a banshee. She throws all of her small body into the fray as if in the grip of St Vitus' dance. If she had the power she would pull her head away and even when Julia has her hand behind that tiny head, quite sure she's firmly clamped on, in just that way the pediatrician told her she must, Kimmy, the baby, still refuses to suck.

Perhaps that's where it started. This is what Julia thinks as she slides into her clothes in Dr da Costa's examination room and checks her hair and make-up in the mirror, thoughtfully provided for that purpose, and helps herself to a tissue to blot at her mouth before she slicks on more lipstick.

'No problems, Julia?' says Dr da Costa. It's the usual rhetorical question but it seems to Julia curiously laughable at exactly this point in her life.

'No, I don't think so,' says Julia.

'When last did you go to your gynaecologist for a check-up?'

'Not for some time now. It's hard to say. You know how it is.'

How can he know? Yet she asks him.

'Do you check yourself for breast lumps?'

'Sometimes I do,' Julia says and the first prickle of

disquiet is there at the back of her neck, in the palms of her hands.

'When last did you self-examine?'

'I really can't say,' says Julia. 'What I mean is, I can't say exactly. Is it important? Have you found something that shouldn't be there?'

'There's no need to be anxious.'

Dr da Costa looks across at her with a smile she imagines is meant to be encouraging but then Dr da Costa has probably said much the same thing many times before and Julia has heard it only this once. She has a feeling that something is coming she won't want to hear. Or does she imagine it? She has a feeling that Dr da Costa is drawing away from her that way people do from the tainted or does she imagine this too?

'Don't look so worried,' he says. 'It needn't necessarily be a problem but I'd like to refer you to a colleague of mine anyway. There's something I think we need to have checked out.'

Julia has been coming to Dr da Costa for quite a long time now. The visits are always visits to look forward too. It's not like going to a doctor at all. Between visits you have the feeling that when you get back the next time he might not be there. Like Caroline's beautiful plants he might have been stolen away in the night and the next time you see him it will be as a Hugo Boss advertisement blown many times bigger than life on a billboard.

He has a nice, informal way with his patients. His chosen companions may be men but no one understands women the way Dr da Costa does. Sometimes Julia thinks that once you have Dr da Costa in your life you don't really need an analyst at all. You can tell him anything. He can't offer advice. That is out of his field of expertise but even so, there's nothing that says he may not listen to what you have to say. He's a very good listener and he's sympathetic. You can see in his eyes that he understands.

'A few more tests. Better to be on the safe side,' he says. 'I have a colleague. He's in the same building and I know if I ask him he'll see you today. Maybe almost immediately, if you're willing to wait just a little while.'

'What kind of tests?' Julia says.

'Nothing alarming. I can promise you that,' says Dr da Costa, getting up from his chair. 'But I think it's best if you have a diagnostic mammogram just so we can see what's actually going on and a needle aspiration to draw off some fluid. You won't even feel it, I promise you. It's just a routine test and it's helpful. When last did you have a mammogram by the way?'

'Some time ago now,' Julia says.

The 'Dread Diseases' policy doesn't cover routine procedures. Doctors are costly enough and the price goes up when expensive imported machinery's involved.

'We'll probably find there's no cause for alarm but there's a small mass on the left breast I'd like to be certain about.'

She feels an impulse that tells her hand to reach for her breast. It takes a conscious effort to stop it, which even in the grip of incipient panic is ridiculous. It's her breast after all. She may feel it as and when she pleases but she won't do it now. She won't do it here.

'I can quite understand that you missed it,' he says. 'These things aren't always easy to find. From that point of view it's good that you came in because now we can have it properly checked out.'

'What kind of "mass"?' Julia says.

'Probably nothing at all,' says Dr da Costa. 'The one thing we don't want to do here is get ahead of ourselves. There are a whole lot of very simple explanations we need to discount before there's any need for actual concern.'

Would he feel that if he had breasts? Would he be standing there so calmly with his arms folded and his beautifully manicured left hand resting lightly on the fine stuff of the arm of his suit jacket if it was his breast they were talking about?

Probing the fibrocytic mass that nuzzles comfortably at the base of Julia's left breast is a routine procedure. It is not an 'emergency'. It can wait until Monday. Julia supposes there is meant to be some comfort in that.

A biopsy will be done 'to put everyone's mind at rest', 'just to be certain'. An anaesthetic will be required but that's nothing to worry about. A small incision, a barely noticeable scar and a good night's rest in a clinic that runs in every way like a five-star hotel and after that, life will go on. Doctors are always happy to give advice but there's no doctor in the world that would venture to suggest exactly what direction it is life might take when it does what it must do and continues.

'I'll buzz through and get my secretary to make an appointment for you. Do you have a practice you prefer? If not, there are a great many good people, I can recommend someone to you.'

'Whatever you say,' says Julia.

'What I'd like is for this to be scheduled just as soon as possible. I'd like us not to leave it. Let's get it done and put it out of the way.'

She likes the way he says 'us'. It makes her smile. It's intended to be kind. She knows that. He does it to make her feel less isolated, to indicate that whatever it is that may be coming her way, she isn't going to have to face it alone. She feels sad for him. She feels maternal. She wants to reach out and touch him and tell him that no matter how much any of us might wish it otherwise, once we set out on this particular journey we travel alone, not because it's what we want. We do it because there's no other way.

Then it's done and Julia, free to go, leaves his office, a very different woman from the one who walked in.

She goes past his secretary, who once, before she became invisible, was a woman not unlike herself until that unfortunate business with the black boy came out and her husband sat behind the wheel of his Jaguar, put a gun to his head and blew out his brains.

Julia walks from the charming old house tastefully renovated into air-conditioned suites for dark-suited doctors. She takes her 'mass' with her and doesn't look back. There it sits quite comfortably in her left breast where it might have been for quite a long time now and nobody but she and Dr da Costa are aware of its presence and she has never felt so completely alone in her life.

ADELAIDE

The garden people have come with the lilies for the pool. Adelaide knows nothing about them. The 'madam' hasn't told her anything. The 'madam' went out this morning in that kind of mood that lets you know that whatever you do that day, nothing is going to be good enough.

Gladstone is not happy either but at least he can complain to the 'boss'. The 'boss' always listens to him and then puts the 'madam' right back in her place but not this time.

This is Gladstone's 'old age' job. He's a 'construction site foreman' not a garden worker but even so he likes the garden and will help out if Mr M asks him to but he will not put on Wellington boots and go down into the river to clean up other people's rubbish. *Ayikona!* Definitely not.

'Oh, yes, you will,' says Julia who after years of

never speaking directly to Gladstone has decided it's time to break this old habit along with the rest.

'It's a matter of respect,' Douglas always says. 'After all, he's an old man now and we owe him that at least.'

'And you, of course, would be the expert on respect and who exactly is owed what and by whom,' says Julia. 'So you can tell him respectfully that I've had enough of it. He's going to get up off his backside, get into those boots and go down to that river and clean it. He can do it or you can. It's up to you.'

Gladstone can complain as much as he likes and Douglas can take any line he wants in the matter. The truth is that these days Mr M's wife sits on his head. He is no longer the 'boss' of this house. When he talks to the 'madam' he may just as well talk to the wind. Everything he says blows past her and is carried away and those powers he once had are swept away right along with it and Adelaide has ideas of her own on the matter.

Adelaide also has thoughts about Julia's parties. She doesn't like the influx of strangers disturbing the quiet order of Julia's house. Over her fresh shampooed rugs they'll go, denting sofa cushions, filling up ashtrays with half-smoked Stuyvesant Lights. They'll finger the silver 'bibelots' (which Douglas always counts just for safety's sake afterwards), ask for iced water and keep their handbags clutched under their armpits like so many sleeping chickens with their heads tucked away. In their wake there'll be a trail of abandoned sun-glasses and the cloudy white rings of wet glass bottoms on wood that are so hard to get out.

There'll be presents as well. They always bring

presents none of which Julia needs. There'll be be-ribboned bunches of flowers waiting for stem-clips and vases of cold water sprinkled with Chrysalis for longevity in the heat. There will be boxes of gold-foiled chocolates and bottles of wine.

Let Gladstone clean up the river for Miss Julia's party. Adelaide doesn't mind. If a woman is good enough to pick up clothes, to scrub floors, to clean out the dishes the dogs and chickens eat from, then surely a man need not lose his dignity for the sake of clean-ing a river.

Tula, with her small feet that could curve over the rocks and keep her whole body steady, would like to go down and help him but her grandmother says 'no'. It is 'man's' work and not good for a woman and any sensible woman should learn, even at a very young age, that she has no need to break her back or get her hands dirty doing a job that's meant for a man.

If Mr M has said the river is a man's job then it must be so. She can ask Mr Malipile and he will tell her him-self. Everything Mr M says is perfectly right with Mr Malipile and she would have said more but then the truck arrived from the Plant Emporium a day early to deliver the water lilies and when Adelaide told them they were a day early, they would not take them back.

'We have a schedule to stick to,' the truck driver says. 'It says here Friday we deliver and today is Friday and we're delivering.'

'The madam didn't say anything about this,' Adelaide says.

'I can't help it if she didn't say anything,' the deliveryman says. 'What I'm telling you are the facts. Either you take them or you don't. If you don't we don't come back again till maybe sometime next week and if that suits your madam it suits me just fine and where is she anyway?'

'Not here,' says Adelaide.

'What about a mobile?' the deliveryman says. 'Let's get her on her mobile and I'll talk to her and we'll sort all this out.'

'No,' says Adelaide and the deliveryman must think this is a very strange house where the 'madam' can't be contacted on a mobile and Adelaide isn't about to explain.

'It's fine with me. If you don't want to let me talk to her I don't mind. It's your job, not mine.'

It's Mr M's fault and now she has to suffer but how can Adelaide tell this man that because of the 'boss' her 'madam' is the only white woman in Johannesburg who can't do her business on a mobile?

Adelaide doesn't say 'yes' and she doesn't say 'no'. She lifts up her shoulders in a way that says she's saying nothing at all, they should do as they please and Gladstone in Wellington boots with a hook on a pole to tug out recalcitrant pieces of rubbish walks past her without looking at her at all.

'Lilies in a swimming pool. What next?' says the deliveryman to the young man who rides with him to help him offload. 'The chlorine will finish them off in next to no time. These people are unbelievable. More money than brains. That's the trouble.'

The lilies stud the water of Julia's dark-bottomed pool. They look at home there, like stars fallen from heaven to give joy for a day, maybe two, but not much more than that.

Tula thinks they're beautiful. She sits on the edge of the pool with her feet dangling over the side, whitened, made larger by the silvery water. She has a drawing book and crayons. She makes a picture for her mother who she hopes will come to fetch her quite soon. She is not wanted here. Mr M's wife has made that quite clear.

'Don't get too comfortable,' Mrs M, her grand-mother's 'madam', says. 'There's nothing that doesn't come to an end and one day, much sooner than you can imagine, all of this will as well.'

That will be fine. That day can't come quickly enough for Tula. Her mother told her something about the people in this house that she hasn't told anyone else.

'They're not the owners here,' her mother says. 'They think they are but they're not. It doesn't matter what they may think. Whether they know it or not, they're just passing through.'

Tula knows about 'passing through'. Since they left Ponte City they've passed through quite a few places themselves.

'It was a dump,' her mother always says when it's time to pack up again and leave quickly. 'They should have paid us to live there, never mind the other way around.'

Tula's mother says she mustn't even think twice about some of the places they've passed through. They're travelling, that's all, in their pretty clothes and beautiful shoes and once you get where you're travelling to no one even bothers to ask where it was you actually came from. All that counts is that you've arrived.

Tula can't wait. She knows she has to but it's hard. All she wants is that day to come when she can go home, wherever her mother says is 'home' for that time but it's only her mother who can make that day happen.

Mr Malipile is not a bad man. He's old that's all and one day he will go back where he came from where the chickens are real and you can catch them and kill them and eat them. He agrees that she knows a lot but she doesn't know everything. Kentucky Chickens, which are all children seem to know about these days, didn't start their life in a deep fry in Doornfontein. They don't come plucked all nice and clean in the packs the 'madam' brings back from Woolworth's. All chickens start their life in the same way and some of them end up as Kentucky and some have other lives altogether.

Mr Malipile says he's surprised that she can tell time. He has a fine wristwatch Mr M gave him for 'services rendered' over the years but he couldn't tell time until he was very much older than she is right now. In the place where he comes from, where he's going back to although nobody here knows it yet, telling time is not all that important. The truth is that it is not you counting time at all, it's quite the other way around and time is the boss.

You can have as many fine wristwatches and clocks as you like; time will still be the one that counts you away. When you are gone, time will go on. He knows that such matters are of no real importance to a young child like herself as long as she understands that for him, it is a different matter altogether.

She doesn't think telling time is such a clever thing

to be able to do. Sometimes she plays a game with herself and says in an hour her mother will come for her. She will ring at the front gate and her grandmother won't like it but she'll open up anyway and wipe her hands on her apron the way she always does when she's expecting someone.

Her mother will come swinging down the path, swaying on her high heels, walking like she's only been away for five minutes, just long enough to put on a new sweater and gold bangles and smooth scented gel on her hair.

Tula knows what an hour is, she knows two hours and she knows three. She can count time passing and she doesn't think it's all that clever. Mr Malipile is wrong about that. All being able to tell time does is make you feel sad and wish you weren't quite so clever after all.

Tula's mother can't phone the house just whenever she likes. The 'madam' doesn't like it, especially now there's only one phone. She's told Adelaide she doesn't want to drop everything she's doing to come and find her and call her to the phone. She doesn't need the only line she has these days blocked up by Adelaide trying to get her life sorted out. The odd phone call if it's an emergency she supposes must be acceptable but if you countenance one call it soon becomes a habit and as rows over phone bills were invented in this very house, it's not a habit this particular 'madam' would like to encourage. She has more than enough to deal with right now. She doesn't need any more.

Sometimes Adelaide does phone Tula's mother but

she has to wait for those times when Julia's out and then she has to send Tula to the terrace doors as a 'look out' just in case her car comes sliding back through the gates earlier than expected.

'Be quick,' she says when her mother actually answers her mobile and she calls Tula to talk to her. 'Hurry up. Say what you have to say and then put the phone down.'

It's hard to be quick and hurry up and get out what it is you've been saving up to say when you're a bit shy. The longer her mother leaves her here the more shy she gets. When she's around her mother and her friends she's not shy at all. She never sits around without anything to say for herself the way she does here. Here she is shy, like the young girls who come up when she and her mother are out shopping and ask her mother if she's really that same person they think she is. Is she really the lady from the TV shows just walking around Shoprite just like anyone else?

The girls are always the same, about fourteen or fifteen years old. They look at her mother and point to her and talk behind their hands and sometimes they giggle out of nerves and excitement. There's always a brave one who gets pushed forward to go ask the question and you can see the question coming for miles because it's always the same. If only they knew, they needn't have worried because Tula's mother always knows when they're coming. She knows when she's being looked at and talked about even if she doesn't look back. She's always ready. That's why she goes out so beautifully dressed in her expensive clothes from Rage and Kookai and the Space Station. She likes the attention. Sometimes she'll even sign

271

pieces of paper for autographs just like a film star.

'Hello, sugar baby.' Her mother says that when she talks to Tula. 'I hope you've been a good girl.'

Tula doesn't know how old you have to be before your mother stops saying this to you. When she hears her grandmother talking to her mother, asking her what's going on with her and what she's up to, she doesn't hear her say this to her own daughter and maybe she should. It isn't being 'good' to leave Tula here like this. Tula knows it. Her grandmother knows it and she thinks her mother knows it as well.

'I'm coming to get you real soon, baby,' her mother says.

'How soon?' says Tula.

'Just as soon as I can, baby girl,' says her mother. 'Just as soon as I get myself sorted out.'

Tula has made up her mind and she doesn't care if her mother doesn't fetch her at all. She doesn't think she'll even go with her mother if she does come to fetch her. She will not wear her neon pants or eat a hamburger at Bruma Lake. She gets her meat and porridge from her grandmother who gives her half off her own plate. She does this because she expects the next fight or the one after to be the 'master' shouting about how much beef bones cost these days and how many mouths he's expected to feed and when it comes her grandmother would like to be ready for him with her answer. In any case, half her grandmother's food is more than enough for her. She doesn't need a 'sorry' hamburger from her mother.

She hasn't said what she's thinking to anyone. Not to her grandmother and not to Mr Malipile and as she may not talk to strangers these are the only two people she could tell. If she'd asked them, they could have told her that this is the way people who have given up hope speak and she's wrong to give up hope as far as her mother's concerned. She hasn't known her mother all those very many years but she has known her long enough to know she always comes back.

When she does come back, her mother comes on the day of the water lilies in just the same way she left, with her high-heeled shoes on her feet and big red lips painted all over her mouth as though nothing in the world is any different.

Once she has heard voices and looked up and seen it is her mother Tula doesn't even have to be there to know how it will be. Her grandmother is cross. She says she wasn't expecting her mother that day. No one is ready. She isn't ready. Tula isn't ready. It's just as well the 'madam' isn't here or there would be trouble. There's a big party on the go at the house tomorrow and plenty of work to do today and she could have sent a message to say she was coming.

'People don't "send messages" these days. They use a telephone but it's hard to use a telephone when what you get at this house is a person who is all milk and honey for "hello". Then when you ask nicely if you can speak to your own mother, the voice changes, just the way white voices always change when the person at the other end of the line just happens to be black.

'But here I am,' Tula's mother says. 'Aren't you at least glad to see me?'

Tula, down in the garden holding herself back, can see and hear everything that's going on outside the back door. She can see that her grandmother won't ask her mother to come into the kitchen. The 'madam' doesn't like 'strangers' in the house. She knows that if her mother had her own way she would walk right into the best room and sit down and even have a mug of tea there. Her mother and grandmother are two very different people but even so she can see that her grandmother, in her own way, is pleased that she's come. Tula is not really wanted here and it's hard for her grandmother to owe a favour and have to keep her face and eyes empty and not be able to show anyone here how she really feels about some of the things that go on.

Tula doesn't move. If her mother wants her she can come and find her. She will stay where she is, down by the pool with her drawing things. She was making her mother a picture of the party flowers floating on the pool. She was going to give it to her mother when she came but she won't give it to her now. This time her mother has kept her waiting too long and she doesn't deserve it.

'Come on, sugar baby,' her mother is calling. 'Mamma's here, come to fetch you.'

It's funny to see her mother, in a yellow dress she knows for sure she bought in one of those expensive shops in Hyde Park and a hat and big sunglasses, walking through her grandmother's 'madam's' garden as if she owns the place but her mother's like that. She couldn't care less. If Tula says the word 'madam' once she's left here, her mother will take her by the shoulders and shake her a little bit and tell her she better not ever again let such a word pass her lips, that is unless she wants trouble. If that's what she wants then she'll have to get herself ready to be shaken much harder so that ugly word shakes itself loose and falls right out of her head. Then they can pick it up off the floor and throw it down from the top of the rubbish chute of the old Ponte City where they used to live, right down to the bottom with all the other rubbish where no one will ever find it again.

'Tula,' calls her mother. 'Come. Get your things. Come say goodbye to Koko. Come say "thank you". We have to go now.'

She can see her mother but she's pulled up her knees and made herself small. She's pushed herself back against the wall of the pool house so no one can see her. If her mother looks down all she will see is the dark water of the pool and the lilies and the stone girl on the fountain bending down over the edge to look in the water.

This girl is supposed always to be looking down and all she'll ever see is her own reflection looking back up at her. She won't see it today. Today she will see nothing but pink lilies gliding along like ballet girls with the pink frill of their skirts sticking out and their feet paddling underneath the water which you can't see at all.

'Where is that child?' her mother says and her grandmother starts calling too, calling to her to come out but she won't. She is a girl who can tell time. She can count one hour go by, she can count two, she can count three and she can pull her drawing book and her pencils under her knees where they won't stick out and she can sit still for a very long time.

'Where is that child?' Tula's mother says and her grandmother is right out in the garden now because

275

Tula is not meant to be outside. She's supposed to stay in the room.

'If this is your idea of a joke,' her mother calls out, 'it isn't funny. I have a new friend outside waiting to take us away in his car and he won't think it's funny either, not if he has to wait too long. Come on, Tula, before Mamma gets cross.'

It's her grandmother walking fast who comes down the steps to the pool. She is responsible for Tula. It's her fault. You hear stories about children drowning in swimming pools. Water and fire are the big dread of a woman who has known life in a squatter camp. Children are easily burnt. One pull at a paraffin lamp or a gas stove and a child can be scalded or burnt, marked with pink burn scars on their skins for the rest of their lives. A shack can burn down. A baby with its back still unsteady can slip and drown in a bath. All it takes is a tired mother with a lot on her mind to turn her back for a minute. Children drown in swimming pools and Adelaide gives her daughter, her granddaughter and Mr Gladstone Malipile the fright of their lives when she throws back her head and cries out loud with a terrible cry.

'My God, Mamma,' says Tula's mother. 'What is it?'

Tula is on her feet and out from her hiding place with her book left behind because she also wants to know what's happening. Adelaide sinks to the ground with her head in her hands wailing for what is to come and all because she didn't know what to do about the pool flowers for the party and took her eyes off a child. Life should have taught her better than that.

Then Tula comes up the steps, seduced by this new

thing that puts her own sulk in its place, to see what's gone wrong.

'Here's Tula,' says her mother. 'Please stop, Mamma. You're frightening her; you're frightening us both. Please stop, Mamma, and tell me what's wrong.'

Adelaide is sitting with her legs stretched out in front of her. Her overall is pulled up so anyone who cares to can see how swollen her knees are. Her head is down so all you can see is the red and yellow floral pattern of her headscarf and Tula's mother has her sunglasses off and Tula has her hands locked together behind her back and her hands pull hard against each other. She thinks it's her fault. She's the one who started this thing and now she doesn't know how to stop it and down in the river Gladstone in the thick-soled Wellington boots he didn't want to wear in the first place has failed to gain purchase on a round rock. His legs fail to hold him and he falls down hard to his knees with a terrible crack. His overall pants are torn and in the bends that cover his knee there's blood seeping through.

'Oh, Mamma!' says Tula's mother. 'Did you think Tula drowned in the pool? Oh, Mamma! What a fright you gave us. What do you think we are? Did you forget, Mamma? Didn't I tell you? Tula can swim, Mamma. She learnt in that old pool we had in Ponte City when we still lived there.'

It's all over and Tula is glad and it takes her and her mother both to pull her grandmother to her feet and Tula can see she's angry with them both. She puts her back straight and pulls her overall straight and turns her wet face away from them.

'Oh, Mamma,' says Tula's mother putting her arm

277

around her shoulders. 'Don't be cross, Ma. We're sorry, Mamma. Truly, we are. Tula's sorry. You're always so good to us. We didn't mean to give you a fright.'

Tula's never seen her mother quite so nice to her grandmother before and she's glad. She could laugh out loud she's so glad. She's glad because all her grandmother was screaming and crying about was because she thought she would drown in a stupid old pool. It would never happen. She has a yellow bikini and plastic fish hairclips to go with it and when she was smaller she had orange armbands and an over-the-head body ring. Many things have happened to Tula, many more things are still waiting to happen but drowning isn't one of them. She couldn't drown if she tried.

'Get your things,' her mother says. 'I want to talk to Koko before we go. Hurry up, please. You've wasted more than enough time already.'

She would like to say 'goodbye' to Mr Malipile but there's no time for that. No one is looking so she holds out her hands and makes 'shoo' and gives the silly chickens a fright so they run in all directions. She will not be here for the party but as she's not wanted here anyway no one will mind. If she's never brought back here to be 'left' again she won't mind that either. Being with her mother is much more fun.

She would have come out from behind the pool house anyway. She'd already made up her mind. They wouldn't have had to call for much longer. It didn't smell nice there. It smelled of pool water and wet wood and the Jeyes Fluid dip you're suppose to dip your feet into down at the Municipal Swimming Bath so you don't get 'vrotpootjie', foot fungus.

Tula is ready. All her things are pushed in a bag and the stupid Silkies high-step away with their heads in the air just like the 'madam' and her friends when she comes out of her grandmother's room into the light. It's a nice day outside and a good day to go and she thinks that if she gets an offer she wouldn't mind eating a hamburger now.

CAROLINE

Caroline has given Ezra, Jemima and Josephine a whole weekend, Friday night to Sunday, 'off', all of them together at the same time so they can be with their families. When it's done, when she walks back from the kitchen past the big winter drawing room, she looks down and walks fast and does not look into the accusing oil eyes of old Cuckoo Bannerman who peers down from the wall with disdain.

She will be in the house, of course, although on Saturday she will go to Julia's party. Flash Security will make their regular patrols and there'll be the duty nurse, the one who comes on at midday and hands over to the next one at eight, by which time Caroline will be safely back home.

The nurse, sent by a nursing service, is new. Her name is Prudence and Dr Stevens has had a 'talk' with her as he does with all the nurses and discussed Gus' condition. Prudence, in Caroline's opinion, will do very well. She has a small, pretty face and her manner is slightly uncertain.

Caroline is not present at these briefing sessions. Who can know Gus' condition better than she does? She doesn't need to hear it all over again. She knows far more than Philip Stevens and much more than any nurse ever could, no matter how scrupulously trained or carefully briefed. Sometimes, in the past, when she's walked through what she thinks of now as Gus' part of the house, she sees dark-suited Philip speaking in the avuncular, professional way he's acquired over the years to whatever nurse happens to be on duty. He always speaks in low tones and Caroline wonders why. If they're so certain Gus is no longer with them and can hear nothing at all, why should they go to the trouble of using a conspiratorial whisper when they speak about him?

In the past it offended and angered her although she's said nothing. She knows their tone. It's the regretful, respectful tone you use when in the presence of those already deemed dead.

She feels herself surrounded by people who aren't at all what they ought to be. Except for Julia, of course. Julia's the same. Jimjam-James she notices speaks these days with a stateless twang, an amalgamation of accents that stop somewhere mid-Atlantic.

He used to say: 'Jeez, Mum, do you know how I "gullah" Dave's mountain bike?' She wonders now at all the time she spent banishing childhood slang, insisting that he speak proper English and not be like the kids on the street who borrow words from all the languages of Africa just as they need them. She needn't have bothered. Life in a new country has succeeded where she failed and he has a new secret language of his own with a new set of keywords which, as far as she's concerned, might just as well be Swahili.

It can't go on. The developer has been back with a set of sketches for a townhouse development and a new set of blandishments that he no doubt imagines will prove irresistible. He's very young. She wonders what he says to his friends when his time with her is over. 'The old duck's still holding out.'

That's probably it and the 'old duck' intends to hold out for just a short while longer.

'You don't have to bother about giving me the details,' Jimjam-James says on those occasions when she's not required to make do with his strange new voice on his voicemail. 'You know what my feeling is. Get rid of the place.'

It's very strange. She feels in control, quite capable of making any decision that needs to be made. She understands that things change. She walks down the thick patterns of the carpets in the corridors of her beautiful house, checking always for order, making certain with each step that everything's in its rightful place and being kept in a proper condition. In a house like this there are things that have been there for a very long time that need special cherishing. No one knows this better than she does herself but even so the permanence that was there once is not there now and she feels the ground move beneath her feet and it feels like the destabilizing swell of the sea beneath the deck of a fast-moving liner.

It's going to defeat her in the end. She can feel it.

The scraping sounds she imagines she hears from the night garden tell her so. It isn't easy. Nothing in this new world is easy. With each day that passes it becomes more difficult. She has set out a path for herself and now she's unsure how she can keep to it.

What to do next. This is what she needs to know.

There are solutions for everything. All you have to do is look for them and sometimes, if you're lucky, you're not even required to look very far. They might even come to you, delivered on a silver tray, in the same way the mail is brought to the desk in the morning room of the Bannerman house and has been for just as long as anyone can remember.

LALLY

'Imagine our being such fools,' Lally says.

They banged and banged at the door. She called out to Rosalie please to open up.

'She's in there,' Silvie says. 'I'm quite certain she is. She hasn't been out for days now.'

'If she's in there, then she must open up,' says Lally with that determined look on her face that Albert has come to detest.

The priest's boy slips by down the stairs. There are bicycle clips on his not-too-clean trousers, which make him look as if he's stepped out of another age, and a satisfied, surfeited smirk on his mouth.

'Pardon me,' he says like one who belongs. 'I'd like to get by if it's not too much trouble.'

He's sallow-faced and unlovely but he hasn't wasted his time. When he opens his mouth out come the perpetually affronted cadences of his master's voice and there's something disdainful in the set of his nostrils that quiver slightly as if something unsavoury has assaulted them.

'Get out of the way,' says Albert to Lally. 'You've already alerted half the neighbourhood.'

'If she doesn't open this door I'm going to call out Emergency Services and have it banged down,' Lally says and Albert slides his arm past his wife, turns the handle and the door yields at once and opens with ease.

'I do wish you'd listen to me every once in a while,' says Albert, openly annoyed when he might once have been no more than slightly grieved, but Lally has no time for this now. Victory is hers and she's into the flat.

'It's Lally,' she announces. 'Where are you, Rosalie? What on earth's going on?'

'You can leave everything to my wife,' Albert tells Silvie. 'Now she's got herself in she'll take charge and sort it all. You can depend on it. She'll see to it all whether it's what's wanted or not.'

MICHAEL

It's the last day of the week, the last day of the month and Michael's at his place at his mother's table just like he always is.

'So? Tell me,' his mother says filling his plate with the same brisket she's been filling his plate with for years. 'I went for a little drive with Rose Levine the other day and I see the sign has gone up for the new casino development. So? When do you start?'

'We haven't appointed the contractors yet,' Michael says. 'But we will. We already know which way we're going. We'll tell them on Monday.'

'It's a nice job for someone,' his mother says.

'Yes,' says Michael. 'I think it will be and maybe, this time, not just for one firm.'

The old hands and the up and comers. The new dilemma but why not, in these new days when both have something to bring to the party, ask two firms to amalgamate? Old companies can learn to be flexible. Those coming new to the game should come willing to learn. The business on offer is big enough. It could accommodate that and there's something else too, although this was not in itself the deciding factor.

Michael feels he owes Douglas something. After all, there was Rosalie.

His mother's become smaller with age but all the old energy is there and there's nothing her son's involved in that doesn't interest her.

On Friday his mother goes to the hairdresser. The only woman in Johannesburg who has to have her hair dyed grey just so when she has something to say her son thinks she's old enough to know what she's talking about.

Those days are past. These days her hair has that edge of blue to it that seems always to be in fashion when a certain kind of woman reaches a certain time of her life.

Michael's mother doesn't do the cooking herself any more. She still has enough food prepared for ten people but there's no more standing over pots through the heat of the day. These days she has a house worker she instructs. The 'maid' she would have called her in the old days. The 'schwartze' when she's being talked about while she's present in the room, dishing vegetables from bowls on the sideboard, handing plates, wondering if her children are home from school yet, hoping they're safe.

That transparent code word that says who she is accompanied by knowing nods and sideways looks and her job is to keep on dishing, just silently dishing, pretending she doesn't know what they mean.

'People look to you for work,' his mother says out of the blue as she jabs at a baked potato and puts it down firmly on his plate. 'It's not an easy thing.'

'It's business,' says Michael and it is but that doesn't make it any easier.

'You should eat,' says his mother like she's been saying for as long as he can remember.

This is his life now. It's not going to change. Rosalie, whoever that woman is she's become, may come to Johannesburg and when she's done with her visit she may leave. It can make no difference to him now. The W.H. Auden: *Collected Works* has had many homes since the windowsill in Bez Valley. It went missing for a while. It found its way to his ex-wife's townhouse where it couldn't have been safer and might have lived out its days undisturbed but he wanted his books back and sent packers to fetch them. It fell out of a box and was so hurriedly repacked the spine was damaged. When he looked again the letter was no longer there.

'What happened to this stuff?' he asks the removal people.

Two boxes of books came undone. Old books for the most part. They were lying on the sidewalk, in the road. There were bits of paper, pictures, all kinds of stuff littering everything.

'Lots of pictures of your kids. Nice kids you've got,' the removal man says, blatantly currying favour. 'Don't worry, we picked them all up.'

He had his 'boys' chasing up and down the street after all the flyaway bits and some of the passers-by helped them. They jammed it all back the best way they could. He's quite sure of that although he can't exactly vouch for what went back where. Still, if he's looking for something it's bound to be there. It'll turn up.

Michael doesn't think so.

He has those same Fridays he's always had, taking his place at his mother's table, making up for all those other children who would have been in the middle of their lives now with children of their own, if only they hadn't failed to arrive.

There are Sundays with his girls and holidays and all the time he can buy from their mother in exchange for as much time as she thinks she needs at any health spa of her choice just so he can spend more time with them until time runs out. Then he'll be doing exactly what his mother does now. He'll find himself sitting at a table with two grown-up women considering fondly the triumphant way they manage to negotiate the day-to-day business of living and where along the way it happened that they learnt to be so smart.

ROSALIE

'Strawberry jam and artichoke hearts,' says Lally dismissively peering around Rosalie's kitchen. 'What on earth possessed her to buy mountains of something so useless? Can you get over what she said to that poor man downstairs? She must be demented.'

Lally is crimson with agitation just at the thought of it.

'Why on earth suggest he might eat her?' Lally wants to know. 'What made her come out with something like that and offering to pay her rent in full if he doesn't? What must she have been thinking of but he took it quite well.'

'People don't eat each other any more,' Albert says. 'At least not around here. Not so far as I know. I can't speak for Brixton. I wonder where she got that from?'

If cannibalism was still *de rigueur* anywhere in their immediate environs, it occurs to him that he might

290

have something rather more toothsome to offer than Rosalie, who's a bit on the thin side.

Rosalie is a woman afflicted. She must have been ill for some time. Certainly for months but perhaps even longer although it would have been hard, impossible to detect at the outset. That is the doctor's opinion.

'What exactly is wrong with her?' Lally would like to know. 'I want you to know she isn't just anyone. She's the brightest and most courageous of women and it's quite disgraceful that it's come down to this. If we'd been told we'd have intervened immediately, of course.'

'We'll have to do tests,' the doctor says patiently.

'What kind of tests?' demands Lally, an educated woman which gives her entitlement. She must have all the particulars. That is her right.

'A brain scan,' says the doctor. 'Some cognitive tests to try and establish the exact degree of deterioration.'

'Do you realize she's still a comparatively young woman?' Lally says.

'I don't think it's a question of age,' Albert says in a hiss. 'That's not what she's saying, if only you'd listen. Dr Padayachee isn't speaking about senile dementia. She's explaining to us about Alzheimer's.'

'I know that,' says Lally.

'Of course you do,' Albert says grimly. What he thinks is that she would do, wouldn't she? After all, Lally knows everything.

Albert and Lally once invited Rosalie on a holiday to a cottage that was offered them down at St Ives.

'We can have her all to ourselves then,' Lally says rather smugly.

This is the last thing in the world Rosalie wants but against her better judgment she goes because people are singling her out for kindness because of the things that happened to her in the Struggle in South Africa and she's aware that they are.

'Do say you'll come,' says long-ago Albert. 'Put poor old Lally out of her misery and let's all have some peace.'

Rosalie will never go back to St Ives. It rains all the time in St Ives and the sea is the colour of slate and Lally talks without stopping and is an exceedingly bad cook.

'Just tune out,' Albert says. 'It's what I do and it helps.'

It doesn't help Rosalie. She lies on her hard bed at night in the single room allocated to her with Lally's voice still ringing in her ears and Lally's voice is persistent. You can't shut it out and then there's that thing that happened with Albert.

All three of them were there. They were walking on the beach quite long distances apart, looking for shells, pretending they didn't mind the hard way the wind whipped at them. Rosalie was wearing rope-soled espadrilles, a dress, when trousers would have been more suitable and a cardigan. The wind was truly cold. She could think of at least a dozen places she'd far rather have been and yet that was the place she found herself.

Her head was bent down. She was concentrating very hard on looking at pebbles, seeking out shells and all she could think about was wishing she were somewhere else. Practically any other place would have done.

Every now and then she bent down more intently as if she saw something interesting when, in fact, she saw nothing at all.

The wind whipped her skirt round her knees and she didn't see Albert come up although when he was very close to her she could feel him.

She didn't like Albert. She didn't trust him. He was timid and bloodless like a bank manager escaped from a Graham Greene novel. She'd found herself, for no reason she could explain, spending a great deal of time avoiding him.

On that day she didn't quite manage it. He came up behind her. One minute he was just another wanderer on a windswept beach. The next she could feel his body heat and his breath, hot and damp in her ear. She found herself cut off, screened by his body from the wind and from Lally who was self-occupied some distance away. With no warning at all, his arm as if from nowhere was around her, encircling her from behind. She never imagined he could be so strong. His arm was like an iron band and his hand, large, white, furred with hair, cupped her right breast and held it fast.

'If you ever, well, you know, if you ever, I just want you to know I'm your man and it would be just between us. We need never tell anyone.'

Then it was over. He released her. He dropped his arm. His hand fell away and her breast sprang free. It was as though it never happened at all. It was so quickly done she thought she might have been mistaken but she knows she was not. She turned around to face him. He had, she saw, a fine tracery of red veins on his eyeballs. His upper lip was damp.

She thought he might be slightly insane but he was smiling.

She knows Lally's here. She doesn't want to go into the tunnel with Lally. That's why she tries to kick her away and at the same time free herself of the sheets and blankets that ensnare her. If she doesn't kick Lally away she will be trapped with her for ever and the idea is so intolerable that it sets her first to keening and then to weeping uncontrollably.

She should be on her way to Julia's house but Lally has said she can't go. No one has told her as much but she knows this is so. She has her white dress though. It's a white dress although it fastens at the back. She can't remember that. 'Always wear dresses that button up the front.' That's what he said in those days when he could hardly wait to reach for her. This dress has turned itself around in all those years it lay in her cupboard but it is the same dress. She can feel her body weighted down with lead, longing to be free, struggling inside it and she will not say anything but it isn't a dress she ought to have chosen because it has no pockets. She's felt. She knows. This dress has no pockets and there's no comfort of the small square of card inside one that will say who she is and help her find her way home. Lally, knowing how cruel this is, might have done it on purpose because now she is truly lost and there's no certainty that anyone will ever again know quite where to look for her and she certainly cannot tell them herself.

CAROLINE

Philip Stevens has come, drunk his whisky, left the almonds untouched, talked to her about the various problems that crop up in the world of medicine these days, and then gone. Every second doctor in Johannesburg is doing a legal or illegal locum in England or in the Emirates or Canada where the weather's impossible but the pay, converted back into Rand, is so tempting.

His colleague, Dr da Costa, although in a different field from his own, has bought shares in a game lodge up in the Sabi area. The discreet face and body lift, this too is the fashion. The five-star clinics are filled with patients who come out for a discreet re-adjustment and healing time at a game lodge tucked away somewhere no one else knows about. They stay a week or two, then go back where they come from with no words sufficient to praise the efficacy of time spent in Africa where the living is easy and the cost little short of a joke.

Caroline, on this day before Julia's party, is in very good looks. Every Friday at almost exactly this time, in this calm old house where everything runs in such an orderly way not even the flower petals fall unless so instructed, Philip Stevens thinks this.

She has done something new and becoming to her hair. The last of the summer light filtering down into the Summer Hall, which stands open at this time of year to the garden, becomes her. It softens her face. The thought comes into his head that she's a good-looking woman at the height of her powers but she's wasted and there's nothing to be done about it which makes it no sadder to see.

'You're not really interested in all the trials and tribulations of the medical profession,' he says.

'Of course I am,' says Caroline. 'Your glass is empty. Won't you have another?'

It's not his practice to have more than one drink on these visits but this night seems to have something particular about it, so he says that he will.

She's lucky to be spared the public health system, he tells her.

'You shouldn't get only what you can afford to pay for as far as health is concerned but that's how it works.'

In the townships medical interns come from every conceivable place you can think of to see injuries, burning from paraffin stoves overturned, gunshot wounds, knifings, things no doctor in a more conventional practice would expect to see in a lifetime. That's what it's like out there these days.

It's strange to be speaking of such things at Caroline's house where things are so different.

At Caroline's house the 'Kreepy Krawly' slides across the floor of the pool in a leisurely way. There are gaping holes by the pool house where the bread trees once stood and the soft shaded lights shine down on the path.

Philip's voice comes and goes and it's nice to have the undemanding hum of a man's voice in the house. She misses someone to share the small events of the day with and there's no guilt about listening to Philip tonight. He speaks soft and slow in the way a man speaks passing time with someone familiar, offering words of no real consequence. It's just that. A float of words dancing between them like the ribbons of light that weave their way across the pool and are gone and she has made up her mind now. This will not go on for much longer and the languorous feeling that seems to surround her, soft like honey, so that he can't really avoid noticing even though he tries, is nothing more or less than contentment.

When Philip leaves she goes up to spend her evening time with Gus and tonight she stays longer than usual. The windows are open and the air coming in from the garden is pleasant and fresh and she breathes in, breathes out, sets her heartbeat in time with his ventilator and lets her mind float.

It's easier now to fill her head with images of Gus, of her younger different self and the good times when James was still Jimjam whose Mummy could be depended on to order his world but times change and the time has come to pull free of the past.

*　*　*

Tomorrow she will be at Julia's party. She has a new dress and a very pretty single string of perfectly matched pearls put together from the famous Bannerman necklace, deconstructed into more simple arrangements of single string necklaces, two small brooches, a clasp for a twin choker, three rings and a bracelet. Much more sensible and infinitely more acceptable to the insurers than the double rope of pearls and the much spoken of clasp from Asprey's she wore at her wedding.

Invitations to parties do not arrive in such copious numbers as they once did but she understands this. She's invited to visit old friends less formally now, for 'family' occasions. At more formal events no one knows quite what to say about Gus. 'Getting along all right then, is he?' You have to say something. What else can be said and it puts a dampener on things and so does the unchanging expression on Caroline's face. Caroline, with her old name, old money, good jewellery and good manners is not rendered invisible quite as easily as Dr da Costa's secretary is. It might be more comfortable for everyone if she were.

On the night before Julia's party, Caroline, who never leaves her bedroom without being properly clothed, lightly made up, with her hair brushed down, put up again neatly and sprayed lightly in place, walks the grounds in her nightgown. Her hair is loose, her feet are bare and there's a dressing gown thrown over her shoulders and why not? It's a fine night. If you go past the pool across the splashes of light that shine down on the path and walk to the end of the property, the view of the city is dazzling and it's quite true what people say. Up here, where anything's possible, it's like wonderland. You feel detached from the everyday as if the usual rules don't apply and the night air is like the caress of a long-ago lover.

High in a white palace was the king's daughter, the golden girl, that Gatsby adored from his distance and Caroline was a girl like that once but not any more.

It's wonderful to stand alone in the dark, in the silence, among sleeping birds and feel behind her the empty, unprotected house, with its doors and windows standing open, vulnerable to the night.

There's no security system tonight because she hasn't activated it. If morning comes and the garden is bare, nothing but raw ground again, the way it once was and the rooms stand emptied of everything, it won't matter at all. It will happen anyway. It has to. It's the best way, the only way now. Tonight it's like old times and old ghosts are around her. Cuckoo with her table napkins that can stand alone, aided by nothing but Robin Starch, and are quite useless for wiping your mouth because they steadfastly refuse to absorb anything. Those napkins that like to slide and will never stay still on your lap.

Here there's still a whisper of Roley Merriman, fresh from the golf club, bright-eyed with drink before his own sister's wedding. Ezra goes down the garden in his white 'house boy's' coat to call Jimjam for supper and here is Gus, so much taller than any of the other men with his fine sportsman's body and that slow way he has of turning his head.

Here is Tish Bailey with her milky white skin in a shoestring-strap dress with the snake of a bangle winding its way up her arm and a little cat smile on her face.

Tomorrow Gus will be alone in the house with the new nurse, the sweet one, so anxious to please. Ezra won't be there, nor will Jemima or Josephine. There will be no one who's ever heard of Julia or knows where she lives or where the emergency telephone card is, stuck on the back of the door of cook's pantry.

There's no one who'll know where the back-up generator, stored out of sight, is or how it can be wheeled out or where it must be plugged in but the new nurse is a most capable nurse. Philip Stevens says so and Philip is a doctor. Doctors know everything. Philip will know but Philip, like the others, won't be here.

You can stand alone in the night and let your spirit ride free and all it will see as it floats out where you cannot go is tomorrow coming towards you the same way it always does. It will get there in its own time the same way it always does. If there's one thing you can depend on it's that tomorrow will come. All it requires is some patience.

Tomorrow at two o'clock she'll be at Julia's house, drinking Krug Grand Cuvée. Douglas will be there and Rosalie, no doubt with charming little anecdotes of her visit to Mr Mandela and nice Graca and people who didn't want to know her at all in the old days will be happy enough to hang on her every word now.

Caroline will wear her new dress and just one string of pearls and her wedding ring. 'How's Gus?' people will say and she'll say, 'Quite well, thank you' and they'll sit by the river under the palms and eat salmon

300

and nice young waiters, all shades of the rainbow, in baggy khaki shorts and T-shirts, will bring plates, then remove them. They'll fill glasses and keep ice buckets topped up and at half past two the Johannesburg City Council, their usually trusty power supplier, will switch off the electricity on the north side of town where Caroline lives so they can check for faults in the system.

The Johannesburg City Council is really very good about it, given the way you've learned to expect things to be in these days. They always slide a notice in the letterbox warning of power cuts between this time and that while maintenance is carried out on the lines.

They want no inconvenience to anyone, particularly those consumers who can be relied on to pay for the service.

If there's one last thing left you can depend on, then this is that thing. In the matter of electricity, the Council at least does its best to see that you're happy. When a power cut's on its way everyone has due warning. All you have to do is make a note not to forget about it.

Julia is serving caviar mousse with small bagel crisps. There's Norwegian salmon with herbed creamed potatoes and undersize green beans drizzled with almonds. There will be fresh fruit platters, so pretty at this time of year. Bright with melon and pineapple, kiwi fruit, grapes and berries and while Caroline tidily finishes her meal Gus' ventilator, pumping air in, pumping it out, will cease pumping at all. Then, she supposes, there'll be a bit of a panic but even if they knew where to find her, she could never get there in time. It just wouldn't be possible. These things happen. Cuckoo Bannerman once said so. No one's to blame.

In the township there are no polite notifications of blackout on the way. In the township the power comes directly from Eskom, the major power supplier and 'Prince of Darkness' is what they call Eskom. At least they do in the township. There everyone either pays up front with pre-paid cards or plugs in as they please quite informally so the power can go any moment, quick as the flash of a faulty amateur connection but that, of course, is just another one of the problems besetting the poor.

Things are different on the north side of town but 'Prince of Darkness' it will be up on the ridge for a change, at those specified times, while Caroline prefers tea above coffee and China above Indian and declines a hand-made truffle with nectarine liqueur at its heart.

ALBERT

Lally and Albert, safely back on their own side of the river where the houses nuzzle tightly together for comfort, talk about Rosalie. Lally has been a lifesaver.

'That woman downstairs knew something was wrong,' Lally says scrabbling for teabags, dropping one each into a pair of hastily washed mugs, where they lie like undernourished mice while she lights the gas and slaps down a kettle of water to boil.

'She certainly knew,' says Lally. 'She just wasn't prepared to intervene and do something about it, that's the problem. We know all about people like that, don't we? When someone like you and I come along it must seem like salvation.'

Albert, sitting upstairs on the side of an unmade bed, wonders exactly how it is Lally manages it. Wherever he goes in the house Lally's voice follows him. A submarine sonar-tracking device would be proud of Lally. Up an octave, down a decibel, her voice seeks him out with unerring accuracy. He is not safe in the bathroom. He's assaulted in the lavatory. When Lally has something to say, it makes no difference where you may be, she demands to be heard.

'I wonder how long they might have left her if we hadn't come along?' Lally says.

Lally is fishing her way through plates rimed with bacon fat in which leftover rind remains defiantly, immovably embedded. 'You can't live with someone going barking mad upstairs from you and simply ignore it.'

She'd be surprised.

'Here's your tea,' Lally says.

'I'd like to have had Milo instead,' says Albert obdurately.

'You should have asked then,' says Lally. 'You've got a tongue in your head, haven't you?'

'Yes,' Albert says. 'It isn't quite atrophied yet.'

'What's that supposed to mean?' Lally says.

'Nothing,' says Albert taking the mug, holding onto it gingerly, and using the forefinger of the opposite hand to wipe a small but discernible smear from the rim.

'She'll have to be institutionalized,' Lally says with authority. 'There's going to be all that to sort out.'

No doubt Lally will have her say in sorting it all out until something else comes along to divert her.

'They remember backwards, you know,' Lally says, giving Albert a start. Can she see inside his head or can she not? 'They can't remember what they had for breakfast but ask them what they were doing the day Princess Di died, they'll remember that soon enough.'

'I don't think Rosalie would,' Albert says.

'I never said Rosalie,' Lally says. 'I mean these people here. With everything that goes on in the world that's the kind of thing they remember. Nothing better to think about, that's the trouble.'

Without his glasses Albert can see very little. Lally is nothing but a babbling blur in a smudge of a room.

'It's a shame about Rosalie though,' Lally says. 'What do you think will become of her now?'

'Oblivion most likely,' says Albert. 'Which, when you think about it, might not be so bad.'

'She'll be forgotten, that's what,' Lally says. 'She's not all that old, you know. She may go on for a very long time but no one will remember that she was someone once. You mark my words. She'll be dumped in some place and she'll be forgotten.'

'I don't know,' says Albert. 'Some of those places are nice, very nice. They're not bad at all. At least the tea's hot and they're clean and the staff can be cheerful enough.'

'Which means what?' Lally says.

'Nothing,' says Albert.

There's a tin of soup for supper. It's thick and white. It belches away happily enough on the back of the cooker scenting the air, Albert's quite sure, with the salty odour of monosodium glutamate despite all assurances to the contrary on the label. You'd think Lally would notice something like that and pen an outraged letter to the manufacturer but Lally has other things on her mind.

The washing-up can wait. It's waited this long; it can

wait a bit longer. In the watery light of a low-wattage bulb Albert is reading page three of the *Sun*.

'That's not a newspaper,' Lally says. 'It's a comic book.'

'That's all right,' says Albert. 'Then I'll look at the pictures.'

He's quite happy to suffer the penitential pinch of his spectacles for this.

Lally is writing a letter. Peace reigns. She writes with great purpose hardly stopping at all.

'Aren't you going to ask me who I'm writing to?' she says.

'No,' Albert says.

'Well, I'll tell you anyway. I'm writing to Nelson Mandela.'

'That's nice,' says Albert. 'Good for you.'

'Someone has to tell him about Rosalie and who do you imagine will do it if I don't?'

'I've no idea,' Albert says.

'No one,' says Lally with great satisfaction. 'That's precisely the point. After all, he did ask about her. I feel I owe it to him to let him know what happened and he'd like to know, I'm quite sure he would.'

'I'm sure he would,' Albert says. 'But perhaps a line or two would be quite sufficient. He doesn't need a full briefing paper.'

'I have some things to say,' Lally says, as if anyone who knew her could ever doubt that. 'Not just about Rosalie. I thought I'd just let him know that if there are things that need doing out there we might just go out and see they get done. Getting on with the work, so to speak. For Rosalie's sake.'

Which means, here we go again, is what Albert

thinks except he's not going anywhere. He's content to sit in this battered chair, inside his own house with the door safely closed and the comforting rumble of a train going past behind the hedge frieze at the bottom of the garden.

As for Lally, she may go where she likes and stay just as long as she pleases. That would suit him just fine.

'I never really liked Rosalie all that much,' Lally says. 'Did you ever guess? I thought she was rather a peculiar woman.'

'You were probably right then,' says Albert. 'Goodness knows, if it's "peculiar" you thought her, she's peculiar enough now to keep anyone happy.'

'Do you think he'll write back?' Lally says.

'Who?' says Albert.

'Nelson Mandela, of course. I mean I have gone out of my way to write to him personally. I didn't have to do that. He may just like to show he appreciates it.'

'I'm sure he'll see it that way,' Albert says.

Who knows, perhaps Nelson Mandela, that most punctiliously courteous of men, might have nothing more worthwhile to do with his time than write letters to Lally. This is what Lally thinks as she self-seals the envelope with a thoroughly satisfied look on her face. So Rosalie has been good for something after all. All that effort they put into her has not been a waste and Lally is happy.

GLADSTONE

Friday night, end of the week, end of the month and Gladstone in his suit, white shirt, shiny shoes is going home later than usual. Mr M likes him to go back to the township early to avoid the rush, especially on payday but cleaning the river is slow work and Adelaide screaming out the way she did for no reason, giving everyone a shock, didn't make the day any better.

His knee hurts and he finds himself shaking a little and he has to go slowly. He doesn't want to fall again. The white children go over the bridge on their skateboards with their safety hats on their heads. The women out walking for exercise walk fast and in pairs. The joggers who come later, when work's out for the day, jog with headsets on and the cyclists go by with chains churning.

The women who live here go backwards and

forwards across the bridge in their cars and the bridge is one-way only so they have to go slow and each one waits for the other to cross before their turn comes. Sometimes there's a house worker in front with the 'madam' going to the supermarket to push the trolley and be right there on the spot to unpack when they get home.

Sometimes the house worker gets dropped at the shop while the 'madam' does something else more important. Sometimes a house worker's 'madam' will give her a mobile so she can phone her up while she's trawling the supermarket and tell her if she's forgotten something that ought to have gone on the list.

This is what it's come to these days. Anyone looking down can see Gladstone at work in the river and some of them do but none of them really 'sees' him at all. All they see is another 'madala', old man, and Gladstone's knee hurts and he goes slowly and stays in the shady part close to the bank until the sun moves. Gladstone works carefully clearing up all the rubbish and while he works what he's thinking is that he's old and this is no job for him. The time has come for him to move on.

He will speak to Mr M. Not about the river or this new mad woman Mrs M has become. He will speak to him about Makhado that was once Louis Trichardt. He will tell him his mind is made up and he must go.

'Makhado?' Mr M will say. 'Where the hell is Makhado? What was its "white" name? What did it used to be?'

No one has any idea where they are any more with all the name changes. Mr M will say that too and perhaps when he says it he speaks for all of his generation and says more than he knows.

Gladstone is worried about his money. Mr M said that room was his room. Now Mrs M says 'no'. He lives in the township because that's what he chooses to do, so how can that be 'his' room? How many people would not be grateful to have such a room and a roof over their heads while he keeps his as a luxury?

'It's like having a holiday flat,' is what Julia says to Caroline. 'Next thing you know he'll be doing what urban whites do and "semigrate" to the country so he can skip out on the crime thing. Then he can keep his room here as a pied-à-terre for when he wants to come back to town to visit his grandchildren and that would be just fine with Douglas as well.'

It is not like this at all. He would like to tell Mrs M this is not the way he arranged things with the 'boss'. He would like to tell Mr M that this is not good for him but he will not tell him it's because of the money he keeps in the secret place between the mattress and the bed in that room.

That money will not be safe there tomorrow. He will have to take it to Soweto with him and that won't be safe either but he knows that tomorrow if the door of the room stands open and strangers can come and go as they like before you look again the money will be gone.

He has a key for the cash box. It hangs around his neck on a string of leather but the lack of a key will make no difference to a thief and Mrs M's made her mind up. Even today the room has stood open.

'I can open it if I want to,' Julia says. 'I want to make sure that when the hire company and the caterers come here tomorrow it doesn't look like a pigsty. You needn't look at me like that. It may be a room in my own house but I never go in there. How am I supposed to know?'

You can say things to Mr M you can't say to his wife. For all his shouting and rough talk he will listen to you and he'll understand but it's Friday. Mr M is not home and nor is this mad 'madam' and there will be strangers coming in and out of the house tomorrow and he can't take the chance of leaving the money in his room.

It's a big thing to decide. It's not safe to carry money out on the streets these days. He thinks he could wrap the cash box in plastic bags and bury it in the garden but if anything should happen to him what good would a buried box of money be to his daughter or his grandchildren?

If Mr M was here he could ask him if he would put it in the safe but Mr M will have something to say. He will ask him how he managed to save so much money. He will make a joke and say that maybe he's been paying him too much all these years. He will shake his head and say this money belongs in a bank and Gladstone will have to stand in front of him and listen to all these things he already knows.

Gladstone's knee hurts and by the time the river is clean it's later than his usual time and Adelaide has refused to bring his tea down to the river. It's in his flask on the pantry table like it always is but if he wants it he has to go up and get it. She doesn't do 'a delivery service', Adelaide says, but something happened to Adelaide today, to do with her daughter, and she isn't happy. It's a steep walk up from the river and he doesn't feel hungry anyway, so he stays

311

where he is in his lunchtime and finds a place to lie down by the riverbank and rest.

It's the end of the month, the end of the week. This is the time when everyone who has any kind of work at all has money even if it's only for a couple of hours until it's spent and Gladstone doesn't like it. The 'tsotsis', the good-time boys who steal for a living, can smell money on a man and this is the time they're out on the streets, waiting at the taxi ranks, pushing their way through the trains.

It's a bad time.

Gladstone takes off his work shirt, folds it up and puts it in his briefcase to take home for his daughter to wash. At the outside sink, he washes the sweat of the day off his face and his body. He pulls off the Wellington boots and washes them clean at the garden tap, absolutely clean, so that no trace of mud is left on them, then he takes them down to the shed and puts them down, neat, side by side, in their place.

He goes into his room, which is no longer his room, to take off his work pants to be taken away to be washed, to put on his clothes, his suit, his white shirt and tie, his socks and shoes. He has his daughter's monthly money in the inside pocket she sewed into his pants to be safe but the other money is too much, it won't go in there. Shoes are a good place to hide money but his feet are swollen from the Wellington boots and there's no place in his shoes.

The money is too much. These days you get R100,00 notes and R200,00 too but he doesn't like big money. He likes tens and twenties and fifties and now they have become too much and the cash box is full of them.

His son-in-law's brother is a cash carrier for Coin Security. He goes in and out in an armoured car with protection over the windscreen. When a security van pulls up outside a bank people move out of the way. These vans are armour-plated with protection wire over the windscreen and men with truncheons carry the money and men with guns guard them. No one wants to be around if there's a 'hit' but Gladstone's son-in-law's brother says that if there's going to be a 'hit' it won't happen there. When a 'hit' comes it comes on the freeway and you can do all the training you like, you can never really be ready for it because the big hits are always professional jobs.

People say it's break-away groups from the old 'Umkonto We Sizwe' freedom fighters who used up their young days training in Cuba, in Moscow, in Tanzania or fighting in the bush back home. For some of them change hasn't come quickly enough and they can't wait for ever and you can't mess around with them. They're trained soldiers. They know how to run an operation and if they want to liberate some money for themselves so they can have some of the good things they fought for, they can do that too if they like.

Cash money is a dangerous business. Your life is nothing when cash is concerned and Gladstone sits, in his suit and tie with his dark socks and shiny shoes on his feet and his cash box full of money is on his lap. He sits on the side of the metal-frame single bed in the room no longer his. He sits there for a very long time and then he makes up his mind.

He goes to the kitchen and fetches old newspapers and masking tape and a pair of scissors from the drawer. He takes all the things he uses when Mr M asks him to do a small paint job and Adelaide keeps her back turned to him and won't even bother to look round. She is peeling vegetables for supper and listening to Kaya FM.

It's not like the old days when there was nothing much to listen to but Radio Bantu, that station on which in an average newscast a newsreader would say: 'In a train accident that occurred in Johannesburg today, two people and a Zulu were injured.'

Today it's different and Adelaide doesn't turn around even though she hears him and he sees from the back door of the kitchen that the door to her room is closed. Her granddaughter is gone.

Gladstone, alone in the room no longer his, takes the key from his neck and opens up the box. He thinks he knows every one of the bank notes by now, he has touched them so often and he lifts them very carefully and divides them into four bundles. He has thought about it and four bundles will be right. He opens the newspaper flat on the mattress and wraps the money up one bundle after another until it's done. He folds each bundle up neatly and sticks it down with tape. Then he looks at the bundles, heavy with newspaper outside and the notes safe inside and he feels satisfied that what he's doing is the best thing to do.

He pulls out his shirt and undoes the bottom buttons and then very carefully and neatly he tapes the money parcels to his body. Two at each side under his arms and he tapes them firm into place. Then he does up the buttons of his shirt and tucks it back neat in his pants and he can feel the parcels of money thick and heavy and the pull of the tape on the skin at his sides.

He puts Mr M's things back in the kitchen drawer where they belong. Then he goes back to the room he was once told was 'his' and fetches the jacket of his suit, a bit shiny with use but still good. He puts the empty cash box back in its old place between the mattress and the metal wire base of the bed and picks up his briefcase which has nothing inside it but his clothes to be washed and his lunchbox with his food uneaten inside it. Then he puts his hat on his head, turns to look back to see everything's in its place and closes the room door behind him.

His knee's very sore but the work of that day is done, it's getting late and his daughter will worry. It's time for him to go home.

JULIA

There are days in your life that stand out from those days that precede them, that will always be different from any day that might come after. Julia, much later home than she anticipated, alone in her house, knows this day will be one of them.

She dreaded the thought that she might come home and find Adelaide in the kitchen, the vegetables prepared for dinner, the table set for two as if there's any likelihood of any two people in this house sitting down together to eat.

Everything's prepared but Adelaide is not there. The door to her room is closed. Everything at the back of the house is quiet. There's no feel of the presence of anyone and even the Silkies settled down for the night are no more than inanimate mounds of white feathers dotted on the dark of the grass.

Julia, who has been keenly aware of an unwanted

presence, has the feeling that Adelaide's grandchild has been collected at last. When Adelaide comes back she doesn't think the child will be with her.

Adelaide has gone to her friends. Because of the party tomorrow Julia has told her she may have the evening off and she's snatched it up with both hands, scenting freedom from grandchild, daughter and always-in-a-bad-mood-these-days 'madam' on the air.

If Julia could stop time she would stop it that moment. The house is at its best in the early evening. The chairs are set out on the terrace. The air's very still. The last drift of evening walkers has come and gone from the bridge before night settles in. No one goes out walking once it's dark, not any more.

Julia can feel herself moving through her own house, putting her things down, brushing her hair, putting on the light in the bathroom, avoiding her own eyes in the mirror.

There's no cause for immediate alarm. Dr da Costa has said so. One must hope for a positive prognosis. There's no point expecting the worst. The worst may never come.

Tomorrow is Saturday. Nothing is happening on Saturday except Julia's party. In the medical world nothing happens at all except emergencies and Julia's 'mass' is not an emergency.

Julia, in the perfect house she and Douglas made, has a terrible feeling she's going to die. It may not be today or tomorrow but if she doesn't change the direction she's going she thinks she will die alone. Not necessarily in a clinic you'd mistake for a five-star hotel where the staff all look like extras from a high-budget film and there's nothing you could ask for that would be too much trouble.

Julia doesn't want to be cheerful in the way Caroline always manages to be cheerful. She doesn't want to be well behaved in the way her mother-in-law, old Mrs Merchant, always was. Julia doesn't want to take whatever's coming her way and bear it with good grace. She doesn't care to make bargains with God the way Caroline does. The garden at St George's may be as carefully tended as Kew and Caroline may try and cut any deal she likes, Julia doesn't think God's very interested. What she thinks is that by now He's probably had more than enough and couldn't care less.

No more old-fashioned 'All Things Bright and Beautiful'. Things are neither as bright or as beautiful as they once were in this place where people once sang with such certainty of how 'God made them high or lowly; And order'd their estate'. A discreet deletion from the hymnal has put paid to all that. Everyone's equal these days and God is free to take his ire out on them all.

If her 'mass' gets too comfortable and has little 'masses' of its own perhaps she'll die. If she dies, perhaps Douglas' endless 'financial problems' will miraculously right themselves and his girlfriend can move into the house. It's been known to happen.

Husbands lie to their wives about money: 'To stop them spending too much.' 'Because if I told you there was any to spare you'd just have a field day.'

This is not the way they'll talk to the wives who come after. The wives who come after will have the world at their feet. They'll have just whatever it takes to keep them happy and it'll be moonlight and roses and best behaviour all round, at least for a while.

She wonders if Kimmy will come back to the house when some other woman has taken that place that once, for a while, was Julia's?

Julia minds that Douglas is still seeing Kimmy. He never keeps it from her when he has. Sometimes she wishes he would. She imagines the two of them together. It hurts her to think that it might be comfortable and happy and just like old times except she isn't a part of it.

She's angry with herself for the way she scavenges through even the smallest details Douglas offers about Kimmy's life now, snatching at any crumb that she can but she can't stop herself. It's just too important.

There isn't very much she can do about anything once she's gone except perhaps haunt and she's not entirely sure how satisfactory that might turn out to be.

GLADSTONE

Gladstone's daughter likes the end of the week, the end of the month. Her food is cooking. The table is set ready for the meal. Her husband will be home soon. The children are out of their school clothes, into jeans and T-shirts. Cable television is blaring Kids TV and someone out on the street shouts out that all the trains are running late again tonight. Once the news was out everyone rushed for the taxis and you were lucky if you didn't get pushed down if you were in anyone's way. The taxis are like wild things all over the freeway. No trains is bad for Spoornet and its customers but it's good business for the taxis. They are jamming in people just as many as they can and racing like cowboys to get back for the next load.

Tonight people will have to get home the best way they can but it may take a long time and even so, her father is very late. He's never so late and she will not serve the supper until he's in the house.

'Don't worry,' says her husband. 'Your father is a man who can look after himself.'

She's worried. Her father is a man of predictable habits. He comes and goes at the same time each day. There's never been a time when he's meant to be there and isn't and that's a cause for worry. She can go outside her gate and the streets are clear now of people coming home, despite the delay on the trains, and her father isn't back where he should be.

She telephones Mr Merchant's house and the phone rings for a long time but no one answers and no machine clicks in to take messages.

The children lie in front of the television in that way children do when they know their mother is worried and they want to make themselves inconspicuous to be out of her way and out of trouble.

At nine o'clock when she's frantic with waiting and her husband has agreed she should telephone the police and ask if there's been any accident or any assaults reported there's a knock at the door and a man stands there who says he has come to tell them something.

He says he saw a crowd in the road outside Dube station and a man lying on the ground they said had a heart attack. There was a woman there, he thinks she might have been an off-duty nurse because people stood back for her and she seemed to know what she was doing. She was kneeling down, trying to give him some space so he could get some air to breathe and asking if there was someone there with a mobile and if they'd call an ambulance.

'They'll take him to Bara,' says her son who's getting to the age where he knows everything.

'Are you sure it was my father-in-law?' her husband says.

'I am sure,' the man says. 'I know Mr Malipile and I saw the man and it was him.'

Gladstone, deprived of his suit and tie, his socks and shoes and his underclothes, wearing only a regulation hospital gown, lies on a gurney trolley in the Emergency Admission section of Baragwanath hospital. There's a drip in his arm. There's a tube clamped into his nose that helps him breathe. He thinks he's been attacked and his money stolen. There's a pain in his chest. This is what he remembers. He remembers the train. In winter you welcome the warmth of another man's breath. In the late afternoon at the end of the summer the heat is stifling. They are rolling along and he thinks he will soon be home and safe and the train stops for no reason at all. It will soon go again people say. This is what they mutter to themselves. They turn around and this is what they say to total strangers just to reassure themselves. It's been a long day, a long week and a long month. They want to get home and it's very hot when the train stands still and the last of the sun beats down on it. All the heat is trapped inside the carriages. People complain. The youngsters force the doors open. They hang out and shout 'What's going on?' There's no air, nowhere to sit and nowhere to move.

Gladstone doesn't know how long he may have to stand there. He's holding onto his briefcase as if it contains gold. All it contains are his end of the week work

322

clothes to take home for his daughter to wash and a plastic sandwich container with his uneaten lunch still inside it.

He thinks now he should have put his watch in the inside pocket his daughter sewed into the front of his trousers. It would have been safe there along with the rent money. If someone sees his watch, in a situation like this they can take it off your hand and you wouldn't even feel it and he does the best he can to keep his hand at his side.

His knee feels red hot. Even in this hot train carriage it gives out a fierce heat of its own that makes his leg ache all the way down the shin and up to the hip. He would like to sit down. He would like to hear the scratch of the brake being released and feel the throb of the train engine as it comes back to life.

Sometimes thieves steel the copper coil wire that keeps the trains moving. There's a market for copper wire but stealing it is dangerous. There are signs that show you this but a man must live the best way he can and for some people it's worth the risk and now the rest of them must suffer.

Some boys have jumped out of the train onto the track. They say they may as well walk. Gladstone is not certain exactly where it is they've come to a stop. He only knows one thing. He cannot walk anywhere. All his life he has walked just as far as he's had to walk to get to his work, to get home, but today he will not be walking anywhere at all.

His knee hurts too much and the fat pads of money make even hotter patches on the hot skin under his arms and he can feel sweat slide from his face onto his shirt collar. He can smell the heat from his own body rising up through the thick cloth of his suit. The rim of his hat is a steel band round his head but he has no option, he has to stand where he is.

He doesn't know how long he stands there. He thinks he managed to stand as far as the station. Then he got pushed off the train along with the others and there was a lot of pushing and shoving. Everyone is hot. Everyone is tired and wants to go home.

He made his way as far as the street but the pain in his chest was very bad and the steel rim round his head much stronger than any hatband could ever be was crushing his head. His knees wouldn't hold him at all; not the one that burned like fire or the one that did not and he couldn't help himself. He fell to the ground and because he is a big man he fell hard.

Gladstone's daughter, her husband, her son and daughter have come to find him but Friday night, end of the month, end of the week payday isn't an easy time to find anyone at Bara when staff are frantic and the hospital's working at full pressure. People are curt when they mean to be helpful. Gladstone's daughter is shouting when she wants to speak nicely. Her husband spells out her father's name so carefully she's afraid that before he comes to the end of it the first letters will already be forgotten and that makes her shout even more. She barks out his name as if at imbeciles who are perfectly well able to offer their help but refuse to.

She wishes now she'd left the children at home with a neighbour to take care of them. She has enough to cope with without herding them along and they seem

324

to be everywhere. In front of her, behind her, staring at everything, getting in everyone's way.

Then, when she's at her wits' end and rasping out at her husband for not making these people stand still so they can get something sensible out of them instead of being passed one to the other, it's her son who finds him.

'Mamma,' he says, pointing into a room of many beds like a pathfinder leading the way on a strange planet. 'Isn't it Ntatemkgulu?' And it is. It's not her father as he walked out of the door that morning, going down the street nice and easy at his own pace, in his suit and jacket and tie but it is Ntatemkgulu just the same.

He may be in a hospital gown far too small for him with a drip in his arm and an oxygen clip in his nostrils. He may be too big for the bed and seem suddenly to have become more like an ordinary man than the ntatemkgulu of her childhood who seemed big as a mountain but it is her father, her children's ntatemkgulu and she knows him. His eyes are open so he can see she's come for him and she puts her hand over her mouth and cries with relief.

It's a kind of nervous excitement now they've found Ntatemkgulu, at least as far as the grandchildren are concerned.

'You just rest,' says their mother.

'We'll find a doctor,' says their father. 'We'll find out exactly what happened to you and we'll make sure you get proper care. You don't have to worry about that.'

He doesn't want to rest. He doesn't want her to go. He wants her to ask the doctor to give her the rent money. On the last day of the month he always comes home and the first thing he does is put her rent money in her hand. She may not need it quite as much as some other women do but he likes her to know that if there's something she can depend on, she can depend on this.

'Don't you worry about that now,' she says.

'What is it?' says her husband.

'He's worried about the rent money,' she says. 'Can you imagine worrying about such a thing at a time like this?'

His heart hurts. His heart hurts in all kinds of ways. His heart is sick. He's tired and his tongue is thick in his mouth and won't make proper words. He can feel himself standing outside himself, feeling the pain this man on the bed suffers and feeling it so keenly it might be his own.

He feels for this man. His heart is tired too. It is worn out by being too long in this world. It is a tired heart that asks to lay down its burden and the 'boss' may say it can although no 'boss' he's ever known has ever been likely to do that. He may have to carry on for just a little while longer and perhaps he may have the strength to do that and perhaps he won't.

His heart is sad because his money is gone. He is too tired to think about that now but it's gone, all that money he saved all his life. He will have to think about it sometime but not now. Something stings in his arm and he's tired. He will have to think of it but today his children are with him and he's in a clean bed in a safe place and he doesn't have the strength to think of it today.

* * *

Gladstone's son-in-law, his grandchildren have found a place outside where they can sit down and a working vending machine where they can slot in money and buy Coke.

Gladstone's daughter has not been able to stop a doctor long enough to get any satisfaction but she's found a nursing sister with the name Gladys Khumalo lettered on a pin in her lapel. She ushers them into a nurse's station and closes the door behind them.

'I have something for you and there are a few things we need to say to each other and I think we'll do it better in private.'

Sister Khumalo is that kind of nurse who just by her presence manages to cow the children into quiet. For no reason she can explain Gladstone's daughter slips her hand under her husband's elbow and he, for no reason he can explain, moves closer to her and covers her hand with his own.

'Your father will be all right,' Sister Khumalo says. 'He's a strong man. His heart's tired, that's all.

'He'll probably stay in for a few days' observation. They'll have a cardiologist look at him and do a few tests, then they'll probably put him on medication and discharge him.'

'Thank you,' Gladstone's daughter says.

'Don't thank me,' says Sister Khumalo. 'I'm not the doctor. I'm only the nurse.'

Sister Khumalo is not a young woman. She has a pointed face and greying hair. Her body is the compact, no-nonsense body of a capable woman and her eyes the eyes of someone who keeps the full content of those things that she knows to herself.

'One of our staff came in with your father,' she says.

'A staff nurse called Joyce Majile. She just happened to be there when he had the seizure. You can be thankful for that. She gave him CPR. She had someone call the ambulance. She stayed with him all the time. If you want to thank anyone, you might like to thank her.'

'Yes,' Gladstone's daughter says. 'I'd like to do that.'

'She gave up an evening with her boyfriend,' Sister Khumalo says. 'They were going out dancing.'

Is Gladstone's daughter meant to feel in some way responsible for this deprivation? Is she being held to task for something she had no control over, or does she imagine it?

It's hard to imagine standing here in this place, that other world where young women go out in bright dresses and make eyes at young men.

'There's something else too,' Sister Khumalo says. 'Nurse Majile handed something to me to return to your father or hand back to the family. Mind you, I must say, I'd have to make up my mind about what kind of "family" I handed it to.'

Sister Khumalo takes a small bunch of keys at her waist.

'I think I can trust you,' she says and what is there that Gladstone's daughter can answer to that?

Out of a drawer come four newspaper parcels, three with masking tape still attached to the paper binding them fast, one opened and closed again but you can see it's been opened because the newspaper is fresh and resistant to being strapped down.

'It's a lot of money,' Sister Khumalo says. 'If I were you I'd have a word with my father. I'd tell him how lucky he's been and advise him to be more careful in future.'

Her time with Gladstone's daughter is over. There are too many other things she must do and she hands over the parcels into her hands, one, two, three and four. She looks down at the round face of the watch pinned to her lapel, looks once at Gladstone's daughter with her unreadable eyes and is gone.

DOUGLAS

From the moment of switching off the ignition it's forty-three seconds from the garage to the front door of the house. Douglas knows because he's counted it many times. Especially on the late night, early morning returns when the house is still and the only light that burns is the one above the front door.

The house is still tonight. He puts his key in the lock uncertainly as if he's entering some place he doesn't know. It's early enough for some supper smell to linger but all he smells is cleanliness, furniture polish and the undertone of the pot-pourri that Julia buys at the Zoo Lake market.

In the young days of their marriage when he came through the door Julia would call out to him. Sometimes she would come in from the kitchen, the terrace, or the family room with the big fireplace where they liked to sit in the winter, to greet him.

He has never liked walking into any house that's been his home with no one to greet him. As a boy his mother seemed always to be there. As a student he lived in a shared house where the door always stood open and the house was filled with people coming and going. It is strange to come back at a reasonable time, the time other men with lives less cluttered than his put their keys in their locks and find silence. He feels like a traveller long gone, who has always thought himself secure in the familiar and come home to find everything changed.

He's home as he said he would be but this new, wilful Julia is capable of anything and he thinks the soft-lit house must be empty. He'd feel a fool to call out in the quiet with no one to hear. He puts his things down on the wooden bench in the entrance hall. The quiet and the soft light suit him well enough. He isn't hungry. He thinks he might sit quietly alone in the half dark, a man waiting to see what will happen to him next because goodness knows he has no control over this any more, and then he sees Julia sitting on the terrace looking out at the night. She betrays her presence by a small movement of her head and a jingle of bangles.

'What are you doing out here?' he says.

'Nothing.'

'I thought you'd be party-organizing. That's all you seem to have been doing for the last couple of days.'

'That's all done.'

'You must be happy then?' he says.

It's time for recriminations, for the tirade about cost. There's just the two of them now and no Adelaide to hear what they say. He can say what he likes but what is there to say that hasn't been said already? Whatever is said, what difference can it make now?

'So you're happy with the way everything's going then?' he says.

'Is that a rhetorical question?'

It's Julia's moment. It is the last day of the week, the last day of the month and Douglas' staff salaries have been met by the bank. His secretary came into his office and said 'thank you' as if for a gift. She looks different. In this last little while she seems to have shrivelled and she's nervous. She jumps very easily. If you come up behind her it's best to make your presence known in advance.

'I'm asking, that's all,' Douglas says.

'Is that it?' says Julia. 'You're asking "that's all"? All right. Let me ask you something then. Are you happy? With the way everything's going, I mean.'

'No,' Douglas says. 'I'm not.'

'Feel like a change, then?'

How can he say to Julia that the only change he feels like is no longer to have any part in this relentless war of attrition? What he feels like is going back in time to that day when he was a young man, when he'd just come in from water-skiing on Loch Vaal, when the water was cool on his body and his skin was prickly from too much sun.

He'd like to go back to that place where golden-haired Julia was standing with the other women at the 'braai' putting together salads on a fold-out table while the smoke of the fire curled up behind her. He'd like to go back to that place where her eyes sought him out and she raised up her hand to wave a greeting. 'There's

Daddy,' she says. 'Why don't you go and fetch him?' and Kimmy runs forward on her little girl feet shouting: 'Hello, Dad. How's the water?'

What Douglas would like to do is start all over again.

'I feel tired,' Douglas says. 'It's been a hard month, it's been a helluva month. In fact it's been a terrible year. You may not want to hear about it but it has and I'm tired of quarrelling. To tell you the truth I'm sick to death of it and I certainly don't want to quarrel tonight.'

The night garden is calm. The night-lights are gentle. In this twilit world the lilies, one day ahead of their time but there anyway, glide across the pool confident as ice-skaters and the stone girl, whitened by night light, bends down intently to look at them.

'What's the party about?' Douglas says.

'If you hate the idea of it so much, why do you bother to ask?'

'I'm asking because it can't make any difference now. If there's any reason at all for this, you may as well tell me. The bank's not going to pay for it anyway.'

Julia, who has other things on her mind that have nothing to do with money, can't see what difference it can make either and so she tells him it's a party for Rosalie and you'd think she'd physically assaulted him. The old irate Douglas is back again, all his energy restored, as furious as ever and the familiarity of it is so overwhelming Julia thinks she might laugh out loud or might cry, she's not quite sure which.

'Have you gone stark, raving mad?' Douglas says. 'What on earth makes you think I'd want Rosalie here, Rosalie of all bloody people? What makes you think

I'd spend an arm and a leg laying out the red carpet for Rosalie? Rosalie's history, don't you realize that, and she was never so bloody marvellous even in those days when she was still hanging around.'

'You were mad about Rosalie,' Julia says.

'I was mad all right but that was blue moons ago. I haven't thought about Rosalie for years. In fact, I have, actually. I came to the conclusion she was an hysteric who'd do anything she could to stay in the limelight and if they'd locked her up and thrown away the key that would have been just fine with me.'

It is said. It sits in a neat block between them. Rosalie, history, should have stayed locked away for ever. It's Julia who summoned her back.

'Jesus, Jules,' Douglas says. 'Twenty-five years and you still never fail to surprise me. I need a drink. A large one.'

'I'd like one too,' Julia says on this strange day when everything's destined to stand out for ever, far away from everything else.

'You'll just have to put a stop to it,' Douglas says. 'Telephone everyone and tell them it's off. Say there's been a death in the family, say what you have to but for God's sake get rid of her.'

She could and perhaps she will and perhaps she won't. Caroline could help her and maybe she'll ask her and maybe she'll just let things take their own course.

Something in Julia has changed. Douglas can feel it. You can never tell with Julia, especially these days, and it's dangerous to take chances. Julia, the biddable wife, the most loving mother, can be a formidable foe.

'Come on, Jules,' Douglas says. 'What's the matter?'

It's easy to say that her mess of a life is the matter. That's what she always says but tonight she's too tired, she's so tired she can't even summon up enough energy to quarrel. Tonight there's another feeling in the air and it's easier to be simple and the truth is always simplest of all.

'I went to the doctor today,' Julia says. 'There's a lump in my breast.'

She would never have imagined that Douglas would be the first person she'd tell but when you've told someone so many things over so many years the path has been made clear for you and it's easy enough to tell one new thing.

'And?' he says and she notices that in the half dark his voice holds steady.

'And I need to have a biopsy on Monday and it'll mean a stay overnight at a clinic and I know we can't afford it, so please spare me that and then some doctor, half my age probably, will tell me my fate.'

Friday night in Johannesburg and the world will turn on its axis just as it always does.

'The money isn't important,' Douglas says and if the world hesitates for a moment and the rest of the universe notices, down here on earth only Julia knows. 'Do you think I'd even think twice about money when it comes to something like this? I'll make a plan. I always have. I will, Jules. I mean it.'

He's no longer the old enchanter who can make magic with words. Does he sound like a lost man whistling in the dark to comfort himself? Should she allow him to touch her with words and feel the comfort she once did? Does it matter?

'It'll be all right, Jules,' he says. 'You'll see if it isn't.'

'I suppose it will be, all right, I mean,' she says. 'It's just that it's a worry just now, not being quite sure, I mean. That's all.'

It is quiet in the garden with the residual heat of the day eddying up from the ground and the night cool beginning to creep in.

The world is a very still place and Julia and Douglas, who have come such a long way from that place they began, might be the only two people in it. To the outside world they are invisible. They might not exist at all. Only the sound of Julia's bangles betrays their presence and the clink of ice knocking lightly against the sides of a glass held in a hand that is not as steady as it might be.

'So?' Douglas says. 'Here we are. What exactly is it we do next? Where exactly do we go from here?'

'I don't know,' says Julia. 'We wait. That's what we do now. We just have to wait and see.'

THE END